SECRETS AND S'MORES

SECRETS AND S'MORES

Aly Hollis

TAWNY
BOOKS

Friends,

In Campfires and Canines, Hazel came to Bracken Creek Pack to visit her uncle, having no clue the little mountain community her father grew up in was actually a wolf shifter pack.

In Moonlight and Mischief, war breaks out between two neighboring packs, and while Bracken Creek tries to help, Granite Ridge Pack takes the opportunity to move against them. The packs have an epic battle, leaving scars on both sides.

This story picks up about a year later, as the peace between the two packs is on shaky ground.

In the end pages, you can find reference pages of character's pack positions and family trees. I hope this helps!

On a more serious note, some content in this book may bother readers who are sensitive to certain triggers. The narrative contains characters drinking alcohol, explicit sexual scenes, use of guns, hostages, serious injuries and (non-main character) death, profanity, and discussion of abuse in a character's childhood. Please protect your mental health!

aly

For girls who love a rebel bad boy who is really a silly cinnamon roll. Onyx is for us — sorry I was so mean to him.

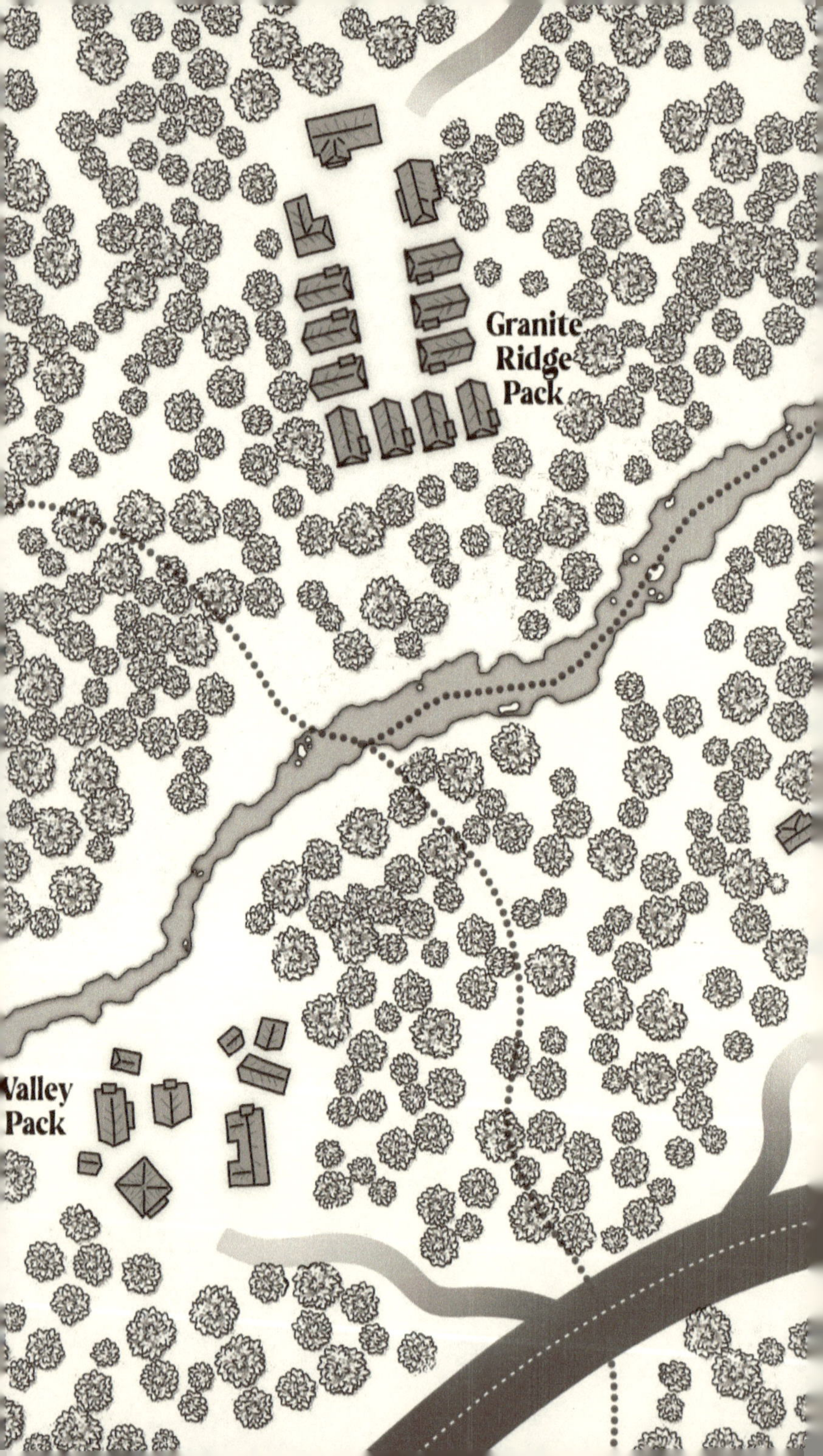

Granite
Ridge
Pack
Valley
Pack

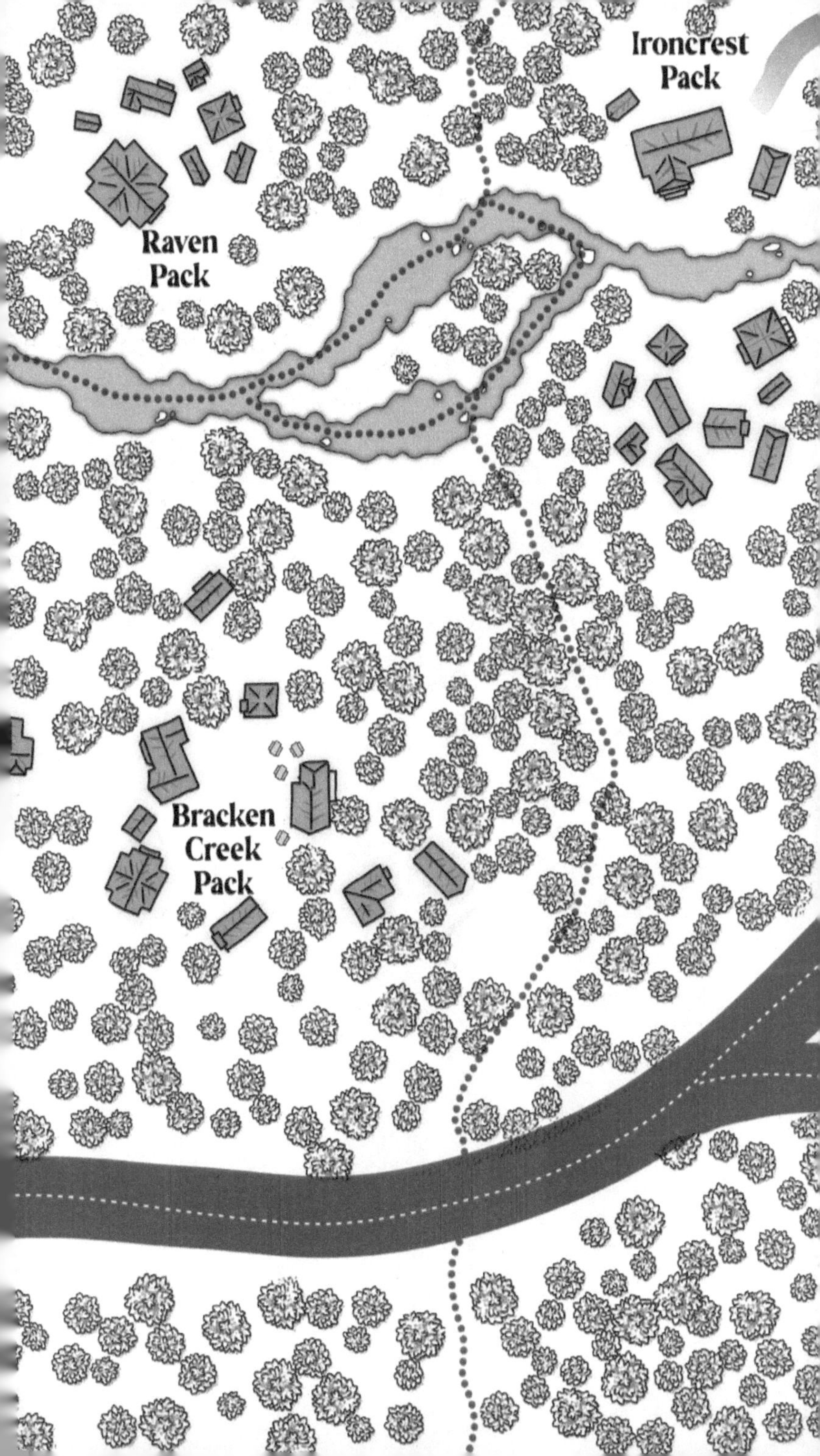

Ironcrest Pack
Raven Pack
Bracken Creek Pack

CHAPTER ONE

TIPSY BAD DECISIONS

Ember

String lights hang low, illuminating a sea of bobbing heads as the crowd of wolf shifters sways to the music. The barn wood is cold against my back as I watch, bitterness souring my stomach as I sip a stolen drink. Young adults from all five local wolf packs dance and drink.

Of all the "pack relations" schemes my brother has devised, this might be the only tolerable one. But as I'm

newly single, my mood is too morose to allow for any sort of fun.

What would Hawk be doing if he was still here? I'm not naive enough to believe he would be dancing with me. He was loyal, but not really romantic. As my *Intended*, he should have claimed me as his mate on my eighteenth birthday. Instead, he returned to his family's pack several hours north of us.

Not that I blame him. The arrangement between our parents didn't account for sudden upheaval. Why would he want to join a pack where one Alpha murdered the other?

The blame lies with Slate, the Alpha of our rival pack and my half-brother. My father was fighting him and my mother took drastic action to protect her child. It's his fault I lost both a parent and later my future mate.

My eyes search the crowd for his dark head. Slate lifts a glass bottle and takes a long drink. His other arm wraps across the chest of his mate who leans against him while she laughs. They look ridiculously happy and it makes me want to claw out my eyes. Hawk never looked at me the way Hazel gazes up at him.

"You should come join us," Jasper says. His lean frame is clothed in black, making his pale hair and eyes stand out. He might be my full-blooded brother, but we are opposites in every way.

"Fuck off," I say, grateful for the darkness that hides

the embarrassed flush crawling up my neck. I'd rather he didn't see me watching his friends like a despondent stalker.

"Someday, you'll get tired of being pissy all the time." Jasper's tone is resigned, and it makes my skin prickle with irritation. Without a glance back, he crosses the clearing and rejoins his friends. His beautiful mate, Marigold, greets him with a sloppy kiss as he wraps his arms around her waist. She is sunshine, strawberry-blonde curls, and everything I could never be.

I can't fault Jasper for defecting from our pack and joining theirs. He seems happy against all odds. If I had someone looking at me the way Marigold stares at him, maybe I would be happy too. But since childhood, I was pitted against my brother, told I was second best. Being four years younger, I never stood a chance when we sparred.

Watching them only worsens my mood, but because I am full of self-loathing, I follow his path until I'm hovering awkwardly a few feet away from that golden circle of friends.

Another of Jasper and Slate's friends, the twin with dirty blonde hair named Onyx, observes me with narrowed eyes. I glare back. He's always watching me at these events, like he's hungry for revenge. His hand moves to his ribs and the scar I gave him the last time our packs went to war.

His navy eyes are heavy across my shoulders, so I straighten and raise my chin. The slightest curl to his lip gives away his disdain. Well, fuck him too.

"Ember!" Marigold cries, pulling free from Jasper and seizing my arm. She tugs me forward into their group.

"I swear, I saw Vale sneak off behind the gym with that girl from the Raven Pack," Hazel says, her words slightly slurred. Damn, how many drinks has she had? I suppose it doesn't matter. With a protective mate at her back, she's safe to indulge. I wouldn't dare to let my guard down by getting noticeably drunk like that. There's no one watching over me.

"Good for him!" Marigold giggles.

"Marigold," Jasper says, his brows furrowing.

"This is exactly what you wanted when you set these parties up," Hazel argues.

Slate's face is buried in her neck, his lips tracing lower over the circle of pale scars that mark her as claimed. His loose t-shirt neckline reveals the edge of his matching set.

The sight makes me squirm. It reminds me of everything I don't have. No mate. No true guarantee of my future ranking. Everything feels like it's teetering on the edge of a blade and if I slip, it'll be the end.

"I don't think he had random hookups in mind," Slate says, lifting his head to smile indulgently at her.

Hazel scowls back at him.

"You don't know it's just a hookup. Maybe we will gain a lovely new packmate. Remember all the shit you guys gave us?" Marigold says, patronizingly.

"Yeah, well, you guys could have just jumped right to dating," Hazel says, crossing her arms and bumping the glass bottle in her hand against Slate's with a jarring clink.

My weight shifts from one foot to another. I shouldn't have come over here.

"Ember, where is your beau?" Marigold asks.

"Not here." I clear my throat. "Hawk went back to his family."

Hazel and Marigold let out sympathetic noises of understanding. Unfortunately, the boys are slower.

"So did you break up?" Jasper asks.

At the same moment, Onyx tilts his head and says, "When's he coming back? Shouldn't you be mates already?"

"Uh, yeah. It wasn't working as an alliance anymore," I say, embarrassment heating my cheeks again.

Onyx lets out a harsh laugh. "He finally realized what a raging bitch you are?"

I'm grateful for the anger that rises in my blood. It's better than the uncomfortable feeling of not belonging. I'd rather be pissed than lonely.

"Onyx, shut up," Jasper growls.

"Don't use that word," Marigold says at the same moment, glaring at Onyx.

A smirk flashes across his face. Those dark eyes, like starless skies, bore into mine as I bare my teeth at him.

"Maybe I'm the one who dumped him." I want to get in his face, draw a weapon to threaten him, do anything to retaliate. But I'm unarmed except for my hidden dagger and this hardly counts as a true emergency. So instead I give him a one-fingered salute and walk away before I make things worse.

His laughter taunts me, followed by a verbal lashing from Marigold.

Seething, I seek out the coolers of alcohol I know I shouldn't have. Grabbing two bottles between my fingers, I stride away to a dark corner where even Jasper won't bother me.

It'd be best if I went home. My mother's new Beta, Orion, is waiting to drive me back to our territory. But he's an asshole too, so he can wait.

I drink just past tipsy, still sober enough to fight, but perhaps not very well. It's stupid, but despite my rage, I remind myself to stay cautious. I can't trust allies to not take advantage of me. My pack was the enemy and I am no favorite.

A simpering girl from the Valley Pack pulls someone from the Ironcrest Pack past me and into the deepest shadows. I can hear a soft whine from one of them. If Hawk had wanted me like that, he would still be here. But if I'm honest, I didn't feel that way about him either.

"Look who's here lurking in the shadows," a low voice cuts through my reflective bitterness. Onyx moves through the darkness like he belongs here. Bathed in dim reflections, his hair is ashen and his skin bronze as he steps closer.

"Maybe I'm trying to be less of a bitch."

"What a noble cause," Onyx says, his eyes scanning me. "Look, I'm sorry. Marigold says I have to apologize.

"I don't want your apology."

"Alright, but I'm trying to do the right thing." His forearms rest against the wall as he leans into my personal space.

"I doubt that. Back off."

I try to ignore him, but his inhale is audible. "You smell good."

"Too bad you don't," I snap, even though it's a lie. I can smell his citrus soap mingling with sweat and something that reminds me of a bakery, like fresh baked bread.

The asshole smiles down at me. I hate that he's a head taller than me. I hate that he's pretty.

"Why are you still here?" My arms cross over my chest.

"Maybe I'm drunk and horny and I like it when

women are mean to me," he purrs.

"You're pathetic. Find someone else to annoy." His eyes light up at my insult. I guess he was telling the truth about liking mean women. Then he's going to *love* me.

"Are you lonely since Hawk left you?"

He's cruel, cold and mocking, and I should not be attracted to him, but all the hairs stand up on my arms at his nearness.

"Like you always feel, since no one wants you?" My whisper is ragged, holding none of the malice I should feel. He should fear being this close to me. The last time we clashed, I made him bleed.

He's near enough I can feel the heat rolling off his skin. My hand presses to his chest, and I mean to push him away, but my intoxicated body reacts without my permission, brushing down the faded fabric and across his torso. Damn, he's a wall of stacked muscle.

"Ah, seems someone does want me." The bastard is delighted at my moment of weakness.

"Fuck off," I grumble.

His hand grabs my wrist, his thumb over my pulse. The contact of his skin scorches me. "Your heart is beating like a hummingbird."

"I'm considering all the ways I'd like to kill you," I bluff. "It's a very appealing idea."

He cocks his head, his eyes glittering with intelligence and mocking humor. "I don't think you are."

His gaze drops down, to where my body has leaned into him. *Shit.*

He lowers his head toward mine and my lungs tighten. "I think you're thinking of *other* things you'd like to do to me."

"I'd settle for strangling, disemboweling, or a simple guillotine." I'm aiming to wipe the smile off his face, but instead it widens, pleased at my threats.

"We both know that isn't what you want."

His warmth is too tempting and it makes me dumb. He dips his head, lips near my ear. "I'm going to kiss you and you aren't going to stab me. Understood?" The touch of his breath triggers a shiver I try to hide.

I should shove him away. I should punch his handsome face. Unfortunately, my willpower is in tatters. A low moan of agreement escapes my throat. I mean it as a growl, but I'm too lost in the feel of him.

"Answer me," his command pulls a gasp out of me and my mouth opens. He reaches up and runs his thumb over my bottom lip.

"I won't stab you right now," I say, though it comes out as more of a whimper. My hands tighten against the fabric of his shirt and pull him against me, and at the same moment, he grabs my ribs possessively, pushing me against the wall hard enough my body jolts.

My vision glazes over. It's perhaps one of the stupidest things I've ever done, but damn if his mouth doesn't feel good against my neck. His tongue licks against my skin and his teeth graze, sending electricity zinging through me.

Something in the back of my mind yells to stop. He's the enemy, and he's made his opinion of me clear. Just because he's sexy as hell doesn't mean I should let him use me like this. But the way his hands run up my side and skims the underside of my breasts has me melting. My anger slips through my fingers, evaporating in the heat of him.

Sighing, I arch my neck as he presses forward. The shadow of a beard along his jaw scuffs my throat and my hands come up to reach for him, wanting more. Like lightning, one hand grabs both my wrists and pins them above my head.

"I still don't trust you," he says, his lips still against my skin.

Good. He shouldn't.

ONYX

Years ago, my brother, cousin, and I went cliff jumping at a river a few hours away. Over and over, we plunged off the rocks, aiming for deeper water, knowing that one slip could mean death. The rush was addictive.

That's what kissing Ember is like.

It's the last thing I should be doing, but I can't resist.

I can't keep my gaze away from the way her dark green hair highlights the emerald in her hazel eyes. Her heart-shaped face glows in the low lights.

My first mistake is getting too close, maybe because I feel guilty or maybe to feel the thrill of irritating someone who clearly would like to murder me.

But when her scent reaches me, all of those thoughts evaporate, and all I can think of is touching her. She's soft wildflowers and the sharp, metallic scent of lightning, so alluring I'm leaning in too close.

She wants me too. The glow of her eyes is a thin halo around her blown-out pupils.

My hand tightens around her wrists, stretching her out for me to taste. She's so pliant, melting against me - the opposite of her prickly personality. It's heady, the way she obeys my silent commands, opening her mouth for me. She kisses back fiercely. Her teeth nip at my tongue, sending a jolt straight to my hard cock pressing against her supple body.

I sweep my mouth to her jaw, wanting to taste more of her. A hushed noise from her throat sends my head spinning. It's walking the edge of a blade and getting away with it, and she feels so good.

"You kiss better than you fight," I whisper against

her skin.

Her chest heaves as she struggles to get enough air to say, "Unfortunately, you don't."

Huffing a laugh at her insult, I use my free hand to tip her chin up so she's forced to look me in the eyes. "Don't lie to me. You've been enjoying this too much for that to be true."

"You're pathetic," she growls.

It's ice hitting my overheated skin. What the fuck am I doing?

My fingers are stiff as I release her and take a forcible step back. The cool air washes over me.

"Better pathetic than a psycho," I mutter defensively. Those startling eyes narrow and then she's moving, stalking off into the dwindling crowd.

Snarling, I adjust myself, gulping down the night air to try and calm the inferno raging through me.

That shouldn't have happened. I try to picture her months ago as she viciously slashed a knife against my side and cut into my skin. That's the woman I just kissed - someone who would gladly gut me.

But now all I can recall from that moment is the way her curves felt in my arms, still naked from shifting. Even then, it had been wildly distracting. That's how she managed to hurt me, or at least that's what I tell myself.

What's wrong with me? That was a fight, not a flirtation. Though I shouldn't be surprised. She's exactly my type - feisty, strong-willed, unpredictable.

Acidic disappointment eats away at me. If I had kept my mouth shut, it could still be on her body. I can feel the ghost of her up against me.

Shaking my head, I return to the dregs of the party to find Vale, the last member of our pack at the gathering. Pink lip gloss smudges his chin and I'm too irritated to tease him about it.

I'm not close with the younger wolf, but he's nice enough. Usually I'd stick with my friends or my twin, Cedar, but he had no interest in attending a party. The two couples headed home when they could no longer keep their PDA to a reasonable level, leaving me unsupervised to make poor decisions in the shadows.

"Have a good time?" Vale asks.

I grunt a non-answer, stalking toward the truck. "You good to drive, man?"

"Yeah, I was too busy to drink." His grin is irritating.

Normally, I wouldn't be angry with a packmate for finding happiness. But after I held a beautiful girl in my arms and then she insulted me and stormed off, I'm not in the mood to celebrate new relationships.

My foot kicks a discarded cup. With a scoff, I pause. The clearing is a mess, with bottles and cups piled by a nearby bin and a few scattered elsewhere.

"Do you know if they have a dumpster or

something?" I ask.

Vale shrugs. "I can find out."

With jerky movements, I gather up the trash liner from the bin and shake it, making room for more cups. It only takes a few minutes to gather up the nearby trash. Vale returns to show me the small dumpster behind a nearby storage building.

It feels good to do something for our allied pack, though it does little to ebb my frustration with Ember.

The door to the truck slams shut behind me with a dull thud. My mood only worsens as Vale chatters about the girl from Raven pack.

As soon as the truck is parked, I leave him behind and head north. My family's cabin is one of the largest in the compound, rising two stories high with a wide porch. And right now, it's silent.

Laying in my bed and listening to my brother mumble in his sleep sounds like torture. My thoughts won't let me rest. I tug my shirt over my head and strip off my sweats, tossing them on the bench beside the front door.

Moonlight streams over my naked body for a split second before I sink into the wolf instincts and charcoal fur sweeps over my skin. Everything falls away, replaced with the animal urges to run, hunt, and protect. With a graceful leap, I land on the pine needles with all four paws.

The night is bright to my canine eyesight. The colors are faded, but every little movement catches my attention. Habit takes over as I lope in a lazy circle around the pack's collection of buildings and homes. Two of my packmates are on guard duty, but they're used to my midnight runs.

The wind ruffles my thick coat. Ember's voice echoes in my mind, breaking through my calm. Pulling back my lips to bare my teeth, I put on a burst of speed and break through the trees into the meadow. Moonlight highlights clumps of swaying wildflowers, with well-worn pathways between them. My paws glide between the newly rebuilt diner and my brother's garden to the north.

The air leaves my lungs in a defeated sigh. Maybe tomorrow will be better, or at least less dissatisfying. Returning to my human shape, I slip into my home and yank on loose shorts before flopping face down in my bed on the far side of the room from my brother. Cedar grunts and turns his head to blink at me, but he knows me too well to ask questions when I'm in a dark mood. Rolling onto my side facing away from him, I listen as he sighs and nestles back into his pillow.

Eyes squeezed shut, I beg my mind to rest. Memories of her warm skin and that floral scent force their way into my thoughts. As if punishing me, my brain replays her words and the way she glared at me.

I shouldn't have liked it so much. There were plenty of nice young women at the party. But none of them made my pulse race like Ember. It was like staring down a beautiful but lethal predator.

Unless I can get my head on straight, it would be best to avoid her. Maybe I'll stay home with Cedar during the next inter-pack gathering. The idea grates on me.

Despite my angst, sleep finally finds me.

Chapter Two

HANGOVERS & HEIRS

Ember

Eyeliner streaks down my face, turning me into a deranged raccoon. Half asleep, I turn on the shower and let steam fill my bathroom. It fogs the mirror, misty gray against the pristine white tile walls. My mother embraced the minimalistic aesthetic while decorating this house, and I hate it.

Twenty minutes of scrubbing later, I feel like myself again. With wet hair clinging to my neck, I yank on

joggers and a sweatshirt before heading to the kitchen.

"Good morning, Ember," Sienna purrs. Others might mistake her tone for charm, but after eighteen years, I know it's a sign she's ready for a fight. She perches on the edge of her seat at the breakfast table, already in heels with her signature crimson lip. Her silk wrap dress hangs loose on her frame, the only sign she's grieved her spouse at all.

I'm surprised she hasn't taken a new mate already. There are a dozen dominant males in the pack who are more than eager, despite the risk, and it would help secure her position.

It's hard to stay Alpha when you murder your mate.

Whispers have circulated the ranks and many of the males are reluctant to follow a single female's leadership. But I suppose that's the consequence of building a pack made up almost exclusively of ruthless fighters, especially ones that aren't particularly bright.

My response is a grunt. I wait for her criticism, but the only sound is the cabinet hinge and the dry rustling of cereal hitting the bottom of my bowl, followed by the clink of a spoon.

Either she's playing at being a good mom this morning, or she's biding her time. *Fantastic.*

"So how was the gathering last night?" she asks after a delicate sip of coffee.

"Fine."

"I'd appreciate a more thorough answer." Her polite smile stays plastered in place.

With a deep sigh, I plop into my seat and shovel cereal into my mouth. The crunch echoes inside my head, drowning out the bleak thoughts that make up my mental playlist.

"Don't you have minions to report to you for these types of things?"

Her dark eyes study me for a moment. I hate that Jasper takes after our dad and I take after her. It's why I bleach and color my hair various shades of the rainbow every few weeks.

"Yes, I do. But no one else spoke with the Alphas of the Bracken Creek Pack." Her words are crisp, only a hint of her disdain toward her former pack shining through. If a stranger were listening, they'd never know that one of those Alphas is her oldest son from her first relationship, before she met my dad.

Leaning back in my chair, I cross my arms and tuck my leg under me. "Look, we barely spoke. Hazel was gossiping about her packmates and Slate was just drinking and groping her."

Sienna's eyebrows shoot up.

I almost regret my harsh assessment. "Not like he was drunk. He just didn't talk when I was there."

Her expression turns analytical and I resume eating my cereal to escape her assessment. "Anything else you'd like to share?"

"Nope." The answer is too quick. I force myself to meet her gaze for a moment, keeping the guilt churning in my gut from seeping into my expression.

No, *Mother dear*, nothing else happened. Only made out with the enemy. Yes, the same one I stabbed. No big deal. just let him suck on my neck while I ground against him like a shameless hussy. And now I'm ruined because every other man I've ever kissed had cold fish lips compared to him. Shit.

"I'm glad you had a good time because you're going to spend several days with them."

My breakfast catches in my throat and I splutter and cough.

"Why?" I choke out.

"I've requested your brother come home for a visit and bring his little mate."

"So?" My coffee does little to soothe me as I wait for her to explain.

"They suggested an exchange in order to ensure their safety, since, as their Beta, Jasper is technically also their Heir until those two have a child of their own."

My brain blanks for a minute. So much for holding my superior position as Heir over Jasper's head.

"An exchange," I repeat dumbly. "Who are you sending?"

"My own Heir, of course." Her manicured fingers

press to her temple as if to ward off a headache.

"Can't you send Orion? Maybe I want to spend time with Jasper too." I know I sound like a whiny child, but spending time in enemy territory sounds unbearable, especially after last night.

"You can catch up with your brother on your own time."

Anger turns my mind sharp. "When would you have allowed that?"

"You had the gathering last night, didn't you?"

A frustrated growl builds in my throat, but acting like a petulant child won't change her decision. I have no autonomy here. Schooling my features to calm, I ask, "What is your goal for this visit? If I'm going to be shuttled off to our enemies, at least tell me what you're trying to accomplish."

Her lips thin, her features appearing predatory. "Daughter, you are going to visit your half-brother and his mate. You are going to be quiet and respectful. And if I require anything else from you, I'll tell you so. Until then, keep your eyes open and your mouth shut."

The icy command hangs between us. Sienna sips her coffee and returns her gaze to her phone. Finally, my emotions calm enough to speak.

"Am I going alone?"

She sets her phone on the table with a snap. "Do you need a babysitter?"

"Of course not." Masking my hurt with sarcasm, I force out a cold laugh. "Hopefully they won't murder me in my sleep. Pretty sure you don't have any other Heirs hidden around here to replace me."

She rolls her eyes and with a dismissive flick of her wrist, opens her phone again.

ONYX

My joints ache as I drag myself from bed. Each beat of my pulse feels like a blow to my temple, and my skin feels too tight. Feet clumsy, I head straight to the kitchen, the smell of my mother's cooking promising some relief.

Four people sit around our kitchen table, my parents and two guests. My mother pops up, grabbing a glass and filling it with water.

"How do you look so peppy?" I ask Hazel with a groan. She sits beside Slate with a tense expression like I interrupted an important conversation.

My father, Fisher, sits forward with his forearms flat on the table and his hands neatly folded. His salt and pepper hair sweeps back off his forehead. Feeling self-conscious, I rake my fingers through my hair and it out of my face.

"Well, we didn't drink like a dehydrated dolphin

last night," Hazel answers with a patronizing quirk of her eyebrow.

The glass of water is forced into my hands. My mother's forehead wrinkles in concern as she discreetly hands me two pain pills. Do I really look that bad? "Thanks, Mom," I mutter before downing the medication and water.

"Come join us," she says, settling into a chair. Her cinnamon hair gleams bronze in the morning light. With a sigh, I slump into the seat between her and Slate.

"We were just discussing a proposal from the Granite Ridge pack," Hazel explains. My hand freezes halfway to the basket of warm pastries in the center of the table. "Not that kind, obviously. Sienna would like Jasper and Marigold to visit them for a few days, and in return, she will send Ember to stay with us."

"What?" I blurt, my mouth hanging open.

Her brows knit together. "Jasper and Marigold will go there, and Ember will stay with us. Like an exchange."

"Is that necessary?" I ask.

"Not really," Slate says. He lets out an audible exhale, his arms crossing. Hazel turns, her eyes narrowing at his reaction.

"You should get to know her. She's your sister." It sounds like an argument they've had before.

"Half-sister," Slate grumbles.

I focus on the pastry selection and grab a brioche

bun filled with blackberries my brother grew. It's a cloud melting into sweet, sticky preserves. Being the son of the pack's baker has its perks.

"So?" Hazel says, her voice rising in pitch. Irritation trickles through the pack bond.

"She attempted to murder you when she first met you," Slate says dryly. His mouth pulls into a grimace.

"That's not exactly what happened," Hazel argues.

My body leans back from her, one of my eyebrows rising. "Let's not forget she stabbed me." My free hand motions to the exposed scar across the bottom of my ribs.

My mother clicks her tongue, crossing the room to grab a sweatshirt. I smile at her fussing and slip it on obediently.

"It makes sense, politically. She's their Heir, and Jasper is yours for now," my father says. Hazel crosses her arms with a pointed look at her mate.

Slate settles back in his seat, acquiescing to his mate's demands.

"Well, we can't have her stay with Hawthorne. Not with how young his kids are," Hazel says. "And Slate isn't comfortable keeping her with us."

"We aren't home enough to supervise her properly." His hand rests protectively on the back of her chair.

"So we're hoping you'll host her." Hazel says,

turning to my father. "You're next in line, as our Delta. You have the space and there will be five of you to keep an eye on her."

My father has taken all of this in without visible reaction, but I can almost hear his brain calculating the risk. As the pack's trainer, he knows our people and our weaknesses better than anyone.

"Four of us," he amends. "We'll send Briar to stay with friends, and then Ember can stay in her room."

"Good idea," Hazel says, turning her sweetest smile on my mother. "Clove, I know this is a big imposition."

"No, it would be an honor."

"I really appreciate that," Hazel says, her eyes crinkling as she smiles.

Brioche eaten, I consider grabbing another pastry. There's a chocolate-studded scone calling my name and the sugar softens my surprise.

"Onyx," Slate says. His tone commands my attention and I fight the instinct to cringe. It's never good when he uses that voice on me.

"We'd like you to take the lead on guarding Ember during her stay with us. Vale can handle your tech duties for a few days, and we'll change up the patrol rotation to free you up."

Is he shitting me?

Thoughts of the scone dissolve as I rub my palm over my jaw. "Am I guarding her from our packmates? Or guarding them from her?"

"Both," Slate says. It's the diplomatic answer. We both know the latter is more likely to be necessary. "Are you up for it?"

"I'll think about it. We don't exactly get along."

"I'm sure you can handle her." Hazel squeezes my wrist and I already know I'll agree. When she turns those big amber eyes on me, I'm a goner. No wonder Slate never says no to her.

"Thanks," Slate says before smoothly transitioning the conversation to training topics. My father and my Alphas trade updates on recent developments and I tune out their voices.

My mind replays the feel of emerald hair brushing my cheek, her soft curves under my hands. It was supposed to be a thrill, just a bad decision in the dark. But now she's coming here and staying in my home. Heat prickles over my skin at the thought.

Something is truly wrong with me if I'm excited by an enemy sleeping in the room across from mine. One with a soft mouth and soulful eyes who would very much like to hurt me.

I'm fucked.

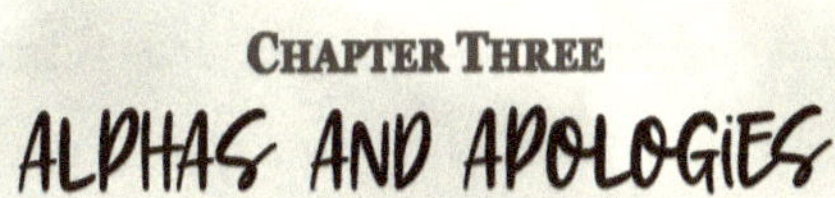

Orion drives me to the parking lot, and I'm left to retrieve my duffel from the trunk before he peels out. He doesn't even bother to say goodbye or make sure I'm well received. The disrespect ruffles me, but there's nothing I can do.

Ahead, only the edge of the training building and the front of two office buildings are visible. Their community is sprawling compared to Granite Ridge's

tight rows of houses and facilities.

A single guard watches me as he raises his phone to his ear. Not exactly the welcome I was expecting. Posture rigid, I fix my stare past him.

My brain whispers that I'm about to be ambushed and imprisoned. It's not logical, but last time I was here, our packs clashed and I was taken away with my hands zip-tied. It's not the kind of thing a girl forgets.

The training building has been refurbished. There are no signs of the destruction we wrought.

The image of Onyx leaning up against the training center's metal wall, making jokes while his hands cover the wound just below his ribs, blood seeping between his fingers, plays behind my eyes. He might be as crazy as I am.

"Ember!" Hazel hollers, striding toward me with Slate at her side. Her smile is welcoming as they reach me, and luckily she doesn't attempt to hug me.

"Alphas," I respond respectfully. My chin dips, though my eyes never leave their faces.

"I hope you have a nice stay with us. We are going to have you stay with our pack's Delta. His name is Fisher and his mate, Clove, is our pack's baker."

No faces come to mind at the names. "Sounds fine."

"Alright, let's head over there and get you settled." She leads us north, past the training building until I enter a meadow blooming with wildflowers. It's gorgeous.

Bracken Creek has been rebuilt. A new cafe sits in the same spot as the old diner we burned down.

Pack members wander around, going between their duties. A few curious gazes follow us, but I see none of the disgust I expect. Surely they know who I am. My family was responsible for invading their home and severely injuring many of their packmates. Eventually, their hatred will come out, and then I'll know exactly where I stand.

With an even breath, I straighten my spine and stride forward with all the faux confidence I can muster.

The Delta's cabin stands two stories with large windows. Split-log steps lead up to the double front door.

A tall woman opens it. A few silver hairs streak her reddish brown hair, pulled into a no-nonsense bun. Lines crease around her eyes as she smiles at me.

Her partner looms behind her. His strong jaw and straight nose feel familiar. Before I can place him, another figure steps into view. Dirty, dark blonde hair swept back into a small ponytail, deep blue eyes that make my stomach clench, a mouth that curves in a mocking smirk. Are you fucking kidding me?

"Ember, this is Clove and Fisher," Hazel says. "And you remember Onyx."

"Nice to meet you," I say, refusing to look at the man who had his hands all over me just days ago.

Clove's warm smile is genuine and I find myself drawn to her, but her mate's expression is colder, holding the suspicion I expect from this pack. Without wavering, I step forward. His judgment is fair and deserved and I won't let it get to me.

"We'll see you at dinner tonight." Slate says, stepping back and taking Hazel with him.

The Alpha female looks between her mate and me. "The pack eats together. Onyx can bring you down to the diner in time." Her shoulders rise and drop, her polite smile relaxing. "I think tonight includes some bread Clove baked?"

"Tonight is fried chicken, so Crickett requested buttermilk biscuits. I finished them about an hour ago," Onyx's mother explains. That explains the nutty flour scent Onyx has.

I draw in a slow breath before I realize I'm seeking out his smell. No way, not going to happen!

"Can't wait. See you all then," Hazel says, swinging her hand clasped in Slate's. He ducks his head in a goodbye nod.

"Here, Onyx, take her bag," Clove instructs.

Instinctively, I clutch the duffle tighter. "I can handle it."

"Just let me be a good host," Onyx argues. With a glare, I allow him to pry the bag from my grip. The brush of his fingers triggers a shiver and I tense my shoulders to stop it from traveling down my body.

Clove leads the way into their cabin. "We eat breakfast in the kitchen, and then bedrooms are down this hallway."

"You have a beautiful home," I say.

The kitchen is clad in blonde wood and pale marble countertops. Open shelving reveals jars of baking supplies. Tubs of chocolate chips and dried fruit. Powders I can't identify, ranging from dark brown to snowy white.

"This is our daughter's room. Briar is staying with friends for a few days, so you'll have privacy." Clove stops at a doorway. A smattering of pink stickers decorate the open door.

The Delta, Fisher, has disappeared, but Onyx still trails behind me. "Don't worry about anything you find in here. Bri's a weirdo."

"I won't snoop," I say, my hands clenching defensively.

"Thank you, dear," Clove says.

At the same moment, Onyx says, "Oh please, snoop away."

With a sigh, she ignores her son and continues, "Briar cleared out her top two drawers, so you can unpack into those if you'd like to."

It's so considerate, I stiffen. If the packs were reversed, I would be tossed into a basement and locked away for my entire stay. Instead, this pack has made an effort to make sure I am comfortable and welcome.

"It's only a few days," I say, my voice too high. "I can manage out of my suitcase. But tell her thank you for me."

"Of course. I'll leave you be. Onyx, keep an eye on the clock. It's only twenty minutes until dinner. I need to head back to help Crickett in the diner."

"Yes, ma'am," he says to her retreating back.

I blink at his respectful response. He's always been so rude or mocking to me, the gracious son routine startles me.

"You can just-" I start, holding my hand out for my duffle. Onyx sets it on the foot of the twin bed but doesn't back away.

"What do you want?" I ask, challenging him. His proximity flitters across my skin like electricity.

For a moment he is silent. Just when I doubt he will say anything, he murmurs, "Did you know?"

"Know what?"

He's lost his mind.

"That you were coming to stay here."

"Well, I obviously figured it out when they stuck me in a car and drove here," I say, obstinately refusing to answer his question.

"That's not what I meant. At the gathering. Did you already know about this visit?"

"I found out the next morning, dude."

He scoffs.

"What? Did you think I was setting up some sort of booty call before this *lovely* vacation?" I press, sarcasm heavy in my words.

"Well," he says with a shrug. His t-shirt rises with the motion to reveal the waistband of his gray sweatpants and a sliver of tan skin.

"You're the one who came on to me," I hiss.

"Are you serious? You grabbed me," he argues, his low voice a caress along my rib cage.

I've been here five minutes and I'm already fighting with this asshole.

"You're delusional," I shoot back.

"You practically pulled me on top of you," he continues, extending his vowels dramatically.

Forcing myself to step closer, I grab a handful of his t-shirt to demonstrate how absurd his claim is. "Yes, I grabbed you and suctioned your mouth on my neck. You had no choice." My biting words seem to weaken leaving my mouth. I'm distracted by the feel of his chest against my knuckles.

"That's pretty much how I remember it," he breathes. No longer angry, his words tease me, sending tingles from my chest to my toes.

"We were drunk," I say. Glaring into his endless eyes, I double down on my lie. "And you're a man-whore." I know it's a cheap shot and probably not true, but it's the only thing that comes to mind.

Onyx throws his head back and laughs, exposing his throat to me. Fuck, he's gorgeous. Unclenching my fingers, I step away, out of the haze of his citrus scent. Gulping down fresh air, I try desperately to clear my head.

The grin widening across his pretty face is a weapon in its own right. Most girls would swoon. I hold my ground, my teeth grinding together as I ignore the way my stomach flutters. Treacherous body.

"I'll see you in fifteen for dinner, Hummingbird," he says before closing the door behind him.

"You are such a dick," I whisper at the closed door. His low laughter echoes in the hallway, barely detectable even with my sensitive hearing.

Heart racketing in my ribs, I survey his sister's bedroom looking for a distraction from my heated skin.

Dried flowers splay in plastic frames along one wall. Christmas lights line the edge of the ceiling.

I would have given anything for a space like this. My sterile room back in Granite Ridge seems like a prison compared to this. Some sort of glossy green houseplant hangs from a hook by the window, the vines draping along the curtain rod.

The duvet is a creamy ruffled confection and I hesitate before sitting on it. The sheets and pillowcase are crisp and smell like detergent.

Curiosity wells up and I fold at the waist to peer under the bed. A low bin overflows with clothing, and beside it sit two soccer balls and a couple of wrinkled magazines. Reaching under, I extract a length of black ribbon, graying with age and dust. With two pinched fingers, I lay it across the dresser.

A stack of newer fashion magazines perches on the desk in the corner. These aren't teen versions, but luxury fashion, like Vogue and Harper's Bazaar. I've never read any of them. But from the creased corners, they look well-loved.

The desk holds gel pens, drawing pencils, and notepads. Under the school books, I find a sketchbook of fashion illustrations. Mostly dresses.

Who's heard of a wolf shifter who wants to design fashion? The thought makes me smile. It will be interesting to see what Onyx's little sister does as an adult.

A door past the desk opens to a tiny bathroom. Dainty white tiles cover the walls up to waist-height, where a wallpaper of teeny sea turtles rises to the ceiling.

Artwork above the toilet features a flamingo in a yoga pose with the words, "Let that Shit Go." Despite myself, I chuckle at it.

A girl could get spoiled in a room like this. Heading back to the bed, I tug open the gauzy curtains and take a deep breath. Maybe this won't be so bad. I can hide in here and avoid Onyx. Yes, that's a good plan.

ONYX

"Planning your escape already?" I ask, taking in Ember's tempting figure before the window. A patch of purple lupine flowers sway between tree trunks visible from Briar's room, their violet petals painted magenta from the fading sunset.

Ember spins, her eyes wide for a split second until her brain catches up and she settles into the wary glare I'm so familiar with.

"If I wanted to leave, I'd be gone already," Her hands go to her hips, eyes alight with a fire.

"I have no doubt." Playing polite host, I hold the door open. "Ready for dinner? You're about to be very impressed. I've been told we have the best food of any pack."

"Good to know," she says, breezing past me. Her sugary floral scent washes over me and I follow after her like a puppy begging for scraps. She's hostile and spiteful, but she smells amazing.

Inquisitive eyes jump to us when we enter the clearing. Most of the pack has gathered, though no one will eat until the Alphas do, per pack custom. We stroll toward my family, Ember doing her best to look unbothered, though I can feel anxiety rolling off of her.

Cedar and Briar stand beside our parents, Briar chattering away and Cedar listening stoically. He nods at me as we approach and Briar gives a little wave to Ember. "Hi, I'm Bri," she says.

"Ember." She smiles, but it looks strained. "I think I'm staying in your room?"

"Yeah, hope you don't mind it." Briar scrunches her nose in a cute half-smile.

"It's nice. Thanks."

If I didn't know better, I would think Ember was just another teenage friend of Briar's who is a little shy.

"Hey." A lanky boy with a tumble of reddish-brown hair joins us.

"This is Indie. He's Marigold's brother," Briar explains to Ember, her hand going to Indigo's arm. Ember looks between them and I wonder if she can see Marigold's features in him. They have the same upturned nose and wide, friendly mouth.

"You're Jasper's sister, right?" Indigo asks.

"Yeah. Nice to meet you," she says, though her tone is flat.

My eyebrow shoots up at the way Indigo's hand comes up to cover Briar's. Big brother instincts kick in and I'm tempted to pull them apart. Only a sharp look from Briar keeps me in my place.

The pack stirs as Hazel and Slate enter the meadow. With a light touch on Ember's elbow, I lead her toward them. She jerks her arm away but thankfully follows my lead.

"Careful, you were almost nice there to my sister," I say, leaning closer to her.

She scowls up at me. "Yeah, I'm typically nice to decent people."

"What does that say about me?" I ask, slapping my hand over my heart with a dramatic sigh.

"I would think that is obvious."

That's a dangerously flirty response from someone who despises me. My pulse thuds faster. Before I can come up with a reply, we're interrupted.

"Ember, I hope you're hungry. Fried chicken is my favorite thing Crickett makes," Hazel says, waving her forward. I trail behind, playing the obedient bodyguard.

Slate reaches out and grips my shoulder, leaning in to talk. "Doing okay?"

"Great," I say, only slightly sarcastic.

Plates clink as we start down the buffet. Ember pinches her lush bottom lip between her teeth as she places fried chicken and roasted vegetables on her plate. I suspect she's hyper aware of the packmates lining up behind us from the way her gaze flickers around nervously.

"See, I told you we have the best food," I murmur as we exit the line. Her dark eyes travel from her plate to me and a hint of a smile curves her mouth before she turns away. Puffing up my chest, I follow Hazel and Slate to their favorite table on the edge of the trees.

Ember hesitantly takes the seat on the end, and I slide onto the bench beside her. Hazel and Slate settle across from us. Even once Cedar sits on Slate's other side, the table feels empty without Jasper and Marigold.

"You guys eat together like this every day? It's like some sort of celebration," Ember says with a curious tilt of her head.

Slate's brows furrow as he looks up at her. "Yes, of course. What does Granite Ridge do?"

"Um," Ember flounders, "It's not a social thing like this."

Hazel grimaces. "Think more prison cafeteria and less restaurant."

"That sounds appealing," I say dryly, not missing how Ember's mouth pinches.

"Ember, how are you liking our pack so far?" Slate asks.

She pauses, turning her fork over in her hand thoughtfully. "I've only seen this area and your Delta's house. But it's nice, I guess."

"Pretty different from Granite Ridge, right?" Hazel asks with a gentle smile.

Ember moves in her seat, her eyes on her plate. "The two packs are very different," she finally agrees.

"I mean, I didn't get to see that much of Granite Ridge either. I spent half my time there locked in a basement," Hazel says with a light laugh.

Slate's jaw clenches. Tension pours through our pack bond.

With a determined frown, Ember meet's Hazel's gaze. "You had dinner with the Alphas, saw most of our facilities, and even got to see the woods between our two territories."

"True," Hazel says, the friendly curve of her mouth looking forced. She expertly deflects the conversation. "So how have things been for your pack in the last year?"

We've gotten reports of how unstable the pack is, which added to Jasper's desire to investigate. Surely, Ember knows about those concerns, but she doesn't choose to be honest.

"We're fine. Rebuilding, just like you guys have done." She nods toward the diner with its fresh metal trim gleaming.

"We only had to reconstruct a building. You lost several of your packmates during the attack," Cedar interjects.

Her dark eyes narrow at my twin, her tone going ice cold. "Well, someone decided to fight with guns instead of tranqs and teeth like civilized packs do."

It seems my little hummingbird has reached the end of her patience. The air feels heavy between us, like everyone is waiting for a bomb to explode.

"Ember," Slate says slowly, "We didn't have much choice in the circumstances."

"How many wolves did you lose?" she snaps without missing a beat.

"We didn't start the fight." Slate is trying to be objective, but he lacks his mate's people skills. A tick in his jaw gives away how infuriated he really is.

"Neither did I, *big brother*," she says, tossing her fork down and stepping over the bench. Hands balled into fists, she stalks away.

"Well, that went well," Hazel growls at her mate. "You're certainly fighting like siblings already."

Slate scowls at Ember's retreating back.

Scrambling up, I'm several steps away from the table before I look back and gesture at our plates. "Can you?"

"I got it," Cedar cuts in. "Go."

"Thanks," I call over my shoulder, jogging to catch up with Ember. She strides into the trees, glossy hair whipping behind her as she shakes her head angrily.

"I don't need a fucking babysitter."

"Just making sure you don't go back and torch my home."

Before I can finish my joke, she's on me. Her index

finger jabs my chest, the pointed black nail pricking my skin through my shirt. "I didn't ask for any of this. I didn't make our packs enemies, I didn't plan to take over your land, and I definitely didn't want to come here."

"I know."

My response must startle her, because she freezes, her eyes still on my chest.

"I don't think it means we have to be enemies just because our packs used to be," I say, offering a tentative peace.

Achingly slow, her hazel eyes trace up my neck, snagging on my mouth and finally reaching my eyes. "But doesn't it?"

"No."

"Everyone hates me. I can feel it. It doesn't matter. I don't need to make a bunch of friends here."

Considering how welcoming we've been, it irks me to hear that.

"I'm not talking about everyone else. I mean you and me."

A harsh laugh breaks out of her throat. "You've made your opinion of me very clear."

"Oh, really?" I say, waiting for her to clarify.

What opinion could that be? And was it before or after I kissed her and pinned her up against a building?

Her hand withdraws, her fingers threading together as she twists her hands absently. "Look, I don't want to spend this whole time being judged or blamed for everything my pack has done, or what I did under orders. I'd like it if we just started over."

"Fine by me. No judging or blaming. I can be civil if you can."

She studies me and I suddenly feel very exposed. Tugging at my neckline, I let out a slow exhale, trying to stay calm under her scrutiny.

"I can be civil," she says slowly, testing each word.

"Alright then, starting fresh as allies," I say, "So do you want to go back to dinner?"

Ember lets out a breathy laugh. "I really don't. But you should go back."

"That's okay. I'm good."

Her arms fold across her, hands gripping her upper arms. "Look, I'm sorry. I didn't mean to throw a tantrum. Slate just got to me."

My mouth falls open. Is she actually apologizing? There's a vulnerability in her eyes when she glances up at me shyly. This is a new side to her, a softness.

Hazel's scent reaches us seconds before she appears through the trees.

"Ember," she calls, her hurried steps closing the distance between us. "Are you okay? I'm so sorry. That was not how that conversation should have gone."

"You don't need to apologize for him," Ember says, her shoulders rising defensively.

"Slate didn't mean it like that. You guys really need to have a long talk and sort this out."

Ember wavers, clearly wanting to decline but respecting Hazel's rank.

"Look, we were thinking about a campfire tonight. I'd really like it if you joined us. It'll be a good time to hang out all together." Hazel tilts her head, brows bunched together in concern.

Ember's expression hardens. "No, thank you."

"I'd like to get to know you better, and I promise it'll be fun. There will be s'mores! Please come?"

She could order Ember to attend and she'd be hard pressed to disobey, but instead, she's asking kindly.

Ember's eyebrows rise. "Fine. Where do I go?"

"Everyone else is still finishing dinner, but then we'll head to Onyx's, actually. The twins have a great fire pit out back."

"Alright," she says begrudgingly.

"Awesome, I'll see you in a bit. Are you hungry? I can grab you more dinner," Hazel offers. I don't miss how Ember tenses, blinking in surprise.

"No, I'm good," she says, her tone softening.

With a hesitant smile and a nod, Hazel jogs back toward the clearing. She's broken through a layer of Ember's armor. Bit by bit, Ember is opening up, and I'm fascinated by the glimpses of what's under all of her anger.

FLAMING MARSHMALLOWS

Ember

was hoping the day was over and I could hide away from everyone, but instead, I'm stuck sitting around a campfire staring at my half-brother and his mate, and my one-time-makeout-partner enemy-turned-ally and his less personable twin. Not my idea of a fun evening, despite Hazel's promises.

She pops open the box of graham crackers in her lap and begins to distribute them in pairs. A square of dark

chocolate joins the crackers, and then I'm being handed a wire rod with the biggest marshmallow I've ever seen stuck onto the end.

No one bothers to explain so I copy Onyx and thrust my marshmallow into the fire.

"So what do you think Jasper and Marigold are doing over with your mom?" Hazel asks. She rotates her marshmallow over the flames and I mimic the movement. The underside has turned a golden color on the edges.

"Who knows? His old house was given to someone else, so they're probably staying in the basement you enjoyed so much," I say. There's an edge to my words, but I can't seem to control myself. Anger and embarrassment are still fresh from our confrontation at dinner.

Shrugging, I continue, "So probably waiting around for Sienna to meet with them. And trying to not get beat up by the wolves who hate Jasper's guts for leaving."

Onyx's forehead falls into his open palm, like he's given up on the conversation. His hair sweeps over his hand and cheeks, shielding him from my stupidity.

"Hopefully it's going better than that," Hazel says. There's a coldness to her tone that I want to flinch away from, but I keep my shoulders back and my chin raised.

"We'll get a report soon enough," Slate reassures her. "I'm sure it's going fine."

Slate removes his marshmallow from the flames

and pinches it between two graham crackers, sliding the stick out with a smooth movement. The marshmallow oozes out the side and he has to rotate it and take a bite to keep from making a mess.

Ah, so that's a s'more - a marshmallow sandwich. It's got to be overly sweet. I've only had marshmallows a handful of times in my life and never these giant ones. I stare as he takes another bite and chocolate peeks between the layers.

"Ember," Onyx says sharply, breaking my concentration.

"What?" I say, my attention snagging on a ball of flames at the end of the stick I'm holding. My marshmallow is on fire. Crap!

"What do I do?" I yelp, all dignity forgotten.

"Blow on it," Hazel coaches. Her words aren't absorbed. Waving my metal stick wildly, I attempt to extinguish the flaming marshmallow with zero success. The flames trail behind it like a burning ribbon.

"Woah, watch it," Onyx warns. He crouches beside me, grasping my wrist in one hand while the other extracts the marshmallow from my grip. His skin is hot against mine and he envelops my entire wrist.

My mind replays a flash of memory. His hand effortlessly holding both of my wrists above my head. My back against the cold, rough wall. His stubble against my throat. Sharp teeth against skin.

With a small shake, I clear my head in time to see Onyx bring the flaming confection toward his face. His lips part and he blows out the flames, leaving a blackened blob.

"Geez, Ember, were you trying to burn the shit out of it?" he murmurs. Maybe it's his deep voice, or the feel of his hand still holding my wrist, but my body is suddenly on alert. My skin feels overly sensitive as his body heat rolls across me. Even under the charred marshmallow and woodsmoke, I can smell his citrus and bakery scent.

"Maybe that's how I like my marshmallows," I say lamely.

With his lips quirked into a half-smile, he grabs my graham crackers and chocolate stack and assembles my s'more. The blackened outer layer cracks and the melted interior oozes through.

"Black like your soul," he teases, offering me the dessert I ruined.

My nose wrinkles as I scowl at him. "I've never cooked a marshmallow like this before," I admit quietly. Hazel and Slate are distracted with their own private murmurings, giving me a false sense of privacy.

"Don't tell me you make s'mores in the fucking microwave," Onyx quips.

"No microwave for me," I say, hoping he'll drop it. A beat of silence hangs between us, his navy eyes unwavering. A choking sensation tightens my throat as he raises a single eyebrow and smirks.

"You've never had s'mores before, have you?" Onyx finally asks.

"Don't be an idiot," I growl, my cheeks flushing under his stare.

Hands raised to pacify me, he backs away until he settles beside his brother.

Cedar still won't look at me, but I have a feeling he clinically analyzed my entire interaction with Onyx. More judgment. Fucking fantastic.

The burned s'mores sits in my palm. I ignore it, instead watching Hazel devour hers like it's a transcendental experience. Slate wipes a smudge of chocolate from her lip and licks it off his thumb. It would be cute with anyone else, but seeing my half-brother do that is gross.

"Perfect," Onyx says, lifting his own marshmallow from the flames. It's smoldering. His full mouth curves as he blows out the flames and assembles a s'more that rivals my own.

I can't help my wince as he lifts the s'more to his lips and takes a bite. His eyes close and he lets out a soft moan. When his eyes spring open, they connect with mine. "I like mine burned too," he says. I would assume he's mocking me, but he proceeds to eat the entire thing.

Frowning down at the cooling s'more in my hand, I

weigh how embarrassing it would be to try it and then realize he was trying to trick me. But no one else watches either of us. With a sigh, I raise it to my mouth and take a small bite.

The charred flavor gives way to the sugary marshmallow. Bitter dark chocolate cuts the sweetness, tempered by the nutty graham cracker. It's divine.

I try to slow my bites to regain some of my dignity, but the dessert is delicious and I can't help but eat every crumb and then lick the sticky marshmallow off my fingers.

Onyx stares at the flames, but his smirk says, *I told you so.*

Hazel lets out a contented hum and snaps off a piece of chocolate to eat on its own. "That's better. I've needed a sugar fix all day."

"Was patrol really that bad?" Onyx teases.

Her amber eyes narrow. "Vale is still obsessed over his Raven girl. I swear, I've never heard the kid say so many words in the whole time I've known him as he did today."

Slate chuckles, his hands skimming down Hazel's thighs.

"Is he seeing her again?" Cedar asks.

"I guess she doesn't have a phone, so he wants to go there and make a big romantic gesture." Her head lolls back against Slate's shoulder. "I need Marigold to come back here and help. I don't know what to do with these teenagers."

"You should have seen Indigo and Briar tonight," Onyx mutters.

"Will you accept a new pack member or have him leave?" I ask, attempting to contribute to the conversation.

"I suppose that's up to them," Slate answers.

"Will Alpha Nyx cooperate in either instance?" My voice quiets.

"She should," Hazel answers patiently. "She's been opening up over the last year. She's even meeting with the Ironcrest Pack soon."

My eyes widen. Surely she misspoke. The Ironcrest Pack and the Raven Pack have been enemies for years.

"Are we okay with this information getting back to Granite Ridge?" Onyx asked softly, tipping his head in my direction.

My teeth click together, my jaw tight. So much for a friendly hangout. Anger rising in my chest, I wait for Hazel or Slate to reprimand him. Not that I expect anyone to defend me, but how dare he question them?

Spots dance in my vision from staring into the flames. I can't take any more teasing from Onyx, or worse, friendly sympathy. My teeth sink into the inside of my lower lip, a poor attempt to contain the chaotic energy battering around in my head.

"It's fine," Hazel says, her tone gentle.

"I suspect they already know. It's not being kept quiet," Slate explains. His calm energy starts to relax me, and I buck against the false sense of security.

Seemingly accepting his Alpha's answer, Onyx sits back. Beside him, Cedar leans forward with his forearms across his knees. "So Nyx is actually willing to meet with them?"

"Yep!" Hazel says.

"I guess she realized hiding in her den is no longer a viable option," I mutter before I can think better of opening my mouth again.

Hazel's head bobs. "Exactly!" Her agreement surprises me, and my lips part silently. "I think the power dynamic is different now with mediation and all the groveling Zephyr has done over the last year."

"Really? Like what?" I ask, feeling foolish for not knowing what was happening with our neighboring packs. It'll be something to correct as soon as I get home.

Slate answers, "He paid to repair all the damage from the fight."

Hazel giggles. "Zephyr seems quite taken with her, actually. He keeps sending gifts and she avoids him. This meeting is a big step for her."

"It'll be interesting to hear what they agree on," Slate says.

"Have you been meeting with Nyx yourself?" I ask.

Slate brushes Hazel's hair over her shoulder, answering without taking his eyes off his mate. "We've had a few calls. Not a lot. Ironcrest is always eager to talk, but both Raven Pack and Granite Ridge are still resistant to meeting regularly."

Hazel sighs. "I wish Sienna would agree to meet with us again, but having Jasper visit is a good step forward."

"So why the exchange? Do you really need me as a hostage to ensure his safe return?"

I wish I could suck the words back into my throat. Four sets of eyes regard me with varying emotions, from surprise to disdain.

"It's not about that," Hazel ventures. "We want to build relationships both ways, and besides, you've never spent time with your half-brother." Her hand tightens over Slate's.

"Right." As if Slate wanted to get to know me. With some effort, I keep sarcasm out of my voice.

"Speaking of," Hazel continues, "We'd really like to have you over for dinner. Just you and us, if that sounds good."

"When?"

"Tomorrow night. I'll make enchiladas."

"Okay." I've never had enchiladas either and I'm not even sure what they are. But considering how delectable dinner was tonight, I'm optimistic they will be delicious too.

"Want me to join you?" Onyx asks. Does he really think I need a guard to eat dinner with the Alphas, one of whom is my half-brother?

Hazel cocks her head, frowning at Onyx. "That's okay. Have some down time."

With a shrug, Onyx lifts another burned marshmallow to his mouth and takes a bite. I couldn't pull my gaze away from his mouth if I wanted to as he licks the sugar off his lips.

Hazel slips off Slate's lap and they rise. "We're calling it a night. See you guys tomorrow."

I return her little wave. Hand in hand, they disappear into the shadows.

"Alright, the lovebirds are off to their nest," Onyx jokes. "Anyone want more s'mores?"

"Um, no thank you," I say, voice rough. I can't meet his eyes after the way I drooled over him eating a marshmallow. "I think I'm ready to get some rest."

"Sure, totally."

The twins make quick work of extinguishing the fire and packing away the graham crackers and marshmallows. I notice the chocolate has disappeared entirely.

Onyx shadows me as I trail across the back patio and down the hall to Briar's room. Instead of going to his own door, he follows me to mine. I spin to face him.

"Can I help you?" I snap.

He leans against the door frame, invading my personal space. In place of the sass I expect, his expression is concerned. "Are you okay?"

"Fine. I mean, your brother is rude, but that doesn't bother me."

His chin dips, his night sky irises searching my face. "He's just like that. He isn't trying to be an asshole. He's just very honest and straightforward."

"Don't bother. You don't need to stick up for me. I can handle myself." My hands rest on the door frame, anchoring myself.

"You know, if you just talked to him, you guys would get along just fine."

"I seriously doubt that."

"But you and I get along just fine and he's much nicer than I am, I promise." He grins at my hesitation. "See? We aren't so bad."

"I didn't say you were bad. I said you were a dick."

"Not disagreeing," he says, that infuriating smirk back.

My pulse flutters in my skin, every sensation heightened as my body reacts to his nearness. Damn it!

Scowling at him, I say, "And you called me a bitch."

"I apologized."

"You said Marigold was making you apologize. You didn't actually do it. That doesn't count."

"What about the rest of what I did to you? Did that count as an apology?"

"Onyx," I warn. My thoughts have gone fuzzy.

"I like how you say my name," he purrs.

I know it's not genuine, but his silky words still affect me. Scoffing, I grip the doorknob at the small of my back and twist. Without breaking eye contact, I step back into his sister's room.

"Good night, Onyx." His tormenting grin is the last thing I see before I close the door between us.

My skin is tingly and hot. Does he enjoy making me uncomfortable? Though from what I can tell, he still hasn't told a soul about our encounter at the party.

Heart racing, I trade my clothes for a nightshirt and slip into the bed. The cool pillowcase soothes my heated cheeks. Eyes squeezed shut, I try to think of anything except the wolf sleeping across the hall.

CHAPTER FIVE

LOOKING A LITTLE STABBY

ONYX

Feeling good, honey?" Mom asks, sliding a plate of banana French toast across the table toward me.

"Yeah." I take a deep breath. The soft floral scent of Ember lingers in the kitchen and the image of her tongue swiping her fingertips as she licks marshmallow from her skin flashes through my head. In one day, she's thoroughly under my skin.

I thought she was a dangerous flirtation, just a thrill. But the vulnerability she showed last night, all my protective instincts rose up, demanding that I care for her. Sometimes the wolf part of me can be such a simp.

With a rough sigh, I shove my fingers through my tangled hair. I need to pull myself together. She's not mine to protect. In fact, I'm quite sure she'd be furious if she knew what was going on inside my head.

"Good morning, Ember," my mother chimes, causing me to startle.

The girl stands on the edge of the hallway, the arch framing her curves. With emerald waves streaming down her back, face scrubbed clean of makeup, and oversized sweatshirt draping over one shoulder, she looks like a goddess.

"Good morning, Clove," she responds politely. Hips swaying, she drops into a chair as far away from me as possible. Could I move seats? No, that would be weird.

"French toast? I've got bananas and strawberries."

"Banana sounds good, thanks."

My mother catches my eye, a pleased curve to her mouth as she hands our guest a plate loaded with sliced bananas over brown sugar custard brioche.

We eat in silence, and my stomach clenches each time I catch her peeking at me through her lashes.

Finally, she breaks the silence. "So what's on the agenda today?"

Sipping my coffee, I regard her, enjoying the dimple in her cheek as she purses her lips impatiently.

"No plan."

Her lips pout as she frowns. In that moment, she looks so much like Slate, I have to cover my grin by taking another drink.

"I can't just sit here all day staring at you," she says with a scowl.

"Sounds like a fantastic day to me."

She huffs and slouches back. "You can't be serious."

"Well, what would you like to do?" I can feel my mother's eyes on us.

"I don't know, Onyx," she says with a roll of her eyes. "But I've gotta do something." She takes one look at my smirk. "Shut up."

"I wasn't saying anything."

Her cutting glare could have murdered me.

"Look, it's Saturday and normally we train on Saturdays. Want to head to the training building and check things out?" Hopefully my dad won't mind a guest.

"Yeah, that sounds interesting, actually."

We finish eating and my mother adamantly rejects her offer to wash dishes. It's another instance where Ember seems entirely normal, even kind, and my heart does a flip that I know will only end badly.

Ten minutes later she reappears in her version of

training clothes. I'm used to women wearing loose t-shirts and sweats or maybe leggings to train. She wears a skin-tight black tank top and bike shorts that show a stripe of midriff.

Peeling my eyes off her skin, I take a slow breath. This would be easier if Ember wasn't so appealing. If she was just mean, I could ignore her, but she's complicated and every time she shows a different side, my defenses start to crumble.

"Ready?" I ask. That dimple reappears in her cheek as she nods.

As we cross the meadow, the three feet between us feels like a chasm, but she walks with her chin thrust upward and her shoulders back. She's trying her best to not look nervous and I respect that.

But there's no reason for her to be anxious. No one here would harm her. Mistrust her, give her suspicious looks, maybe, but no one would lay a hand on her. She's under Slate and Hazel's protection as their guest, not to mention our pack is generally peaceful - especially compared to the brutal way her pack operates.

She hesitates at the door to the training building. Last time she was here, we were battling and she was dragged out with her hands zip tied. Jaw set, she pushes the door open.

My father looks up. Most of the teenage wolves in our pack circle around him, including my sister. Indigo straightens beside her, puffing his chest out. With a wave of his hand, my father dismisses the students.

"Dad, we were hoping to join training." I keep my eyes on the ground in a sign of respect. As I walk closer, I'm pleased to see Ember falls a half-step behind me, allowing me to take the lead.

"I don't think that's entirely appropriate. Do you?" he says, clearing his throat.

"Sir, I can't just sit alone in a room the whole time I'm here," Ember argues, "Let me test myself. I'd like to see how I stack up against your wolves."

My father pauses, and I look up to see him studying Ember. She is stone, unwavering under his judicious stare.

"Alright, but no weapons. The Alphas led patrol out a few minutes ago, so you'll have the place to yourself. But I'll be out back with the pups."

"Thank you Dad," I say, shoulders dropping in relief.

"Can I use a small dagger or maybe a staff?"

Has she lost her mind? I didn't expect my dad to allow her to participate at all, and now she's asking to be armed?

"Hand to hand or go back to the cabin," my father says over his shoulder. With a few motions, he ushers Briar and her friends out of the building.

"Yes, sir," Ember grumbles to his back.

At the door, he twists and fixes me with a hard look. "Onyx, I'm expecting you to enforce my rules. I'll be right outside if there is any trouble."

"Not a problem." I hope it's true. Ember scowls as he props the door open, and I suddenly wish that all of our weapons were behind locked doors. At least the firearms are inaccessible. She looks ready to draw blood after what my father said.

Her voice drops as she draws closer to me. "Do we really have to obey him? He seems easy going."

"Don't let him hear you say that. He's been our pack trainer for twenty years and I can promise he isn't remotely easy going," I caution her.

Ember shrugs, hands flattening along her hips. "My pack's Delta is always yelling and hitting anyone who doesn't obey fast enough. Your dad isn't like that. I can't see him hurting anyone."

"You know there's other ways to gain respect other than violence."

"Ineffective ways."

"I don't think you've had very good trainers."

"Come fight me and find out."

"Do you have any weapons on your person?"

"No." The words are light, flippant. Somehow, they ring untrue.

Eyeing her figure, I can't see where she would have tucked a knife or other weapon, but after several battles and serious injuries, I know to trust my instincts. "Are you lying?"

Her face brightens into a true smile, although it's more a devious grin than something joyful. I'm still shocked by the difference. She's stunning. "Come find out."

It takes all my self-control to not launch myself at her. But the possibility of injury lingers in the back of my mind. "Ember, I don't want to get stabbed again. You're looking a little stabby right now."

That smile reappears, like a punch in the gut. It'll be impossible to fight her when I'm distracted by it. "Look, I promise I won't stab you."

I hold out my hand, the littlest finger extended in a childhood ritual.

"Really? A pinkie promise?" she asks, but she takes my finger with her own. With a light shake, we seal the vow.

The second my hand leaves hers, she attacks. Considering the girl comes up to my collarbone, she is shockingly aggressive.

Her hands grab my shoulder, jerking me forward while her knee comes up to hit the inside of my thigh. Too close to my balls for comfort. Between the pain and the instinct to curl up protectively, my body goes down hard. She shoves me to the floor at her feet, and I roll over to look up at her smug smile with that enticing dimple.

Struggling to draw in breath, I push myself into a seated position. "Damn, I did not expect that."

Ember gives a little shrug and offers her hand. The need for revenge pulses through me. Instead of allowing her to help me up, I yank her down, hooking my foot behind her ankle and drawing my knees up to pull her feet out from under her as she tries to compensate for the pull of my grip.

With a snarl, she lands on her ass, hands catching her before she falls entirely flat. "Dick," she growls.

"You didn't fight fair. Why should I?"

"How was that unfair?"

We sit facing each other, our glares more playful than malevolent. After a few deep breaths, I push up to my feet and offer my own hand. She swats it away and rises gracefully.

"You really think you can handle me?" she taunts, beginning to circle me. My feet move without thought. I may not have the discipline or skill that comes from daily effort, but I was raised by the pack's Delta, and the basics are built into my blood. When we were kids, I could best Slate easily, though he outpaced me somewhere around age twelve. In the last year, I've taken my training seriously now that I hold a pack ranking.

Ember darts in, swinging with a closed fist. My arms are longer than hers and I hold her back with a hand to her chest, right below her neck. Her wide eyes blink at me for a second, and I use the pause to slide my hand up to her throat with a soft grip.

Her mouth opens, eyes dilated. Her expression is distracting, and I run my thumb along her skin. In that instant, Ember leans back and kicks forward, the bottom of her foot connecting with my stomach. Stumbling back, I struggle to find my footing. She doesn't wait for me to recover.

Teeth bared, she leaps at me. Twirling out of my grasp, she slams a fist into my ribs. Instead of letting her get enough distance for another hard strike, I grab her waist and drop to the mat.

On the ground, I use my size to pin her, carefully restraining her wrists. She growls up at me. "That would never work in a real fight."

"Maybe," I reply. "What's this?"

Gingerly, I slide a small knife from her waistband.

"That's just for emergencies," she snaps. "Give it back!"

My brows pinch at the fear in her voice. "Ember, you don't need it here."

"I don't trust anyone here. Don't you dare," she snarls.

My grip on her weapon tightens. "After all this time we've spent together, you don't trust me?" I mean it as a joke, but some part of me is actually hurt.

"Why would I?" she spits.

"You said you didn't have a weapon."

"I told you to find out."

"Well, I did. And I think I'll hold on to this for now. You can have it back afterward. I wouldn't want you to slip and hurt yourself. Or me." Her eyes blaze as I set it to the side of the mat. Considering how angry she looks, it's not safe to let her keep it. I like my body without knives embedded in it, thank you very much.

Ember rolls to get her feet under her and I move with her to stay close, my head dipped toward her's. The second we are further apart, she will punch me in the face. I can sense that truth with every bit of my intuition. The result is that we stand chest to chest, her dark hazel eyes looking up at me in surprise.

"Is this how training is done in Granite Ridge?" I ask, casually drifting to the side so we can begin to circle one another.

She closes her teeth over her bottom lip and I don't expect an answer. Finally, she says, "Not really, we do more drills, and then when we spar, it's usually a competition."

"Do you guys do that a lot?"

"Yeah." Her tone is flat and cold.

"Are there prizes?" I ask with a forced grin.

"Usually whoever does well gets dinner, and those that do poorly get the shit beat out of them."

"Are you serious?" I ask, my feet halting.

Without warning, she surges forward. My shock costs me a fraction of a second, but it's enough. Throwing my weight onto my back foot, I grab her arms so I can push her aside, but I can't get a clean hold on her. We go down in a tangle of arms and legs.

Her nails dig into my forearm and she pins me with a defiant sneer. I could knock her off easily. She doesn't have the weight to hold me down. But the look of triumph in her eyes gives me pause.

It's not until I feel metal against my ribs, where my shirt has pulled up, that I realize what she's doing.

"Ember, don't." My words are more plea than warning.

Bold hazel eyes stare back and her hand trails up until she grips her knife tight to her breast. "Onyx, just let me have this. I never go without it. It's for emergencies and I promise not to use it unless my life is in danger."

Relief courses through me. She isn't about to disembowel me.

"I think we're done training." I try to keep my tone neutral, but disappointment tinges each word.

She pushes back as I sit up until she's hovering over my lap awkwardly. Already, her knife is tucked away, and she gathers her hair into a twist at the nape of her neck. I find the line of her jaw and the curve of her mouth fascinating as she glances away from me.

"So what about wolves who aren't ranked? In your pack's competitions," I ask, trying to bring back our conversation.

Ember shrugs and sits back on her heels. "Everyone holds a rank in Granite Ridge. If they can't fight, they don't have a place with us."

That doesn't make any sense. How does their pack operate? "What about seniors?"

"We don't really have any," she says, cocking her head at me, as if she's unsure why I'm questioning her.

"What about kids? What age do they have to start training?"

"Um, twelve-ish? I think I started at ten, actually. But we don't have a lot of kids. We occasionally take in strays, so there are a few teenagers."

"Your pack isn't exactly normal. You know that, right?" I blurt without thinking. Mentally kicking myself, I shove my hand through my hair and brush it away from my forehead.

"So I've been told." There's that lip curl again. I'm not sure if she's showing disgust at her own pack or defensiveness at my judgment.

"Do you ever want something different?" I ask, unsure of what I'm trying to gain in this conversation.

"Why is *this* considered normal?" She questions me, opening her hands in a sweeping gesture. "Just because you grew up with it?"

"Well, no," I argue.

With a haughty laugh, she tucks a leg under her and rises. Anger shines in her eyes and the tightness around her mouth. "It's amazing you guys ever stood up to us."

"Excuse me?"

Her eyes rove down my body as I stand to meet her. "Your pack is weak."

Hot anger floods my blood, drowning out the empathy I had for her. My tone is harsh and I can't help it. "We aren't weak. And we don't beat each other half to death and then starve our packmates as punishment."

"That's not how it goes," she says, her arms crossing. A beautiful flush rises up her neck.

"Tell me I'm wrong. You're always expecting a fight. Why is that?" I push forward, demanding an answer with my direct gaze.

"Of course I am," she hisses.

"Why?" I won't let this go. I need to know what drives her.

"Because I have to fight for everything I have. It makes me stronger." Her pose is regal, chin up, shoulders back.

"You shouldn't have to," I argue.

A flash of teeth almost pushes me back a step, but I hold my ground. The green glow to her eyes is threaded through with gold.

It wouldn't surprise me if my own eyes were that

cool blue they turn when I'm upset or turned on.

"Not all of us have a fairytale childhood."

My hands go to her upper arms, keeping her from turning away from me. She doesn't seem to notice, her tongue darting out to wet her lips.

"My pack saw me as a punching bag. If I wasn't tough, I'd be dead." The cold resignation in her words makes my heart pound. No wonder she's so defensive.

Instinctively, I pull her into my chest. She stiffens and with a dry cough, she asks, "So, are we about to fight or fuck?"

My laugh is raw. "No, I'm comforting you."

"Well, it's weird," she protests while settling against me. I could rest my chin on the top of her head if I wanted to. She fits against me perfectly.

"Do you want me to stop?" I ask.

"In a minute," she murmurs. Slowly, her muscles relax.

Taking in a deep lungful of air, I lose myself in her scent. It's a walk in the meadow in the moments before it begins to storm. Electric, sweet, and heady.

The door bangs open and Ember leaps back, as if we were never touching.

Patrol pours in, chatting while they head for their lockers. Hawthorne nods at me in greeting, his eyebrows rising as he takes in Ember's flushed skin. Thankfully, he leaves us alone.

With a sigh, I uncap a water bottle and offer it to Ember. She hesitates before taking it, and doesn't drink until I've had half of the second bottle.

"I think I'm ready for a shower," she says, making a face, "You got your sweat on me."

The distance between us shrinks as we walk northward toward my home, our arms almost brushing.

The house is quiet. Before we go into our separate rooms, Ember pauses. "Look, I shouldn't have told you any of that about my pack. I was being kinda emotional and it wasn't very accurate."

The lie stings.

"Really? It seemed true when you said it. And I like hearing about your life," I say.

Her eyes narrow. "Don't worry. It won't happen again."

"Ember," I say, hoping to stop her from disappearing. It doesn't work.

She begins to close the bedroom door between us, but before it clicks shut, she says, "Just forget it, Onyx."

Chapter Six

SAUCY BURRITOS & HALF BROTHERS

Ember

i'm grateful to be having a private dinner tonight, even if it's with my half-brother who hates me. The suspicious stares of Onyx's packmates follows me all afternoon, making me sick to my stomach. It was a relief to head northeast toward Hazel and

Slate's cabin. Onyx walks with me, his careful glances monitoring my emotional state. Since when is he part-babysitter and part-therapist? I want to push him away, but the attentive concern is something I've never had before and it's oddly comforting. Ever since he held me after our fight, he's been quiet.

Onyx raps his knuckles on their door. A soft squeal and garbled voices inside tells me Hazel is way too excited about our dinner.

The door swings open with a soft creak. "Hi, Ember," Slate says. "Thanks, Onyx. See you later."

My guard hesitates, his eyes bouncing between me and my half-brother. "Bye," I say, hoping he gets the hint and leaves. All of these moments between us are getting confusing and muddying up my thoughts. I'm looking forward to clearing my head, even if it means spending time with a sibling who hates me.

Jaw clenched, Onyx finally turns away and steps off the porch.

"Thanks for coming," Slate says, stiff and polite.

My arms cross defensively. I don't want to be here and I hate pleasantries. It would be better if he would air his grievances and we could deal with it. Although that might lead to me being chased out of their territory. Not the worst thing that could happen.

"Ember, do you want some soda?" Hazel calls. Slate holds the door open as I step into their home. The cabin feels old with warm wood trim running along the floor and the ceiling. The front door leads into a cozy living room with a set of leather armchairs and matching sofa. Further in, Hazel buzzes around a small kitchen. The shiny appliances stand out against aged, worn cabinets. The cabin is decidedly a mix of vintage and masculine design styles. Framed sketches dot the walls throughout.

"I'm good with whatever," I answer, pausing in front of a drawing of a waterfall. The pencil is blended until the gradients are smooth, making the flow of the water in the foreground ethereal. It could pass for a photograph but somehow it portrays more emotion than a still photo ever could.

Hazel appears at my side, holding a chilled soda can in a koozie printed with a wolf wearing sunglasses. It's the most ridiculous thing I've ever seen.

"Slate is an amazing artist. It seems to run in the family." Her smile is sweet and genuine, and it feels unwarranted. I'm not deserving of her kindness, of anyone's kindness, least of all the girl I saw as an interloper needing to be disposed of when we first met.

Shrugging, I look back at the artwork. "Yeah, it's nice."

She watches me, waiting for me to volunteer personal information, but I have nothing to say to her. Her human upbringing is obvious at this moment.

"Ember, would you like to see the rest of the cabin?" Slate asks. Hazel sends him a look of gratitude as she heads back to the kitchen to finish some sort of salad.

Slate shows me the office through a door beside the kitchen. The room is set up with a drawing table and a computer desk. Tattoo equipment covers two shelves above the desk.

"What's with the tattoo gun?" The question slips out of me before I can reign it in. Slate's arms are covered in tattoos, down to his wrists, so clearly he likes them.

His mouth curves into the first real smile I've seen. It feels familiar, and I realize he has the same smile as Jasper. My heart tugs at me, reminding me that I miss my idiot brother. I'd trade Slate in for Jasper if I could.

"I did a tattoo apprenticeship a few years ago. I'll tattoo you if you want, some day." Slate offers. The stern Alpha persona is gone and he's putting out a calming charismatic energy. I feel drawn to him and I don't like it.

"No thanks," I say cooly, but then curiosity gets the better of me. "Did you do Onyx's tattoos?"

"Yeah," he answers. "I've done everyone's tattoos. Jasper even got his first one a few months ago.

"What?" My brother let Slate tattoo him? It feels a bit like a betrayal. Another sign that Jasper has fully integrated into this pack and left me behind.

Slate heads back to the door. "Yeah, Marigold's wolf

with sunflowers. Ask him to show you when he gets back."

"Maybe."

Upstairs holds only their bedroom, with a wide king bed covered in an old quilt, and a line of bookshelves on the wall opposite the windows. I would guess Hazel is the reader, since Slate seems to be the artist out of the two of them.

"Dinner's ready!"

Back down the staircase, Hazel sets a casserole dish with a vibrant red sauce on the round table. I leave the empty seat to my right between Slate and myself. His arm goes to the back of Hazel's chair possessively.

In short order, my plate is loaded up with a sauced-up chicken burrito and a pile of salad sprinkled with tortilla strips and tomato. The enchiladas are delicious.

Swallowing her first bite, Hazel smiles sweetly at me. "So, Ember, are you artistic at all like your brothers?"

"No really. I don't draw or anything."

"What do you like to do?" Slate asks.

"Um, not much. I listen to music, I guess."

"Oh, like what kind of music?" Hazel's voice brightens.

"All kinds. Two thousands rock is good. Nineties rap. Anything with a good beat. I'm not picky."

"I love that," she says. "It would be fun to trade some music. Do you ever read? Marigold and I have a little book club."

"Not really."

"Okay, well if you want to join us, you don't even have to finish the book. We'd still like you to hang out with us."

"I don't think there will be time before I go home," I say with a tight shrug.

"Of course. But you could always drive over for the day," she suggests.

"My mom wouldn't like that."

After a minute of silence, Hazel runs her hand along Slate's forearms and squeezes his wrist. They exchange looks.

Slate clears his throat. "Look, Ember, I wanted to apologize for yesterday. I know the conflict between our packs was difficult for all of us, and I'm really sorry you lost your dad."

I could have choked on the bite of meat in my mouth. Swallowing forcibly, I dab my mouth with my napkin, desperately sorting through the conflicting emotions caused by his confession.

"It wasn't your fault," I settle on. It's tempting to blame him. I have for a long time. But after spending time here, I'm questioning the truth of it.

Slate's voice drops. "I honestly don't know what possessed her to do that."

It's painful to meet his gaze. "You're her child too."

His mouth curves into a grimace. "She picked him over me a long time ago."

It feels too close to bonding, having a vulnerable conversation, sibling to sibling. I don't want to be close with him. Some day we will be Alphas of separate territories and may have to face off.

"Well, I hope you feel special now." The words are ice daggers.

Hazel sighs, her mouth turning down at the corners. Good. I'm their political hostage, not a long lost sister to embrace. So why do I feel so wretched?

Hazel fills the rest of dinner with small anecdotes about Jasper's time with their pack over the eighteen months. It sounds like he's had a lovely time building a life with them and his new mate. Without me.

It's a relief when they wish me goodnight. Probably a relief for them too, since I wasn't contributing anything to our conversation. They even trust me enough to allow me to walk back to Onyx's cabin unsupervised after I assure them I know the way.

The moon illuminates the leaf-strewn pathway from their cabin to the central clearing, and it's not hard to find a smaller trail from the underbrush leading south toward the Delta's cabin.

It's cool and quiet, and I feel my tension unwinding. Drawing in a lung full of pine air, I let the stress of that dinner trickle away. Starlight illuminates the boughs of fir and maple trees as I wind my way toward my temporary home. The forest is lush south of the river, and my territory seems dry and devoid of life in comparison.

It's not far to the two-story cabin I'm staying in. The evening is so quiet and lovely, I sink into a chair at the fire pit to decompress.

A dark gray shape moves through the trees ahead. My hand goes to my blade, just in case. A wolf approaches, walking with his tail curled upward and his gait friendly. That citrus scent hits me.

"Onyx," I say. He rests his muzzle on my knee and my hand goes to his head without thought. The fur around his ears is silken and I can't help but dig my fingers in. A low rumble emanates from his chest.

Too soon, he pulls away and trots a few feet away into the forest. "Did you even go home? Or have you been hanging around this whole time?" I ask, even though he can't answer me right now.

His dark eyes watch me reproachfully over his shoulder.

"What are you waiting for? Go run. I'll head back to the cabin. I can make it on my own."

He chuffs, swinging back toward me and nudging my hand. Before I can pet him, he pulls away.

"Fine." Giving in, I tug my shirt over my head and drape it over the chair. "But you're coming back to get my clothes. I like this outfit."

He answers with another chuff. As I strip off my leggings, he watches me boldly. He's seen me naked before, but it feels different now.

As soon as my clothes are piled together, I shift. Black fur overtakes my pale skin and I drop down onto four paws. The forest lights up around me, bright as daylight. Onyx wears a charming smirk on his muzzle. He's a fine looking wolf, dark gray with black across his back. Lighter gray-brown peppers his chest and down his belly.

With a wag of his tail, he bolts. My wolf instincts surge, ready to chase him. It feels so good to give in to that urge. My paws dig into the soft earth and launch me forward, wind threading my fur like a caress.

Onyx weaves through the trees ahead, and I duck my head and increase my speed to catch up to him. He zips forward, just out of reach.

Trees whip past, and I spot a dark trailer to our right. Onyx turns, curving our path eastward. I cut the curve and playfully snap at his tail as I get closer.

Wolves are meant to run, and my body floods with feelings of contentment. My instincts whisper that this is right where I am meant to be.

He never lets me catch him, and being a smaller wolf, I can't close the distance. But utter satisfaction soaks into my being as we lope back toward his cabin. His granite wolf scales the porch steps and shifts back to human, grabbing a shirt off a stack of clothes set out.

I turn my eyes away from his body. "Ember," he murmurs, "shift back." Peeking, I realize he's holding up an oversized shirt for me instead of dressing himself.

It takes me a minute to focus enough to shift back. The naked man standing here waiting for me doesn't help my concentration. With one hand crossing my breasts, I accept the shirt from him. Like a gentleman, he focuses on dressing himself while I slide the soft cotton over my head. It drapes down to mid-thigh.

Onyx stands in sweatpants, chest bare. Endorphins linger in my blood, and I can't help but smile at him. He stares at me, a stupid grin spreading over his handsome face. We are a pair of idiots. Especially him, opening himself up to his enemy. But we don't feel like enemies right now, and I can't wipe the smile off my face.

Silently, he pulls the door open and we pad toward our bedrooms. His door hangs open and I can see Cedar sprawled across one of the two beds. Onyx follows my gaze and then rolls his eyes.

Instead of going to his own room, he follows me to my door. I twist toward him, wondering what he's thinking. He moves forward into my space until I'm leaning back against the closed bedroom door.

"Did you have a good time at dinner?" he whispers, his lips moving to my ear. The skin across my cheek and ear light up like he's touched me, though I can only feel his breath.

"Not really," I say honestly.

"I didn't like it either," he says. "I prefer when you eat dinner with me."

My hand flattens against his chest and I mean to push him away, but can't bring myself to do it. He takes it as an invitation to touch, and one hand goes to my hip. His thumb digs into my skin through the thin cotton shirt.

"Onyx," I say in warning.

"Ember," he answers. The rumble of his voice skitters goosebumps across my skin. "I like you in my shirt," he says. His mouth drops to my shoulder and he gently bites my shoulder through the cloth.

"You're running high off your shift," I choke out.

His navy eyes shoot to mine, his head coming up so fast his dirty blonde hair flops over his brow. He ignores it, all of his focus on my face. I want to shrink under the intensity.

"No," he starts, "I can't stay away from you." The draw of his brows and the downward curve of his mouth tell me he doesn't want to feel this pull toward me. I'm a guilty pleasure.

"You're attracted to angry women who hurt you." It's a statement.

His eyes narrow and my heartbeat picks up. "I'd rather fight with you than be with anyone else."

"Don't say things to me like that," I hiss, pleading. "You don't actually like me."

His brows furrow, mouth curving into a slight frown. I wait for whatever cutting barb is coming my way.

"I like you too much."

Pushing off the door frame, he walks away from me. Cold washes down my chest and stomach in his absence. He likes me?

His door clicks closed, and I numbly let myself into Briar's room. Adrenaline from his touch still rages, compounding the hormones already in my system. It's too much. Exhaustion seeps in, and I curl up in the bed. Before passing out, my fingers twine through the wide neckline of the shirt, bringing it up to my nose. His scent is faded after going through the wash, but it's still there. It seeps into my lungs and into my very being as I lose myself to sleep.

Chapter Seven

Cheesette & Cheddarbelle's Fabulous Day

ONYX

Soft laughter floats through the cabin, pulling me from sleep. My arm covers my eyes, and I lay there listening and trying to sort myself out.

Last night after dropping Ember off with Slate and Hazel, I shifted and circled their cabin. With my sensitive wolf ears, I heard flashes of their conversation and it didn't sound pleasant.

Slate has been my ride-or-die since we were kids, but he is failing to connect with Ember and it makes me heated. She deserves a brother who supports her. And besides, she's the future Alpha of an ally pack.

But last night, running with her, I knew I was in trouble. She's going to go home soon, maybe tomorrow, maybe today. And I'm addicted to her. Every wolfish instinct I have pushes me to get close to her. Those animal instincts don't understand that she's leaving.

When I make it to the kitchen, wearing only sweatpants low on my hips, Ember isn't sitting at the table where I expect her to be. Instead, she's at the kitchen counter with a round of bread dough in front of her. Flour dusts her palms and across her loose t-shirt.

My mother leans over her, murmuring encouragement and instruction as Ember folds the dough and presses it flat with the heel of her hand before turning it and repeating the process.

Her eyes are bright, a soft smile on her lips. This is not the same girl who I kissed at the party. The difference is staggering. I was hoping to draw her attention by showing up half-dressed, but instead she's got my jaw hanging down as I stare at her.

Scrambling for something to ground myself, I grip the kitchen table and drop into a chair, unable to take my eyes off of her.

"Morning," she says, glancing over her shoulder at

me.

My voice doesn't catch the first try, but I manage to return the greeting. "How did you sleep?"

"Good," she says, already focused back on her kneading.

My mother hands her a small knife and draws lines in the dough showing her where to cut. Ember makes three slices up the dough, stopping just short of the top, and then braids it. With a flourish, my mother tucks it into a baking dish and sets it aside to rise.

"Fantastic. You are a natural at this."

Ember's eyes widen, as if this is the first praise she's ever received.

"What did you make?" I ask, dying for a scrap of her attention.

Ember dusts the flour off and slides into the seat across from me. "It's just a brioche. Hopefully it's good."

"It'll be delicious," my mom interjects. "You've got at least two hours before it needs to go into the oven. I can keep an eye on it for you." The microwave beeps as she reheats a leftover breakfast sandwich for me. She uses sourdough to make her English muffins, and I've loved them since I was a kid.

"Thanks, Mom." The sandwich is cheesy and greasy with bacon, and I immediately follow it with one of yesterday's scones, a banana, and a tall glass of milk.

Ember watches me, picking off little chunks of a

scone and popping them into her mouth with an amused expression in her eyes. "So what are we doing today?"

"Since I don't have any patrol duties, I'm not sure." Rising, I tuck my dishes into the sink. "What do you want to do?"

"You can always help Cedar with chores," my mother calls from down the hallway.

"That sounds interesting," Ember says. Her arms fold over her chest and I'm not sure if she's being sarcastic or not. I know Cedar isn't her favorite person, but he's my twin and she's ... something I'm not ready to label.

"Let me show you his garden and we can see if there's anything fun we can help with."

She glances at the brioche rising on the counter with a damp kitchen towel draped over it. "I'll think about it." That small smirk is back. "Why don't you put some clothes on? Not everyone wants to see your abs."

Leaning back in my chair, I grin back, loving every second of this exchange. It would look like nothing at all to anyone else, but I see her opening up and enjoying herself. It's everything I hoped for.

"We both know that's not true, but I will anyway, just for you," I snark back. Striding to my room, I'm surprised her soft footfalls follow me. My heart speeds, but I keep my movements casual.

Stepping into my room, I leave the door ajar, and I

can feel her lingering in the hall. "Hoping for a peep show?"

Ember rolls her eyes, stepping into my room. It's strange seeing her in my space.

"I'm happy to show you anything you want," I say, twisting and flexing as I reach for a shirt from my dresser.

"You're delusional," she says, the beautiful pink tint to her cheeks betraying her, "and messy." She's not wrong. There's a visual divide between my space and Cedar's. Gingerly, Ember steps over some clothing strewn across the floor.

"I had a feeling you liked video games," she mutters. While she examines my shelf of game discs, I tug my shirt over my head.

"Would you want to play some time?" I ask, coming up behind her to look over her shoulder.

She tugs a disc from the shelf. "What about this?" It's a car racing game.

"Really?" I ask.

She tucks the game back with one finger. "Maybe."

"What about this one?" I yank a zombie game from the shelf.

"No way," she says, wrinkling her nose and shaking her head so emerald hair cascades over her shoulders.

"Okay, what about..." Holding out Minecraft, I raise an eyebrow.

She tilts her head and stares at it.

"It's a building game. You really didn't have much fun growing up, did you?"

Her shoulders slump the slightest amount, but I'm so attuned to her body language by now, it's a meaningful change.

"I only got to play whatever games Jasper was given," she says, sighing as she steps back from the shelf.

"We can fix that! We could play today. I have a pair of cat ear headphones that would look great on you."

That earns a laugh. "Why do you have those?"

"I'll have you know, I look great with cat ears," I say with a grin. "With this game, you can make anything you want. There are different kinds of blocks and-"

"I think I'd rather play the racing game. Those were my favorites," she says, cutting me off.

"Sure. I'll get it set up," I say, reaching for my controllers.

"How about after we do our gardening?" she says, though I see a flash of a smile as she turns away.

Her fingers trail along my shelves as I finally pull on a black hoodie. "Alright," I say, "I'm all set. How do I look? Like the most handsome man you've ever seen?"

She exhales a laugh, shaking her head as she walks out of my room. I follow her back to the kitchen and we wash the breakfast dishes and wipe down the counter. It feels good to work side by side with her.

"Ready to garden?" I ask her.

"If you insist."

We find Cedar in the center of his vegetable garden, where the long beds are covered in a tunnel of mesh to protect the most delicate of his produce.

"Mom wanted us to come help you."

Cedar looks up from his work and scowls at us. "You can't help with this."

"What are you doing?"

With a dramatic sigh, he brushes the dirt off his hands and stands to face us. "I'm transferring seedlings into the garden. It's tricky. Their root systems are delicate."

"Fine, sorry we wanted to help."

"Would you guys feed the animals?" He eyes Ember curiously.

Her arms hug her waist defensively, but she nods and takes a measured breath. "I think we can handle that."

"Great, Onyx knows what to do. Let me know when you're done."

I could smack him on the back of his head for being rude, but he gave Ember a chance and she seems interested.

"Alright, let's start with the chickens," I say. Ember's hand flies to her mouth at my words. "Did you not know we had chickens?"

"Yeah, I did. I mean, I heard them. But I didn't think about visiting them." Her expression stays neutral but I can sense the excitement bubbling up behind her rambling words.

"The chicken coop is here," I point to the larger structure beside Cedar's storage shed. "Come on."

Her arm brushes mine as we walk the narrow path, and for a moment I almost reach for her hand. Before I can, she moves away.

"Wow, look at them," she says, peering through the chicken wire.

"Here, grab that bucket," I say, pointing at a feed tub. "We do two scoops of grain feed, a cup of vitamin powder, and a cup of their supplements." She holds the bucket while I fill it with scoops of chicken food.

"Now how do we give it to them?" she asks, peering down into the bucket in her arms.

"They have a feeder we have to refill. And we can't forget their treat." With a wink, I pull out a bag of dried mealworms.

Ember leans away, nose scrunched and mouth downturned. "Bugs?"

"Yeah, they love them!"

The hens cluck when we duck through the low door and close the wire gate behind us. With practiced movements, I unlatch and pull the lid off the feed silo. Ember bites her lip as she tips the bucket and pours in the hen's breakfast.

"What do we do with the worms?" she asks, warily eyeing the hens waddling to the feeder.

"Just scatter them," I say, offering her the bag.

With a grimace, she takes the bag and tips it down so a few mealworms scatter across the floor of the coop. Before she empties the bag, half a dozen hens zero in on the worms and rush toward her. Their wings slap her as they scramble for their favorite treat.

"Onyx, they're attacking me," she yelps. Despite her distress, she stays still, letting the feathered chaos batter her calves.

"You're okay. They aren't hurting you," I say in a low, soothing voice. Stepping closer, I plunk the lid back on the feeder and reach for her. My thumbs rub small circles into the curve of her waist while she watches the hens peck the ground around her feet.

"See? Friendly chickens," I say finally.

"Are they always like this?" she asks, her voice clear despite her eyes being wide.

I can't help the chuckle that escapes me. "You haven't been around animals that much, have you?"

"Why would I?" she snaps. "Can you get me out of here?"

"No." My grip tightens on her waist. "You can do this. They're just silly, fat birds. And you haven't finished giving them their dessert."

"Seriously?" Gritting her teeth, she rotates, emptying the bag out in a wide circle. The rest of the coop joins in on the madness, pecking and clucking excitedly.

It takes a few minutes for the girls to calm down. Ember's breathing evens out as she stares at the flock.

With one last squeeze, I let her go. "Picada," I call, looking for my favorite chicken. She sits in a nesting box and watches us, standing when I call her name. Gently, I scoop her up and turn back to Ember.

"This is Piacatta. Here, pet her. She's very sweet."

Tentatively, Ember strokes Picada's feathers.

"See? Nice chickens. They were just excited about breakfast."

"Do they all have names?" A smile tugs at her mouth and she looks down at the chickens bustling around their little coop.

"This one is Cutlet, and here's Cacciatore," I say, pointing out the chickens I've named. "Kiev, Curry, Satay, Fricassee, Alfredo, Teriyaki." Ember lets out a small laugh, but she smothers it with the back of her hand.

"Here, let's refill their water and go feed the goats."

She strokes Picada one last time. I set the hen back in her box, murmuring thanks to her for being such a good girl.

I use the hose to refill the girls' water before leading Ember over to the goats' pen. She stops at the fence and rests her elbows against the top.

"The smaller one is Cheesette and the bigger one is Cheddarbelle," I explain. Cheddarbelle trots over, her soft, brown ears swaying. "They're Nubian goats. Either Cedar or my dad has already milked them today, so we just need to refill their food and water."

"You milk them?"

"You haven't seen my dad's cheese kitchen have you?"

"His what?"

"Yeah, he makes goat cheese. You've eaten some already. But it's really messy, so Mom doesn't let him use the normal kitchen. He's got a whole set up. I can take you there later."

"You guys are so weird," she mutters, the slight curve to her mouth giving away her amusement.

After I refill their water, we load up on feed and treats and let ourselves into the goat pen. Cheesette walks out of their goat house and swings her head around to stare at Ember with her rectangular pupils.

"They're a little creepy," she says, her voice hushed as if the goats would be offended if they heard.

"Not my baby girls," I joke, holding my hands over Cheddarbelle's ears. They're so long and floppy, they swing below my hands. She shakes her head to knock me away.

"I'm sorry," Ember says to Cheddarbelle. Pure delight shoots through me that she's playing along.

"Here," I thrust an apple slice into her hand. "They'll love you forever if you give them treats."

I refill their food while Ember feeds carrots and apple slices to Cheddarbelle. Everything is fine until Cheesette joins in.

"Hi, pretty girl," Ember coos, petting the smaller goat. Cheesette tosses her head and lurches forward to ram into Ember. "Hey!"

There's no way I can reach her in time before her ass hits the dirt. Apple slices spill out of the container and both goats help themselves.

"Onyx!" she cries, waving at where Cheddarbelle's back hoof pins her shirt to the ground. "This is worse than the chickens!"

Shoving the goat aside, I pull Ember up. Half way, she lets out a shriek. "She's eating my hair!" I freeze, horrified as she wrestles a thick piece of hair out Cheesette's mouth.

"It's because you dyed it green. It probably looks like grass to her," Cedar calls from the fence. He watches our circus with a small smile.

"It doesn't look like grass," Ember protests. I can't help my guffaw at her outrage. She pushes Cheesette away. "No treats for you, you little shithead."

"Aw, she didn't mean that," I say, feeding a carrot to the smaller goat. Ember scowls at me.

"No accountability for being rude to guests? That

tracks," she snaps.

"I'm *sorry*," I drawl.

Her hands shoot up. "Go back to babying your goats."

Cheesette shoves her nose into my palm, demanding more attention. I feed her my last carrot and give her a good ear rub.

Ember stands at the fence with a small and utterly smug smile on her face. Before I can question her, Cheddarbelle knocks into my back with her front hooves. I stumble forward and catch myself, but both girls are knocking into me with their hooves, trying to climb my back. Twisting, my ass hits the dirt.

"Hey!" I yelp, covering my head with my arms. But the goats both stick their noses in the scoop of my hoodie. Reaching in, I find a couple of apple slices. After the treats are removed and fed to the greedy goats, they leave me alone.

"Did you seriously put apples in my hoodie?" I ask, and Ember bursts into laughter. I vault the fence and grab her around the waist. "I can't believe you tried to get me mauled by goats."

"But they're so sweet, they would never maul anyone," she says, her voice high. As she laughs, her head tips back. I'm inches from her neck. Dark green waves tumble over her shoulders and down her back. She's so gorgeous it hurts.

Her hands go to my shoulders to steady herself, and then she's looking up at me with those eyes framed in dark lashes. She's stunning when she's angry or serious, but laughing - laughing Ember is something else entirely.

Despite the fact we are in the garden in the middle of the morning and anyone could see, I can't help myself. I'm pulled to her. She tips her face, a silent invitation, and our lips meet.

She's soft and warm, her mouth sliding over mine until her lips part. I love how she tastes like sugar and chocolate. Her fingers thread into my hair and I growl at the light tug as she pulls me closer. Her hips press into mine as I back her into the fence.

I'm lost to the feel of her. It's everything I remember from our first kiss and more. Pleasure and need mingle with affection. Her nails scrape my scalp as she clings to me, pressed between the fence post and my body.

One arm wraps around her waist to hold her up as her knees weaken. The other goes to the nape of her neck so I can angle her to kiss deeper. She lets out a breathy moan in her throat.

Her leg hikes up on my hip, like she's trying to climb me. Without thinking, I push my thigh between her legs. She squirms, grinding against me. My hand travels down to her ass, lifting her until she's half straddling me and my knee hits the fence post.

My mouth goes to her throat, nibbling as I lick and suck my way to the crook of her neck. "Onyx," she whimpers.

Her hands go to my shoulders, pushing me back. I release her, stumbling back a step as her feet hit the ground again. She grips the fence behind her to stay upright. Her glazed eyes find mine, her chest heaving as she pants.

What did I do wrong?

"We can't," she gasps. "Your brother is right over there," she gasps, tipping her head towards where Cedar is back to transplanting seedlings in the center of the garden. She steps closer again until her breasts brush my chest. "At least we can't do this here in the middle of your pack's garden."

Every thought is wiped from my mind. I want her so badly. This flirtation has built and built until she's all I can think about.

"Let's go back to the cabin," I say, breathless. She nods.

As we walk back to my family's cabin, I watch her. She glances at me, a small, sweet smile on her face. Her heart-shaped face is flushed and I want to kiss that blush from her nose down her chest.

I want her to stay. She can be happy here. I'll do everything I can to make sure of it. But she'll never want to stay when everyone is being cold and judgmental to her. If they can see her the way I do, that might change. She's already won over my mother. Hazel and Marigold won't be a problem. Mentally, I make a list of what I can do.

"I smell like farm animals. I'm going to go shower, but I'll see you after, okay?" she murmurs, slipping into Briar's room. I stare at the closed door dumbly.

I take the fastest shower of my life, and when I get out, Cedar is back. My mind races with everything I need to say. He sits at the kitchen table dipping vegetables in ranch.

Sitting across from him, I lean forward to get his attention.

"What's up?" he asks.

"I need you to be nicer to Ember," I say, trying to keep my cool.

"I am," he says, frowning at me.

"You've kinda been an asshole to her, questioning her every chance you get." Anger seeps into my tone.

"I'm not doing anything."

"Oh really? You've upset her at least twice, and you're definitely not being welcoming."

He watches me for a moment. "Why are you so upset about this?"

"She doesn't deserve it." My hands flatten on the table, trying to resist knocking the carrot out of his hand as he crunches another bite.

"She tried to kill you last year. She tried to kill Hazel the year before. She's been unkind to everyone since she got here," he says thoughtfully.

He doesn't see. He's taking everything at face value.

"She's trying. She's just reacting to how we are treating her. She's been really kind to our sister, to Mom. She's opening up to me."

Cedar gives me a long, critical stare. I raise my chin and narrow my eyes, daring him to say something stupid. It's been years since we actually fought and I'm itching to hit something.

"You're attracted to her. It's clouding your judgment."

The urge to smack him overwhelms me, but I know it's logic that will work with my brother. Slowly, I recount what's happened the last day. "The kind girl who baked with our mother this morning and then helped me with chores, that's the real her, and if everyone weren't so fucking judgy toward her, that's who she'd be all the time."

"I'm not sure about that."

He's impossible.

"Cedar, I swear, if you don't back me up on this," I leave the threat hanging. We both know I'd never actually hurt him, but I don't have a better way to express how important this is to me.

His arms cross and his brows furrow. "Alright. I'll do

my best to be nicer."

It's not much, but Cedar always follows through on his promises. If he gives her a chance, he'll see what I see.

The shower noise from Briar's room cuts off.

"Thanks, man," I say to my twin.

"This is really important to you," he observes.

"Yeah."

Ember wanders in, wet hair against her neck and fresh clothes on her body. She winces as she slowly lifts the kitchen towel, and then smiles to find the brioche fully risen and ready to bake.

"What temperature?" she mutters, looking for the recipe card.

"Three-hundred and fifty, for forty minutes," Cedar says without looking up.

Ember swivels and blinks at him. "Thanks," she says hesitantly.

The oven beeps as she sets the bake temperature. While it preheats, she sits beside me.

Cedar crunches on a piece of celery. "Do you want some veggies?" he asks.

"Um, thanks," she says, accepting a carrot stick from him.

"Our mom makes the ranch too," I say, grabbing a celery stick for myself.

Crunching and chewing are the only sounds for a painfully awkward two minutes. I stare at Cedar, willing him to say something. Finally, he does.

"So, did you like the chickens and goats?" he asks.

Ember smiles weakly. "Yeah, they're cute."

"They're great for fresh eggs and milk," Cedar says, clearly unsure of how to hold a conversation with a girl.

"She met Picada," I say, proud of my favorite chicken who answers to her name.

"She was sweet," Ember agrees.

"I saw what you did with the apple slices," Cedar says, his mouth curving into a smile. "Pretty funny."

"Oh," Ember says, her cheeks tingeing pink again. I'm sure we are both having the same thought - was that all he saw? When did he go back to his garden?

We're saved by the oven chiming. Ember shoots up, peeking into the oven before she slides the brioche in. I can't help biting my lip as she bends at the waist to center the loaf pan on the oven rack.

Cedar crosses his arms, eyes narrowed at me when I look up.

"So what now? We've got thirty minutes," she says, dusting off her hands.

"Want to pick out a video game?" I suggest.

She props a fist on her hip and raises an eyebrow. "I believe I was promised a tour of a cheese kitchen?"

"If you want to."

It's not a quiet bedroom, but I can work with a cheese kitchen.

Ember follows me through the laundry room and into the addition my father built years ago.

"This is not what I expected," she mutters, the sunlight from the sky lights highlighting her cheekbones and the delicate tip of her nose.

We're squeezed into a narrow kitchen, standing on sealed concrete floors. Gleaming stainless steel lines the walls, including a commercial triple sink, a wide 8-burner range, and two refrigerators - one to store ingredients and one to age cheese.

Slipping my arm around her waist, I guide her forward, past the row of pots so large a small child could sit inside them.

"Honestly, I don't know anything about how cheese is made," she says, slowing her gait so she presses back into me.

I'm surprised at the euphoria that shoots through me at her nearness and the way she smiles at me. I'm thoroughly ensnared, and the danger of who she is and what she's done is fading away.

"It's pretty simple. We take the milk, it's stored in this fridge," I thump my palm against the closer fridge. "It gets cooked with rennet, which is actually a kind of mold, I think. Cedar can explain that better. Anyway, it forms curds, and we press out the whey which is like water until the curds are solid. It gets dried, aged, or whatever depending on the cheese."

Her lips part as she listens to me ramble. "That doesn't sound very simple."

With a rolling laugh, I herd her closer to the fridge to see what cheeses we can sample. She peers over my shoulder as I pilfer my father's current stock.

"Here, try this. It's fresh farmer's cheese, totally plain." Prying the lid off of a round plastic container, I grab a spoonful of the spreadable cheese.

Ember hesitates, pressing her lips into a line while she leans away.

"It's not bad, I promise."

With a little coaxing, she opens her mouth and takes a small nibble.

"So what do you think?"

"It tastes like milk." Her eyes open again, flitting from my chest to my face. "I can see how that could be good in a recipe."

"Yeah, it's not really a snack cheese," I agree.

"Got any others to try?"

We try a hard cheddar, a brie-style round, and some mozzarella.

"You can make all these different cheeses from goat's milk?" she asks, popping another pearl of fresh mozzarella in her mouth.

"Yeah. I mean, there's a flavor difference. But it all depends on what you add and how you treat the milk."

"Wow," she says, watching as I sprinkle salt flakes

over the last bite of mozzarella and offer it to her. She eats it off the end of the toothpick and runs her tongue over her top lip to get the extra salt.

An alarm buzzes from the house, and Ember's eyes brighten. "Ready for some bread?"

"Go ahead, I'll be right behind you," I say, shoving containers back into the fridge before I can follow her. I'm just in time to watch her tug the oven mitts off of her hands.

Steam trails off the bread loaf, filling the room with the warm, nutty smell. My brother is nowhere to be found, and I'm grateful I don't have to share this moment with anyone else.

Her eyebrows are raised in a soft expression seeking my approval. Stepping closer, I make a show of inspecting the brioche before saying, "It looks perfect."

Closing her delicate hand over my bicep, she squeezes excitedly and my heart skips a beat. "Can we slice it right away?"

"It might deflate because it's really soft right out of the oven," I say. "Can you wait five minutes?"

She turns, her lip pouting as she frowns. "Fine."

With a chuckle, I gather up butter, the cutting board, and a bread knife while she watches her bread, hands clasped tightly behind her.

"Alright, it's probably been long enough," I concede after a few minutes.

Her teeth press into her lip in the most distracting way as she concentrates on flipping the tin over and dropping the bread onto the cutting board.

"Do you want some?" she asks, dragging the knife through the edge of the bread.

"Abso-fucking-lutely!"

Forget cheese - Ember holding out a slice of fresh bread slathered in butter is one of the most gorgeous things I've ever seen. My mouth waters.

Her eyes widen as she watches me take my first bite. Eyes closed, I tip my head back in ecstasy, exaggerating yummy noises so she never doubts how good it is.

She takes her own bite, her cheeks flushed and a shy smile on her face.

"This is the best thing anyone in the world has ever baked," I say, groaning as I take another bite.

"You're ridiculous," she says with a soft chuckle, wiping crumbs away from her mouth with the back of her hand.

"I'm serious. So good," I add with another groan.

"Yeah, but I'm so full now," she says, rubbing her belly. "I need a nap." A yawn proves her point.

I gaze longingly at the steam wafting off the hot bread.

"You can have more bread, Onyx," she says, smirking. "I know how much you enjoyed it. You could always take a second slice back to your room for some private time. I don't mind," she teases.

"Hey!" I scold, my laughter following down the hallway as she disappears.

I can't resist the second piece she offers, but I eat it over the sink and then wipe the crumbs from our first slices into the trash.

On the way to my room, I hesitate at her door. Her breathing sounds even, so now's not the time to bother her, no matter how badly I want to.

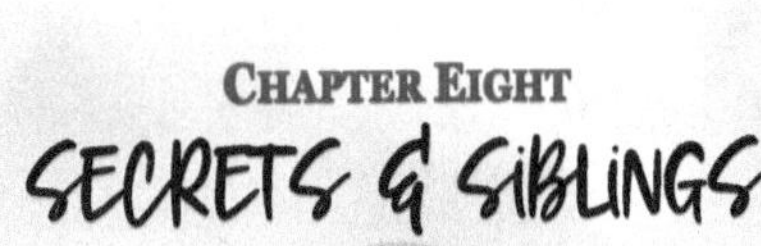

The taste of bread still on my lips, I lay back on Briar's bed and replay this morning's kiss in my mind. The first time we kissed, we were tipsy and it was hot and angry. This time was light - stars bursting behind my eyes, electricity zinging over my skin. It was bright and scorching. It felt like he could burn away everything in my life and leave only him and that moment.

I want to let him. I want to forget the first eighteen years of my life and never leave this small window of time with him. I can even deal with the coldness from his packmates, if it means going back to his warmth.

But that is a daydream, and I know if I did something drastic like give up my ranking in my pack, I would resent him. I've worked for eighteen years to gain power, and I am one step away from being Alpha where I can control everything around me and no one will ever dare cross me again.

If I continue to get closer to him, it'll hurt worse when I leave. Or I could seize the opportunity and enjoy everything I can with him. Either way, I'll be heading home in the next day or two. If he gets me alone again, I don't think I'll have the willpower to resist him. The way he was devouring me with his eyes in the kitchen, I don't think I want to.

It might be worth it. I'm used to pain. I've got scars to prove it. So why not take advantage of this chance with Onyx? I can deal with the fallout when I leave. And if I'm insanely lucky, we can continue to meet up and spend time together even after I go home.

Mind made up, I lay there in a t-shirt and underwear and pray that he comes to check on me.

A light knock on the door sends a thrill down my spine. "Yeah?"

"Sweetheart, your brother is back. Do you want to

come see him?" Clove's voice calls through the door.

All thoughts of Onyx shatter. Jasper and Marigold have returned, which means I am going home. It's over before we had a chance to start.

My throat burns as I pull on a pair of shorts and stuff the rest of my clothes back into my duffle. Onyx and Cedar meet me in the hallway, looking confused.

"What are you doing?" Onyx asks.

With a steadying exhale, I steel myself. "Jasper and Marigold are back, so I'm going home."

The look on his face guts me. His lips part and his brows rise. "Let's talk about this."

Cedar brushes past us, following their mom out the door.

"We knew I was only here for a couple of days. Since they're back, I'm going home."

"Wait," he says, reaching for me. I allow him to take my duffel and set it by the door. "What if you stayed?"

Frowning, I prop my hands on my hips. "I can't do that. It wouldn't be allowed."

"Fuck that," he hisses. "It's your choice. If you want to stay longer, I'll do whatever's needed to make it happen."

His low voice caresses my skin, and I feel my neck arching in submission. He shouldn't have this kind of power over me, but I love it. Closing my eyes, I focus on what I need to do. And it's not running away from my life because a hot guy flirts with me.

"Let's just go see what's going on, okay?" I say, my voice gentle while I take his hand. He threads our fingers together and it feels so natural that I'm momentarily stunned.

"Promise me you will think about it," he whispers. His pleading squeezes my chest and goosebumps break out over my arms. He doesn't know I've already been day dreaming of staying with him. That's how dangerous his influence over me is.

"Alright," I say simply. Stiffly, I pull my hand from his and he doesn't protest.

The silence is full of unspoken desires as we walk south, toward my brother and my way out of here.

My mother's red sports car stands out among the ivories and sage green trucks in the parking lot. Alarm bells go off in my head. Why would she drive them herself?

She's the first one I notice, with her dark hair in a classic chignon and her eyeliner so sharp she could cut someone. She stands beside Jasper and Marigold who speak with Hazel and Slate, but my mother's posture makes it clear she is not a part of their group.

Their hushed tones are impossible to hear over the birds chirping and the crunch of gravel under our feet. Onyx's father, Fisher, and the Gamma, Hawthorne, join the circle, and more hushed words are exchanged.

Fisher's arms cross over his chest as he watches Jasper and Slate gesture while they speak.

Jasper looks up at me and I want to run to him. But the divide between us is too great. Dark circles smudge under his eyes and he looks paler than normal. Beside him, Marigold clutches his hand in both of hers tight against her stomach.

Sienna looks down her nose at Hazel, and the younger Alpha nods. Slate wraps his arms around his mate's waist, his eyes dark. My instincts whisper that something is wrong. The concerned curve of Hazel's eyebrows stand in contrast to the polite smile on her lips.

My mother gives a curt nod and turns on her stilettos. She's back in her car before I can reach them.

"What is she doing?" I snap.

Jasper cuts across my path, blocking me from her car. "Ember, wait!"

"Wait, what–?" My question breaks off as our mother reverses and peels out of the parking lot without me.

"It's fine," he says, "you're going to stay a few more days." His familiar voice soothes me and it's all too easy to submit to his will.

I bare my teeth at him, fighting against his influence. "Why?"

My brother stands his ground, facing my growing anger without visible reaction, though his gaze jumps to his mate. Marigold steps closer and takes his arm. "Your mom has a few things she wants to settle before you go home. And we wanted to spend some time with you."

"Why didn't she discuss it with me?" I growl, throwing my arm out to gesture toward her tail lights.

"You know how Mom is," Jasper says dismissively.

"I am her Heir, second ranked in my pack," I say, bolstering myself despite the bitter taste in my throat. It feels like a lie. "Not a child to be sent away whenever she gets tired of me."

"Let's just enjoy a couple days together and then you'll head home." Jasper sounds exhausted.

The rational part of my brain questions everything. Why does he look so bad? If he was a guest of the Alpha, it should have been a luxury vacation. But my feral instincts push those thoughts out of my head with the overwhelming sense that I'm being lied to.

"We are going to unpack and relax for a bit. But could we plan on spending tomorrow together?" Marigold asks with a sweet smile.

"Whatever." I spin, keeping my pace to a quick walk despite how badly I want to run.

As I pass Onyx, he turns to follow me, keeping pace at my side. Jasper's eyes burn into my back, but I ignore everyone.

My feet take me towards my temporary home without my guidance, which only serves to irritate me further. As we step into the quiet cabin, I hiss, "Are you happy now? You got what you wanted."

Onyx halts, his eyes dark when I finally look at him.

"Are you kidding? You're hurt. That's the last thing I wanted."

I ignore his words, unsure of how to take them. "Something is clearly wrong and I'm being treated like a child."

It only makes me feel more childish but I let him pull me into his arms. Cheek against his chest, he kisses the top of my head. I'm able to release some of the tension threatening to break me.

"I'm sure we will find out everything that's going on. And it'll be fine. I'll do whatever I can to help. And in the meanwhile, you get to stay a few more days with me."

His arms tighten around me. I know he's just trying to comfort me, but I can't help but take it as an invitation. Tipping my head back, I kiss his jaw. His stubble is rough against my skin.

"Ember," he rumbles. "We should be finding out what happened, not..." He trails off.

"Later," I whisper. I can't deal with my pack or my mother right now. Not when Onyx's body is pressed against mine. "Distract me. Please."

"You're going to be the death of me," he groans against my temple.

"Despite evidence to the contrary, no, I'm not," I

tease, slipping my hand under his shirt to run the pads of my fingers across his scar. With a grin, he hoists me up so my legs wrap around his waist. He carries me through the kitchen and down the hallway to his room. Before I can protest, he tosses me down on his bed and turns back to click the lock.

"Are you sure you want to do this? I'm still leaving eventually," I ask, needing him to realize the situation.

"Even if you were leaving today, I would take every second you gave me." His words are punctuated by kisses up my neck as he crawls over me. "But do you? Because this isn't a distraction for me."

His expression is vulnerable, offering up a piece of himself to me. And I know I shouldn't, but I can't help myself. I want this and I want him.

With a nod, I tighten my legs around his waist again, reveling in the feel of him against me.

"You are stunning," he murmurs, sliding my shirt up to uncover my breasts. I gasp as his mouth closes over one. His hand goes to the other, softly stroking and running his thumb over my nipple. His tongue rolls across the other one, and I press my head back into his mattress.

Bunching his shirt up in my fists, I writhe under him. "Onyx," I moan. His response is a hum against my breast that nearly undoes me.

He moves to the other, his tongue licking over me.

The arm not propping him up moves down, tugging at my waistband.

His head comes up, eyes silently requesting permission as his fingers trail under the edge of my waistband.

"Yes," is all I can manage. My hands tug at his shirt, and he shrugs it off so I can run my hands down his chest. His ab muscles tighten as he lowers down and slips out of reach. My hands skim up over his shoulders, feeling the cords of muscles flexing as he tugs my shorts down with his teeth.

Every molecule of my body is strung tight, feeling his breath against tender skin. Skin no one else has touched. He takes his time, slowly running his fingers and then his mouth lower.

"We are needed in a meeting," Cedar calls right before the door handle jiggles.

We freeze, his breath panting against my skin.

"Shit," I whisper. "What do we do?"

He slides my shorts back up my hips and rises up to a kneel between my thighs, looking disoriented. The door handle clicks as Cedar tries again.

"I'll go, deal with the meeting. You go back to your room after we're gone," Onyx says. The look he gives me is pure lust. His navy eyes glow dusty blue, like moonlight. His full lips are slightly parted, and I want them on my body, but we are out of time.

"Wait," I hiss, words clicking into place in my brain. "They're having a fucking meeting without me?"

"Maybe it's something totally unrelated," he reasons. "But I'll tell you whatever I learn, okay?

"Fine." I say.

"Onyx?" Cedar interrupts.

Onyx leaps up, yanking his shirt back on. As he unlocks the door, he blocks me from view, pushing his brother back. But Cedar's hand goes to the door to keep it from closing. The two males posture for a moment as Onyx tries to make Cedar back down, but the lighter-haired twin peers over his shoulder and it's too late. He sees me with bare shoulders, Onyx's quilt pulled over my breasts.

"Not a word," Onyx snarls at him.

A crease forms between Cedar's brows. "This is not a good idea. I warned you."

The door closes and I can barely hear Onyx's angry words as he leads Cedar away.

Heart racing, I slip my shirt on and peek into the hallway. There's no noise in the house, so I dart across to Briar's room and shut the door. Want and need rage through me, and I faceplant into the bed with a frustrated groan.

ONYX

Jasper looks like this is the last place he wants to be. He rests his forehead against the heel of his hand. Marigold leans against him, her cheek to his shoulder. Both look exhausted and decidedly grim.

Slate sits across from him, his mouth a thin line. Hazel runs her fingers over his wrist, drawing swirls with the tips of her fingers. To Hazel's left sits Hawthorne and then my father.

The pack bond resonates in the room with so many wolves gathered together. I can sense frustration and resignation rolling off my friends.

Cedar takes the chair past Jasper and I take the one beside Marigold. It makes me nervous to have my twin further away, knowing his inclination for sharing information without tact. Of anyone, he was the worst person to have caught up - except perhaps Slate or Jasper. They are going to be furious. Ravishing the Heir of another pack was definitely not in the job description when Hazel asked me to guard Ember.

Marigold sits up and squeezes my forearm. "Are you having an okay time?" she asks quietly.

Swallowing, I bob my head. She turns and smiles at me. I can tell the second she breathes in and catches

Ember's scent on my skin. She goes still, her eyes flickering from my face down my body like she might find the girl tucked in my pocket. Her brows crease. Anyone else, I wouldn't worry. They'd assume it was because I was on guard duty. But Marigold snuck around with Jasper for weeks before they admitted their relationship to us. I'm screwed.

"Okay, let's deal with this," Slate says. His exhale is heavy.

Jasper sighs too, the half-brothers looking more alike in that moment. "So things aren't looking great in Granite Ridge," he begins. "Sienna has been ruling alone for the last year, and their pack is largely male."

"She hasn't taken a new mate and doesn't intend to," Marigold amends. "I think she really loved Ferris."

Jasper's jaw clenches. "Well, the talks among the pack members are starting to turn ugly. She's had to squash a few rebellious discussions already, but it's only a matter of time until someone challenges her."

Hawthorne's hand rubs his jaw thoughtfully. "And do we think she can win a challenge?"

"Against those fuckers they've got in that pack?" Slate says, his tone harsh.

"This is the consequence of building up a pack of brutish men, training them like a militia, and then telling them they are the superior pack. For years," Hazel says, emphasizing her words. "Sienna can't control them without Ferris."

"So what if she loses her pack? Who is likely to challenge her?" Hawthorne presses.

Jasper runs hand through his hair, already tousled from his anxious habit. "It'll probably be Orion or maybe Aries. And they're bloodthirsty. They won't hold our alliance. They'd probably attack Raven pack first, especially if they could get Zephyr to turn on Nyx. Then we would be next."

"We should prepare for a fight, then," my father says. Beside him, Hawthorne raises a pacifying hand.

"It would be best if Sienna wasn't ousted," Hazel says, shaking her head like she can't believe she is supporting her mate's mother who hates her.

"Well, what can we do?" Slate asks Jasper.

Jasper rubs his hand down his face. "I don't know."

"If we send any sort of support, it'll just make her look weaker. Short of going in and assassinating a third of her pack, I don't see anything we can do," Marigold says.

This is going from bad to worse, and I can't sit silently.

"What about Ember?" I blurt.

"She's staying here," Hazel says. "At least we can keep her out of whatever carnage is about to happen."

"Who is telling her what's happening?"

Slate's eyes bore into mine, his dominance pressing

down until I drop my gaze. "We aren't going to tell her."

"Why?" I ask as respectfully as I can manage.

"What do you think she'd do if she knew?" Marigold asks softly.

Fear and anger swirl together, making me sick. "She'd want to go home and do something to help. But that's her decision to make. She's an adult and Heir of Granite Ridge."

"She's my sister, and I won't get her thrown back into that pack as it self-destructs." Jasper's words cut into me. "I know you don't care if she lives or dies, but I won't see her torn apart."

"Of course I want her safe," I snap. "But she has rights. I'm sure if we talk to her about the situation-"

"Have you ever talked with Ember?" Jasper interrupts me, his sky blue eyes blazing bright cyan. Marigold grips his arm, and I have no doubt she's feeding calming emotions through their mate bond. The rush of his anger lessens.

"I've talked with her a lot this week," I say, unable to stay quiet. "She's gotten a shit deal, but she's trying to do the right thing. And everyone is holding her pack's mistakes over her head."

"Onyx, I know this isn't fair to her. But we can't risk her running home and getting herself killed. If she's safe here, Sienna can focus on dealing with her pack. It's the only thing we can do to help. So you can't tell her anything." Hazel's dominance feels different than Slate's. Slate's is like a physical force pressing down on my shoulders. Hazel is like a warm blanket wrapping around me, drawing me toward what she wants and coaxing me to cooperate. I know if she wanted to, she could push harder, but she's gentle.

"Yes, Alpha," I say. The soft pressure releases me and the wolves around me relax in unison.

Ember is going to be furious when she finds out they kept this from her, but I'm powerless to help the situation.

"Please be extra vigilant. Whenever you aren't with her, make sure someone else is. Jasper and Marigold will take her whenever they can," Hazel says.

"Clove and I can take some of that responsibility on as well," my father adds. Hazel nods, looking between us.

"I'm staying in contact with my mother, so I'll provide whatever updates as soon as I have them." Jasper grips his mate's hand.

"Hopefully this resolves soon and she can go home," Marigold adds sweetly. Her words churn in my stomach. I want Ember to be safe and have everything she wants in this world, but I also want her with me. And staying here in Bracken Creek accomplishes several of those goals, though it denies her position as Heir. Somehow I know she would trade her safety and happiness if it meant taking up the mantle of Alpha in her pack.

Slate dismisses us and I head back to my cabin, leaving my father and brother behind to talk with Jasper. Not caring about etiquette, I head straight to Briar's room.

Ember sits up on her bed, her expression open and vulnerable. It almost breaks me. I open my mouth and then close it, unsure of what I can say.

Gracefully, she rises and approaches me. Her hands rest against my stomach. I'd love to bypass our discussion and push her back onto the bed and kiss her until neither of us know which direction is up. But she is expecting an explanation.

"Jasper and Marigold were sharing about their visit, but they didn't say much." It's the truth.

Her brows furrow as she looks up at me, but she's patient for more of an answer.

"I guess your mom wants you to stay with us. Well, Jasper was the one who wanted it. Honestly, I don't know."

"Nothing else was discussed in the meeting?" she asks, gently requesting more information.

I drag my hand through my hair. "There were a few things the Alphas ordered us to keep quiet about. I'm sorry."

Understanding washes over her face. Her lips part

for a moment, forming an "o" shape. I pull her to me, hands on the small of her back, but she leans away.

"I'd like some space. I thought I'd get some answers, but you can't, and it just confirms they're keeping something from me." Her tone is even, but it feels like the quiet before a storm.

My hold loosens and she pulls away. "Please don't push me away," I plead.

"It's been an emotional day," she says. "I think I need some actual rest. Can you close the door on your way out?"

"Ember," I say, wanting nothing more than to touch her. Her eyebrows shoot up, and I know she's made her decision. "Talk to Jasper or Hazel." It's the only thing I can say to help.

"I will." Her arms cross, and she watches me with a focused calm that scares me more than her anger ever has. Each step away from her feels like needles stabbing my skin, but I make it to the door and give her one last pleading look. Her gaze is distant, lost in thought.

Hating everything about the situation, I close the door, turn my back to it, and sink to the ground. My forehead rests on my forearm across my knees. She's hurting behind this door, so I sit outside and wait until she's ready to let me back in.

WHO DID THIS TO YOU?

Ember

Dinner sounds unappealing, so I continue to lay in my borrowed bed and brood. Tears burn in my eyes but never fall. I want to fight, hurt someone, but not him.

Somehow in the last few days, Onyx became someone important to me. Someone I would protect, even refuse to hurt if we were on opposite sides of a conflict. He's more than a friend. The feel of his hands on my body sends goosebumps over my arms.

Even as disappointed as I am that he couldn't tell me what they said in the meeting I was excluded from, I can't be angry with him.

Tomorrow, I will confront my brother. But right now, there's someone else I can question. With a grimace, I pull out my phone to text my mother.

> What the hell? Why did you leave me here?
> 9:10PM

> I decided it was best you spend more time with your brothers.
> MOM 9:11PM

> And you couldn't be bothered to talk to me?
> 9:10PM

> I'm busy and you need to be respectful. I am your Alpha.
> MOM 9:11PM

> And I'm your Heir, but you aren't treating me like your second.
> 9:10PM

> I will be sending you instructions tonight. I want you to gather some information while you are there. Be ready.
> MOM 9:11PM

I leave her text on read. Maybe she means asking questions, but I have a feeling she means spying. That's not going to happen. My position here is already precarious, but if I'm caught stealing information, they would imprison me truly.

Emotional drain melts into exhaustion, and I doze. A knock on my door wakes me.

"Go away, Onyx," I rasp, clearing sleep from my voice.

"I've got dinner for you, honey," Clove says.

Popping up, I rub a hand across my face and say, "Oh, thanks. Come in." The door handle starts to turn but stops.

"Mom, let me," Onyx mutters.

"Not a chance. Sit back down, or better yet, go clean yourself up," Clove scolds. Onyx's grumbles fade and once it's quiet, Clove opens the door fully.

"Thanks," I say, accepting the plate. An oversized croissant overflows with chicken salad studded with grapes. Another novelty for me. Taking a bite, I savor the creamy sauce and the bright crunch of celery.

"When did you have time to make croissants?" I ask between bites, smiling weakly at Onyx's mother.

Clove waves her hand. "Puff pastry is such a pain. I usually make huge batches and then freeze them. It's easier to make in the winter when the butter doesn't want to melt."

I nod, taking another bite. My stomach gurgles in appreciation.

"I appreciate you teaching me how to bake." The words get caught in my throat, but I force them out. "I'm going to miss you."

"You're welcome to come back any time."

"I don't think that's very likely. My mom is pretty controlling."

"Yes, I suppose she is."

"I need to find out what's going on. I can tell Jasper was lying to me. Do you know what they were meeting about?"

Clove's hand brushes over my hair, the way I always imagined a mother would do. My throat aches and my eyes sting.

"I'm sure Jasper will explain everything tomorrow. It'll be okay."

"If it wasn't a big deal, they wouldn't have kept anything from me," I mutter.

"Maybe," Clove answers. "But I have a feeling this is going to be a transformative time for you and your pack.

They may need you, but you also need space and independence to grow. A little separation from your mother isn't a bad thing."

The truth of her words grips me. I would have given anything to be away from my mother's control and scrutiny. But it's the feeling of helplessness that turns my blood to ice. It's something I fight every day in Granite Ridge when wolves disrespect my ranking and my mother speaks down to me. If things go wrong, I don't have the power to stop it. Something deep inside of me knows that's why my mother didn't want me there. I'm too weak to be of any help.

"Ember," Clove says, pulling me from my spiraling anxiety. "Try to enjoy the time you have with us. Everyone here cares about you. You're safe. Make sure to rest and recharge."

"I will, after Jasper is honest with me." I'm not ready to let go of my anger, though Clove's kindness softens it.

"If that's what you need to do," she says, standing. I let her take my plate.

"Thanks, Clove."

"Good night, love." She opens the door and I hear Onyx scrambling out of the way. After she leaves, I listen to him settle back against the door. Ridiculous man.

My body itches to go open the door and let him in. I've already used him as a distraction before. But that wasn't wise. This time, I won't be opening the door and falling into his arms. I can't figure out how to deal with the situation when I'm distracted by his mouth.

I sleep fitfully, my heart aching. A deeper sleep takes me some time in the early hours and when I wake, it's late morning.

Scrubbing myself helps marginally, as does blow drying my hair smooth. A little extra eyeliner and I feel ready to face everyone.

When I open the door, Onyx falls back onto my shins. He smiles up at me sheepishly.

"Have you been here the whole time?"

He scrambles to his feet and shrugs. "I went to the bathroom once or twice."

I almost laugh, but remember the divide between us. He's just following his Alphas' orders. But being left in the dark is somehow worse when he's unable to help and clearly wants to.

"Where's my brother?"

"I'll take you to him after you eat some breakfast."

"Onyx," I warn, my nails digging into my palms.

"Breakfast," he answers in the same tone, the twinkle in his eyes the only sign he's teasing me.

With a scowl, I march to the kitchen and allow him to present me with some of the brioche spread with butter and jam. It's just as delicious cool, and despite my irritation, I eat the entire plate.

"We made this jam, you know." He scrapes the knife against the jar to capture a smudge of jam to spread across his last bite of bread.

I don't have the energy to respond. My cold anger gathers up inside of me as I mentally rehearse my discussion with Jasper, ready to unleash when my brother inevitably refuses to answer my questions.

"Everyone is at training. My dad and Slate ordered double training for the next few weeks, including weapons." My ears perk up at weapons.

The meadow is quiet. It's Monday, maybe the children of this pack are in school. A little spike of curiosity urges me toward the school to see if it's Marigold in the classroom, but I ignore it. My pack doesn't have a school. I did online classes, like my brother. But maybe someday, Marigold can help me set up a proper school for my pack when I'm the Alpha.

Onyx pushes open the door to the training building, and I'm surprised at how many wolves occupy the space. The garage door on the back side is open, and more wolves train in the dirt beyond.

A group of females grapple in a ring, while a few people lift weights along the wall. I hone in on Jasper, who stands in a line with a gun pointed at a target in the trees. He tenses and shoots, his shot landing off-center. He was always better with knives.

"Ember," Hazel says, using a towel to wipe her

sweat off.

"I'd like to talk to my brother," I say, unwilling to look at the Alpha who is withholding information from me.

"He's finishing up some training. Can you wait a minute?" she asks. Her tone is casual, but there's an underlying command that prickles at me. With a jolt, I realize she's using dominance on me. From the soft brush of it, it's most likely unintentional. I wouldn't even notice if I was her pack. As soft as it is, it feels different than my mother's, and therefore alien.

Turning, I narrow my eyes at her. "Are you trying to start a fight?"

Hazel glances between me and Onyx, her cheek sucked in where she bites it. "No, but maybe it's a good idea to work off some of your aggression before you talk with Jasper? Just a bit of friendly sparring."

A minute later, we replace the sparring women in the ring. Onyx stands at the edge nervously. He's joined by a few pack members I don't recognize.

My focus narrows to Hazel. We've fought before, when she was human in the woods. She had a knife and I took it from her. Only Jasper's arrival saved her. But there are no knives here. Mine is tucked in my room, for once. And I have no reason to kill her. Regardless, I still want to win.

Hazel steps closer, hands up defensively. I'm a

couple inches shorter than her, so I lower myself as I dart in, attempting to land a strike on her ribcage. She's incredibly fast, grabbing my wrist and twisting. I fall to a knee, snarling.

Hazel presses her advantage, trying to force me to the ground. Ignoring the pain, I grab her closer thigh and shove into her. She struggles to maintain her balance, throwing her weight onto me.

My wrist wrenches and my shoulder pops. We both fall sideways.

With a horrified expression, Hazel releases my arm. "Sorry!" she yelps, attempting to sit up. The pain in that arm is blinding, but I'm used to ignoring pain. Using my good arm, I slam into her collarbone, pressing her into the mat.

I press into her airway, observing the ways her eyes widen. She slams into my cheek with her fist, and I have to duck my head. Her weight shifts, her feet getting under me before I can drop lower, and then I'm flying over her to land on my back. All the air whooshes out of my body.

Hazel crouches over me, one hand rubbing at her neck. "Are you okay?" she asks, sounding distant.

Other faces join hers, but I can only focus on Jasper's glowing pale eyes. He hauls me up with rough hands, dragging me away from the crowd and into the trees.

Hazel's voice echoes, "Jasper, she's hurt!"

As I suck in air, my mind clears. My brother's face is twisted in fury.

"Is this what you've been doing here? Attempting to assassinate our brother's mate?" His words are barely above a growl.

"What?" I ask, holding my aching arm and trying to figure out how to pop it back into place.

"She tapped the mat. You could have strangled her!"

"I didn't see," I admit, my eyes dropping to the ground. "I didn't think an Alpha would ever tap out."

"She did it because you were hurt!" he hisses.

"I'm sorry! But she's the one who wanted to spar. If she couldn't handle it, she shouldn't have asked me!" Anger surges back into my body, turning up the pain in my arm until I'm choking on it.

"You should show her some respect. Hazel is the only one keeping you safe right now." I want to argue that I can take care of myself, but it hurts too much to form words.

"Stop it," Onyx growls, prying Jasper's hands off of me. He shoves my brother back. "She's hurt, you asshole."

Jasper looks me over and I bare my teeth at him.

"Dammit, Ember," Onyx mutters. He comes up beside me, using both hands to grip my shoulder and popping it back into place. I turn my face into his chest to muffle the small scream I can't contain.

"We need to talk about this," Jasper huffs when I look up.

"Yeah, there's a lot of things to talk about, since you're refusing to tell me what the hell is going on," I say. Neither of us moves so Onyx stays a weight against my good arm. His hand goes to the small of my back.

"You can't demand answers when you behave like that," Jasper yells. "You are so fucking lucky it was me there and not Slate."

It's too much. She's the one who wanted to spar. Yes, I lost control, but she beat me! Why is he acting like I tried to murder her?

Maybe because I did exactly that in the past.

I could tell him why. But I already seem weak. I'd rather have his anger than pity.

Memories assault me. Our mother glaring into my eyes, explaining we have to break Hazel. That she will either rise to the occasion or we have to kill her. Telling me to hurt her.

The sight of her blood across the floor.

My breathing accelerates and the world seems to blur. I have to get away. I tug my shirt over my head, and leap right out of my sweats as my black wolf takes over my body.

I lose myself in my canine instincts and let the

chaos fall away. There's just the earth under my paws and the scent of little creatures in the woods. I'm in another pack's territory and I need to get away to be safe.

My sensitive hearing tracks another wolf following me, but I consider it with the detachment of a predator. They'll leave me alone once I'm out of their territory. I'm running as fast as I can. No reason to worry or change my path.

The land slopes downhill, and I thread through the trees expertly. My smaller wolf has the advantage, and my pursuer has to slow down. Finally I burst through the trees and leap into the creek. It's shallow here, but still wetting my belly as a wolf. But something tells me to stop. I shouldn't go into my pack's territory either.

The reality of my situation filters in, and I lose my wolf shape. Fur reveals skin, and I'm standing in knee-deep water, without any clothing.

A twig snaps, and I whip around to face Onyx. He raises his hands to show peace, but then lowers them to retrieve a clothing stash. I should walk to him and accept clothing and we can talk about this. But I'm so damn tired.

I sink down on a wide rock and hang my head. It's hot under my skin, but it doesn't matter. The water is icy as it swirls around my shins. The contrast grounds me.

"Hey," Onyx says, wading through the water. He's pulled on sweats and scrunched them up over his knees to keep them dry. It's worth raising my head to admire his bare chest. The spiky neo-tribal tattoos arc across his skin like black frost. I've never let myself stare at his tattoos before, only quick glances, but now I drink them in. The lines remind me of tiger stripes.

"Do you want clothes?" he asks.

What's the point? I drop my head again, the shock of my fight bleeding me out until I'm nothing but a husk.

"Ember," Onyx says. His voice is lower, darker. His shadow moves across me, and I don't realize until it's too late. His hand grips my shoulder as the other runs down my back over old scars from beatings. "What are these?"

I scowl at him, and even that seems to take too much effort. "I told you. When you do poorly at training, they beat you. Remember?"

He traces down to the scars on the sides of my thighs. "Can you tell me which wolves did this?"

Grimacing, I snag the shirt dropped over his shoulder and tug it over my head. "It doesn't matter. It's just how things are."

"It matters because I need to know who to kill," he says, the calm in his words scaring me more than any growl or snarl.

Shoving to my feet, I face him. "Oh, get over it. You're not going to save me. Just because I wanted you to fuck me doesn't mean you owe me anything, or that this is a relationship."

His stormy eyes only narrow. This isn't casual, fun Onyx. The intensity radiating off him takes my breath away.

"You know it's more than that. And I don't care if you say stuff like that to push me away. It's too late for that to work. I know you. And I'm going to do whatever I can to keep you safe." I gape at him. He lowers his head until his mouth nears mine. "And I'm going to do everything in my power to make you happy, because I think you've had very little of that in your life so far."

His grip is possessive, his fingers splayed over my skin under the shirt.

"I need to know the truth about what's happening with my mom and my pack," I say softly.

"Okay," he says. I freeze, staring at him. "If you promise to not leave until you've discussed things with Jasper and Hazel too."

"I don't want to talk with him," I argue.

"I'll make sure he's calm," Onyx promises, his eyebrows high as he waits for my response.

"Deal."

ONYX

Ember stands knee deep in the water with only one of my t-shirts on and she's so beautiful it hurts. She ran all the way to the boundary.

Jasper didn't follow us, but I can feel worry through the pack bond. I try to relay confidence to keep them at bay. I'm about to do something that will make him very angry.

If we aren't honest with her, she'll disappear and do exactly what they are trying to prevent. And now that I've seen the scars, I know her packmates have no problem hurting her. How could Sienna and Ferris let this happen?

When she becomes Alpha, it'll be harder for her to control those wolves since they've beaten her in the past. These wounds weren't from struggling and proving herself, they're punishment for being young and not yet strong enough to stop it.

I have to convince her to stay until things are safe. Until Sienna changes things in that pack and drives out all the people who would hurt Ember. I don't care if I have to go up there and take out those people myself.

"Some of the pack members are giving your mom a hard time and she wants to deal with them while you're here safe and can't get pulled into it."

She stands silently. If her mother is overthrown, she loses her ranking and potentially her membership in the pack. A dark part of me wants that to happen.

"I want to go home."

"I know," I say. "That's why I made you promise to

talk it over with Jasper. He can tell you more. You going home right now might make the situation worse." I'm not convinced her mom cares about her safety, so it's likely true.

Her arms fold around her and she looks very fragile. "Alright."

"Alright," I echo her, running my arms over her shoulders and down her back. She melts into me. Moisture drips onto my chest, and I realize she's crying. "It's going to be fine."

When she looks up at me, the tip of her nose is red and her lashes clump together. "No, I fucked up. I showed how crazy I am and hurt Hazel. Slate will either lock me up or kick me out."

"Hey," I say, my hands rising until I cup her face and force to look at me. "Do you think maybe you fight like that because in your training, losing meant more than just a loss. It meant..." I trail off, one hand brushing over her shoulder blade.

She looks away, unable to meet my gaze. "If I can't control myself, I'm a danger to everyone."

"So you don't fight. You stay with me, bake bread, help with the garden, do whatever you want to do. Forget everything else."

For a moment, it feels like she'll agree.

Her hand tugs on the back of my neck and guides me down until our lips meet. The kiss is slow and soft, and I force my hands to stay still. She needs comfort, not a mauling.

She breaks away and whispers, "Thank you for telling me the truth." She pauses, and I can almost hear the thoughts in her head. "We should go back."

I pull her in for another kiss. "How about later. We're alone out here."

"They'll come looking for us soon, won't they?"

Groaning, I rest my forehead against hers. "When will we ever get some privacy?"

Ember's exhale is uneven, and I know she's thinking of all the reasons we shouldn't be together. But as far as I'm concerned, it's a done deal. I'm in this with her.

CHAPTER TEN

TEENY TINY CHICKENS

Ember

Onyx holds my hand on the walk back. My mind spins with the implications of the situation. I want to go home and help my mother protect our position of leadership. But she doesn't want me there. I'm a liability in this situation - the young, female Heir in a pack of assholes. It's why she paired me with Hawk. A strong male as my mate fortifies my position.

But I can't help but wonder, what if that mate is

Onyx?

The thought makes my stomach clench. It's too much to think about a future with him. I'm already indulging in this fling with him. It's all more than I deserve.

But what if?

When the woods thin and the fresh scent of his packmates reaches me, I squeeze Onyx's hand. "Hey, I don't want to talk with them about my pack yet. I need time to think. It's enough to just know."

His dark eyes study me and I feel like a bug under a microscope. "You'll still talk with them about it before you do anything?"

"Yeah. I promise."

His head bobs. "Okay, well, we still have to talk with Jasper and Hazel about today."

"I understand."

As we approach the training building, I keep waiting for Onyx to drop my hand. But he doesn't. My heart beat speeds up until my blood pounds in my ears. Memories of being zip-tied by these wolves and dragged away like a prisoner replays in my head until I'm squeezing Onyx's fingers so tight he stops walking.

"Hey, it's going to be fine. We can just explain, and I'll do all the talking if you need." Using our joined hands, he pulls me against him.

His citrus scent soaks in my lungs, calming and

centering me.

"No, I need to own my shit."

He kisses my knuckles and we resume our walk.

Jasper meets us in the thinning trees on the edge of the pack's compound. He looks calmer, but his shoulders still tense at the sight of me. Dread weighs me down until each step feels like I'm knee deep in mud.

"This is interesting," he says, crossing his arms. His gaze is cold as he looks at Onyx and then our joined hands. Onyx squares his shoulders and faces my brother.

"We need to talk to you about what just happened."

"Meet me at my cabin in five minutes," he says before turning away and striding back toward the building. I watch his receding form, my dread turning to cold fear.

"I don't know where that is," I tell Onyx.

A hint of a smile softens his expression. "It's close. I've got you, don't worry."

I shouldn't need him, but I cling to his arm anyway. Jasper's threat that Slate would kill me seems all too likely. Hazel might want to dispose of me herself. It's only their code of ethics that keeps me from turning and running. They'd restrain me and return me to my pack, which is roughly the outcome part of me hopes for.

Marigold opens the door of the small log-style cabin. She's wearing a floral sundress with her strawberry blonde hair piled on top of her head. Her cabin smells like sugar and tropical plants. Golden oak lines the interior with warm plaids and accents of sunny yellow. A collection of houseplants grow across the large window in the living space.

"Hey, Goldie. There was an incident during training and Jasper asked us to come here to discuss it privately," Onyx explains.

"Oh, is everything okay?" she asks me. I have no idea how to answer. No. It's a wreck, just like it's been since the minute I arrived here. She must read my expression, because Marigold pulls me away from Onyx and wraps her arms around my shoulders in a tight hug.

Tears threaten again and I take measured breaths to keep them away. When she releases me, she looks me in the eyes and says, "It's going to be fine. You are family."

I have to look away. She leads me to the sofa and I settle beside Onyx while she gathers refreshments in her little kitchen.

By the time Jasper, Slate, and Hazel arrive, Marigold has set out a plate of cinnamon cookies. Jasper sits in the arm chair beside the sofa, and she perches on the arm. Hazel and Slate stand, and my hold on Onyx's hand tightens.

Slate's gaze narrows on our joined hands, and his frown deepens.

"Jasper told me what happened," Slate finally says. I note he says Jasper and not Hazel. She fidgets in her seat as he says it. "What is your side of the story?"

Swallowing, I take a deep breath. "I was really upset because I could tell something was wrong with my mother and my pack, and no one was telling me anything." Onyx runs his thumb over my knuckles, encouraging me.

"I went to find Jasper, and Hazel asked to spar. I don't know what happened. I got hurt and just snapped."

Despite my confession, Slate's expression doesn't change.

Hazel sighs. "I wasn't injured. Honestly, I could have pushed her away sooner but her arm was dislocated and I didn't want to hurt her worse."

Slate's grasps the back of the armchair as he frowns at her. "Jasper said she was out of control and choking you. Even when you tried to end the fight, she wouldn't stop. I'm scared of what would have happened if you hadn't gotten the drop on her."

"I wasn't in danger," Hazel argues. "I wouldn't have sparred with her if I wasn't confident I could protect myself. You guys are over reacting."

My gaze connects with Hazel and she gives me a small smile. For the first time, it really feels like she's on my side.

"I can't have you... snapping, like you said," Slate says, fixing me with a hard stare. "What's your plan for preventing that from happening again?"

"I will make sure I don't lose control," I say solemnly.

"Trying harder isn't the answer." Slate rubs his jaw, locking me in place with his emerald eyes. "You won't spar again"

"But-" I start to argue.

"With anyone." He cuts me off. "If you were a pack member, there would be a consequence."

"It's not her fault," Onyx blurts. My muscles tense as everyone turns their attention to the man beside me.

"She needs to take responsibility for what happened. And she is. What's the problem?" Slate asks.

"She reacted that way for a valid reason," Onyx argues. "She wasn't trained properly. I think with enough time with my dad, that can be fixed and she'll be fine."

"Granite Ridge's training methods are brutal," Jasper agrees. "But I was trained the same and I've never lost control like that."

"Funny you should say that," Onyx growls.

It's like my blood is turning to ice, my heartbeat fluttering out of control. I'm not sure why, but I don't want them to know. To know how weak I was.

"What do you mean?" Hazel asks, her eyebrows pinching in concern as she regards me.

"You need to tell him. I'm very interested to know if he was aware of what was happening," Onyx says, dropping his voice. Rage sharpens each syllable.

"No, I don't," I say, my voice barely catching as I tuck my legs up under me.

"Ember," Jasper says, his voice softening. "What's going on?"

All eyes are on me. My tight breaths aren't getting enough oxygen into my lungs, and they begin to sting and ache. The edges of my vision blur as I study the floor.

Silence stretches on. Fabric rustles and Jasper squats down beside me, getting low until his hands come into my view. Onyx's hand tightens around mine.

"What do I not know?" he asks. Something about his tone loosens my throat. There's no way to keep the tears from my voice, but perhaps I can speak.

"Onyx saw some scars from the trainers from when they'd hurt me as punishment after I lost fights." Hardly more than a harsh whisper, but the words are out there.

Every line of Jasper's body tightens and his jaw grinds. With clipped speech, he asks, "You were included in those?"

All I can do is nod. The movement causes a tear to escape. My movements are jerky as I wipe it away with the back of my hand.

I wait for him to call me a liar. When we were children, he always won. He was four years older than me, but that didn't seem to matter to the trainers forcing us to compete. And then he was safely at home with our parents while I faced the consequences.

Hazel slips out of her seat and returns with tissues.

"What are you guys talking about?" Slate asks.

Jasper stands, his hand brushing my shoulder as he steps back. "Granite Ridge likes to pit wolves against each other, and the loser will often get physical punishment as motivation. Some trainers take it too far."

"Yeah, far enough to scar," Onyx adds, his voice a physical rumble against me.

And there it is, out in the open for everyone to see. I don't think I can take their pity. I'd prefer their judgment.

"That's why you react so violently during a fight," Hazel fills in.

My panic swells again, and I rest my cheek against my knees, focusing on Onyx's stony face. Dark ocean eyes stare back at me, the residual glow of his emotions finally fading.

"I'm sorry," Jasper says, his voice rough. I can't look at him, but I can hear Marigold murmuring under her breath and running her hands down his back.

"Onyx is right. If you stay longer, Fisher can work with you to get control over your reactions. But absolutely no fighting any of my wolves."

"Okay."

"Thanks," Slate says, sounding more like a brother than the Alpha of a pack in that moment.

"That was a lot. We should all take a break and decompress." Marigold stands. Jasper follows her, his face full of tension.

"I think that's a good idea," Slate confirms.

Onyx doesn't release my hand as I stand, anchoring me as I sway on my feet.

"Hey," Hazel says, giving me pause. "What's going on with you guys?"

"You'll have to be more specific," Onyx says dryly.

"You're holding hands," Slate points out.

"Oh." My mouth parts, but I can't put words together. This wasn't something I had picked a label for yet. I didn't expect anyone else to know, but under the circumstances, I'm grateful he didn't let me go.

"We are seeing each other," Onyx says calmly.

My heart skips a beat before it begins to buzz against my ribs.

"You're dating my sister?" Jasper asks, eyes narrowed.

"Yes, when two adults are attracted to each other and enjoy spending time together-" Onyx says.

Slate cuts him off. "Are you sure this is a good idea? You are from different packs. Unless one of you wants to change that?"

Questioning my actions toward Hazel is one thing, but he has no right to interfere in my relationship with Onyx.

"It's none of your damn business. Look, I didn't ask him to be my mate. We are just figuring out how we feel. If it gets serious, I'm sure Onyx will consult you," I snap, though it's weak with exhaustion.

"Have you really thought this through?" Jasper questions, looking to Onyx.

"It's not up to you," he snarls.

Slate's jaw ticks, his eyes alight as he rises to meet Onyx's anger. But Hazel takes his arm, running her hand down it to claim his hand, soothing him. "Guys, this is great. Two people we care about are dating. It's not an international incident." The tension breaks, the entire room letting out a breath.

"Okay," Slate concedes.

"This reminds me of how you guys reacted to Jasper and me," Marigold says with a laugh. "Everyone needs to relax. One crisis at a time."

Everyone ambles toward the door, small looks exchanged between partners as we end our meeting. Footsteps slow as we reach the front door.

"How long am I staying here?" I ask, taking the opportunity to question the Alphas.

"I'm not sure. We are waiting to hear from your mother," Slate says. "We discussed maybe a week."

"Okay," I answer, something in the back of my mind reminding me that they are still keeping things from me. But after the emotional turmoil of the last hour, I can't find the energy to have that conversation.

"I'm glad you're staying longer," Hazel says. "I think we should do something fun to get your mind off things. Would you like to join us for a girls night?"

"I don't thi-," I start to say.

Marigold claps her hands. "No, it would be so fun! It's exactly what you need, and we need to spend more time getting to know you!"

"I can host," Hazel adds. "I promise we won't braid each other's hair or anything weird. Just hanging out and lots of snacks."

Usually I would decline, but something about Hazel's kindness eats away at me. Maybe I should try something new.

"When is this girls' night?" I ask.

"How about tonight?" Marigold asks.

"I'm down," Hazel says.

"Oh, wow. That's soon." I glance to Onyx, but he shrugs. "No reason to wait, I guess."

"Great! Come over after sunset." Hazel's nose wrinkles as she smiles, her head tilting towards her mate.

Onyx squeezes my hand as we follow them out of the cabin.

We grab a late lunch in Onyx's kitchen, and then I crash for a nap before my evening with Marigold and

Hazel. Onyx seems to know that I need space to decompress. Today was humiliating, and I still have to face an evening with the two women mated to my grumpy brothers.

Time races by and I find myself standing on Hazel's patio. Onyx watches from the trees, though he's promised to go home and not patrol the cabin in his wolf form.

"Ember!" Hazel greets me, swinging open her door. "Come in, I've almost got drinks ready."

A small fire crackles in their fireplace, filling the cabin with warm light. Marigold gives me a little wave from the kitchen. She's emptying bags of chips into bowls.

I drift behind Hazel across the living space to the kitchen. "Here, let's take these to the coffee table," Marigold instructs, and I pick up two of the bowls - one of cheese puffs and one with BBQ chips. She adds a bowl of dip and a dish of chocolates.

The blender pulses as Hazel finishes our drinks. A bottle of non-alcoholic margarita mix sits by the sink. I take one of the armchairs, and Marigold sinks onto the sofa and tucks her feet under her. She tosses a cheese puff into her mouth with a grin.

"Here," Hazel says, handing me a wide goblet full of frozen pink margarita. She settles into the other armchair and helps herself to the glossy dark chocolates.

"This is so fun. Why don't we do this more often?" Marigold asks. Hazel just shrugs.

"Hazel, I'm really sorry about this morning," I say, feeling the weight of my mistakes still hanging over me.

She frowns. "You don't need to apologize. I get it. And it's going to get better." She states it as an inevitable fact, leaving me unsure of what to say.

"Hey, we are here to have fun and relax. No apologies needed." Marigold slides sideways to lounge across the sofa. "I really want to hear about you and Onyx."

"Oh, no," I say, burying my face in my hands.

"Oh, yes." She grins wickedly. "He was such a pain in the ass when Jasper and I got together. This is more than fair."

"Why? What was his problem?"

Marigold sighs dramatically. "For a long time, I had a crush on Cedar." She waves her hand in the air. "But he had zero interest in me. I think Onyx had always pictured us getting together some day, and he didn't take it well when he realized that wasn't going to happen."

"He has a big heart," Hazel says, her eyes crinkling as she smiles fondly. I squirm uncomfortably in my seat. "So what happened between you two? And when?"

"This is so embarrassing," I mutter.

Marigold giggles, taking a long drink of her margarita.

"Okay, I'll tell you about me and Jasper, would that be fair?" Marigold says.

"No, that's okay. I don't need to know about that."

"Then how about this? I'll spare you details about your brothers if you tell us about you and Onyx," Hazel teases. Scowling at her, I press my lips together.

"Please? I'm dying to know. I need details so I can tease him," Marigold whines.

Taking a fortifying sip of strawberry slush, I begin. "Remember the last pack party?"

"Um, yeah. It was last week," Hazel says.

"We kinda had a thing."

"A thing?" Marigold is almost bouncing in her seat.

"Yeah, he was annoying me, and next thing I knew, he kissed me." My cheeks burn against my palms as I attempt to hide my face.

"Holy kitty-titties, are you serious?" Hazel says, leaning forward in her chair. "So you guys make out, and then we ask him to watch over you while you stay with us." Her words tumble into laughter. "What are the chances?"

"Well done there," Marigold adds, grabbing another handful of cheese puffs.

Tentatively, I reach for some chips. They're delicious, and they give me an excuse to pause my story.

"So what about after you arrived? How did you go from a random kiss to saying you're dating?" Hazel licks the sugar off the rim of her drink.

"I don't know. We were just spending time together. He's such a flirt," I whine.

Hazel laughs. "Yeah, he really is."

"Ew," Marigold says, pulling a face.

"When I was upset, he was sweet. He comforted me."

"I bet he was *comforting*," Marigold mutters.

"So yesterday we were feeding the chickens and goats, and I kinda pranked him," I say.

"Oh, we should prank the boys!" Marigold interrupts me, swinging her feet down to the floor as if she's about to jump up. "Sorry, continue, I want to hear everything, please."

Despite my embarrassment, I can't stop smiling. "I just stuck apple slices in his hoodie and the goats were all over him."

"Good one," Hazel says with an approving smirk.

"That still doesn't get you to dating. When did he make his move?" Marigold says.

"We kissed right after that."

"Ooh!" she squeals. "And he confessed his feelings?"

"Actually, Cedar caught us making out," I say, unable to meet their eyes.

Marigold sets her drink down and leans forward. "Dammit, I thought I was the first one to know!"

"What? You figured it out?"

"Honey, he came in smelling like you so strongly, I knew he had been all over you."

"Oh, no." I would melt into the cushion if I could.

"Jasper and Marigold did the same thing, don't worry," Hazel says, rolling her eyes at Marigold.

"Ew, that's my brother," I reply without thinking. Both girls dissolve into giggles.

"Your brother is a total Casanova," Marigold says with a grin.

"I'm really happy for you guys," Hazel says, turning the conversation back to me and Onyx. I cringe under the attention, but it's better than hearing about my brother's romantic escapades.

"There's just something about him I really like," I admit. "But I don't see how we can make it work. I don't want to hurt him, but I'm going back to my pack soon."

Both girls stare at me for a few seconds.

"Would you want to join our pack?" Hazel finally asks.

"I can't," I say. "I've got a responsibility as Heir, and Jasper already ran off. I'm all our pack has left."

"You can," Hazel says quietly, all her laughter gone. "Your pack isn't a healthy place to be. You deserve a safe and loving home. More than just Onyx. Jasper is here. We are here."

"But that's the thing, if I'm Alpha, I can change my

pack," I say.

"What if Onyx went with you? We would hate to lose him, but it's not like it's far away." Hazel asks. I can't believe what I'm hearing.

"He has all his friends and family here. I couldn't do that to him. My pack is a miserable place to be right now, and it could be years before that changes." It hurts to say those thoughts out loud.

"So are you just going to be in a relationship even though you can't be together very often?" Hazel asks. Marigold grimaces.

"I don't know," I say.

"Okay, this is a fun girls night and we got all serious again. Everything is going to be fine. Love conquers all obstacles," Marigold says in a sing-song voice.

"Alright, it's your turn then," Hazel says with a wink.

"I don't think Ember cares," Marigold says.

Normally, I wouldn't want to hear any of it, but after what I just went through, it seems fair. Narrowing my eyes at her, I say, "Actually, I'd love to hear the story."

"Fine." Marigold cracks her knuckles and folds her hands over her knees. "I asked to be his roommate, and we got really close." Her tone is dreamy and I almost forget it's my brother she's talking about.

Hazel jumps in, "And you guys kept it all secret from us, sneaking around."

"We hadn't really figured it out," Marigold shoots back.

"When was this?" I ask.

"Last year, like three or four weeks before the whole invasion thing," Marigold says lightly. I tense at the mention of the pack conflict. It was the fight where I lost my father and then I hurt Onyx during the following struggle.

"He took me on a date out for coffee and let me drive his car and then we made out on the side of the road," she confesses with a manic giggle.

"You guys were ridiculous," Hazel says, rolling her eyes.

"Hey, your first kiss with Slate was right after he tattooed you, and you didn't even know he was a wolf," Marigold says.

"We don't have to talk about that," Hazel says, wrinkling her nose. "So, Ember, what kinda of stuff do you like?"

I blink at her sudden question. "Stuff I like?"

"What are your hobbies?" Marigold adds.

"Oh, I don't know." I shrug. "Listening to music, I guess. And I've been playing Jasper's video games that he left behind."

"Onyx loves video games." Hazel says.

"I know," I say with a smile I can't help. Her grin widens until she's beaming at me.

"I didn't see it coming, but I think you guys are good for each other. He can be kinda wild, but he's hilarious and really sweet and I think that's a good fit for you." Hazel concludes, looking satisfied.

"I appreciate that, but-" I start, but Marigold stops me.

"Hey, we are here for fun. No more worrying about problems. Everything will work out, and we are here for some girl bonding. So, I say we prank the boys."

"Slate was going to take them all out on a run," Hazel muses.

"I have just the thing. I thought they were so funny, I ordered them for an art project or something," Marigold says.

"What?"

Ten minutes later we're sneaking into Marigold and Jasper's cabin. It's empty and no sneaking is required, but the girl bonding energy has gotten ahold of me and I can't stop smiling.

Marigold comes out of their spare bedroom with a little baggy of tiny plastic chickens. She pops the bag open and pulls a few out to show us. They're about the size of my thumb nail, and absolutely adorable.

"I was going to make something with them for Cedar," she says quietly. "But this is better." We each take a handful and begin moving through the cabin, stashing them in partially hidden places. Marigold takes the bedroom and tucks them into Jasper's pockets. I tuck one behind the masculine looking bath products and then another behind the toothbrush that isn't bright pink.

"Alright, I'm all done here," Hazel whisper-yells.

"Me too," Marigold answers.

"Alright, who is next?" I say, feeling ridiculously excited.

Fisher and Clove look a little puzzled when we arrive, but Hazel is honest about the prank and Clove laughs for a while before she can nod her approval.

Hazel picks her way through the rest of the house to find anything specific to the twins, while Marigold and I take their bedroom. We tuck little chickens into the shirt pockets of the plaid work shirts Cedar prefers for gardening. She places one on top of his gaming console. I slide a couple into each boy's pillowcase and then tuck them up on the higher display shelves in between the various knickknacks from their childhood. One of them had a thing for painting pet rocks at some point, and they make the perfect platform for a chicken.

It's odd being in his room without him. I've been in here before, but last time it was heated. The sheets are wrinkled and I remember the feel of his mouth against my lower stomach. Despite all the reasons I shouldn't, I want him. More than just his touch. I'm quickly getting addicted to his thoughts, both the snarky ones and the kind ones.

"Okay, I think we're done here. There's only a few left to use on Slate," Marigold says, snapping me out of my thoughts.

We walk back to Hazel's cabin, and Marigold links her arm through mine. I stiffen, but then force myself to relax. It's strange having female friends, but they're sweet and seem supportive. As long as I don't make any mistakes, maybe I can keep these friendships.

Hazel laughs her head off while she tucks chickens in Slate's art supplies and then into his closet. Marigold drags me back to the sofa and we help ourselves to the snacks. I finally try a chocolate and it's divine. Just as I'm reaching for my second one, my phone buzzes.

> I need you to get some information from that pack without them knowing.
> Mom 9:06PM

What? Does she seriously want me to spy on them? They're our allies and they're trying to make good on that promise. Gritting my teeth, I type back.

> That's not a good idea. We need their alliance.
> 9:07PM

> That's why I said without them knowing.
> Mom 9:08PM

She sends a list of reports, like the locations of their security cameras and the schedule of patrols. Everything they'd need to raid the pack.

> Don't ask me to do this. It's not right.
> 9:10PM

> This is your duty and it's an order.
> Mom 9:11PM

> Why? How is this going to help the shit show you're dealing with?
> 9:12PM

> Do not question me. This is necessary, and you're going to do it.
> Mom 9:14PM

"Everything okay?" Marigold asks. I click my phone off and stow it away.

"Sorry, my mom is being annoying," I say, quickly picking up my half-melted margarita and sipping it.

"I know the situation with her sucks. But I'll second

Onyx's offer for you to stay."

"Chickens are deployed and I'm starving!" Hazel announces, plopping down. She grabs the entire bowl of chips and starts to shove them into her mouth.

The conversation stays light, and Hazel laughs while telling us about Slate's initial flirtations and then about how they finally got together. It's sweet and makes me feel hopeful.

Footsteps on the porch announce Slate's arrival.

"It's late, let's head home," Marigold says to me.

Hazel wraps us in a tight hug before we slip out.

"Did you have fun tonight?" Marigold asks.

"Yeah."

"No, seriously," she says, giving me a hard look.

My arms cross over my chest. "I've never really had friends like this before, which sounds totally pathetic. But there aren't a lot of women in our pack and none of them are close to my age. So this was really nice."

"Again, this is why you should stay." She smiles, hoping I'll suddenly change my mind and agree.

"Thank you for everything," I say, waving at her as we split paths. She heads south toward her cabin with Jasper, and I climb the steps to the porch of Onyx's home.

Cedar greets me with a simple, "Hello."

The shower roars behind the hall bath's door, so I guess Onyx is occupied. Pushing the disappointment down, I close the door to my room. It's late and I really am tired. Despite the comfortable bed, my mind buzzes with everything from the last two days. The problems in my pack. My new friends. My mother's awful texts. But mainly, my new boyfriend.

My phone beeps with another message from my mother, demanding my attention. My stomach churns as I turn my phone to silent and place it face-down on the dresser, far from my bed. Tomorrow I'll have to face her demands. But not tonight.

CHAPTER ELEVEN

VIDEO GAMES & VIOLENCE

ONYX

Ember gets home from her girls' night late and goes straight to bed. I listen from the hallway as her breathing evens out. It might be desperate, but I can't help myself.

The next morning Ember bakes scones with my mother while I watch from the table. She listens to everything my mother says and asks intelligent

questions. Her green hair shimmers as she laughs.

"What do you think?" she asks intently as I take a bite of the blackberry scone smeared with butter. It's still warm and the pastry is tender.

"You are an incredible baker. And don't tell my mom, but you might be even better than she is," I say. Mom smiles from the doorway before she heads out, giving us privacy.

"What should we do today? Since I have another free day being an unwanted and involuntary guest," she says.

A grin spreads across my face. "Want to play some video games?"

To my delight, she agrees.

She settles on the sofa in the family room while I run to grab a few video games. When my hand reaches for the case on my shelf, something small rolls under my fingers.

What the hell?

Pinching the item, I open my hand and frown down at a tiny translucent orange chicken. Frowning at it, I spot a second one sitting higher on the shelf, tucked behind a figurine. This one is green.

The chickens tumble in my palm as I wander back into the family room.

"Whatcha got there?" Ember asks. There's something more than casual curiosity in her voice, and I narrow my eyes at her.

"Do you know anything about tiny chickens?"

A beautiful flush rises up her neck as she buries her face in the cushion to stifle giggles.

"Seriously?" I ask.

Wiping at her eyes, she takes a deep breath to steady herself and says, "To be fair, it was Marigold's plan."

"Girls are weird," I grumble, tucking the chickens into my pocket.

Her amused smirk makes my stomach clench. She's stunning.

It takes a moment to focus with her so near, but soon I'm showing her the controls for a racing game.

She sits cuddled up against my chest. My arm is around her waist, so my controller sits against her hip and her head rests against the hollow of my neck. Having her soft figure pressed against me is distracting, and I crash my race car on the first round.

Before we can race again, Cedar clears his throat. He leans against the archway that leads to the hallway. "Hey, did anyone lose a tiny chicken?"

With a frown, he holds up a teeny purple bird between his thumb and index finger.

We dissolve into laughter and I drop my controller onto the rug.

"What?" he asks.

"I have no idea, dude," I wheeze. "But that's fucking hilarious."

Shaking his head, Cedar disappears back to his room.

"I hope he likes them," Ember whispers. Turning my head, we're nose to nose. "Cause there's a lot of them hidden in his stuff. Marigold primarily got them for him."

"So am I just a casualty and you guys mainly hit Cedar?" I ask, just as quietly.

When she shakes her head, her emerald hair shimmers. "Nope, all you boys got chickened."

Chuckling, I grab her chin and tip her mouth up to mine for a brief kiss.

With a wicked grin, she pulls away. "I think we were in the middle of a race."

It takes concentrated effort to take my hands off her and return to our game. But feeling her laugh vibrate through me as she plays the video game is another type of paradise.

Ember races recklessly, crashing her car and swerving off the road every few seconds. She scrunches her eyes closed and laughs. I could stay like this with her forever.

As my car races by with a first place banner, I pull her up until I can kiss against her neck, below her ear. She shivers against me.

"Have I ever told you that green is my favorite color?" I murmur, twining a lock of her hair around my finger.

"Hey, I'm trying to drive here," she says, rotating her shoulders.

"Is that what you were doing?" I ask, nipping at her skin. I've had enough video games with her intoxicating scent invading my senses.

She twists to face me and glares. "Maybe if you weren't so distracting."

"Game's over. Want to go again?" Her pupils dilate at my words and I smirk.

"Maybe in a minute," she says. She drops her controller onto the cushion beside us, and I set mine aside too. Achingly slow, her hand comes up to my neck and her fingertips slip below the neckline of my shirt. Why am I wearing a shirt again? More importantly, why is *she* wearing a shirt?

My eyes close at her touch, and I can feel her moving closer, her chest skimming mine. Kisses feather down my jaw, and I raise my chin to give her access. Her soft growl of approval nearly undoes me, but I let her control everything, my hands loosely around her hips.

Her other hand threads in my hair and she pulls, moving my face to where she wants me. One tentative kiss, and then a harder one. Her tongue licks across my mouth and I open. Her wildflower taste is the only thing

I want in the world. Without breaking our kiss, she climbs over me until she's straddling me, her thighs over mine.

My hold on her hips tightens and I slide one hand up under her shirt and up her spine. The other goes to her ass. She's perfect.

Her phone in her back pocket buzzes. I pull it out and she jerks back, grabbing it from my hand. Biting her lip, she powers it down and tosses it aside. "Sorry, my mom is driving me crazy."

I don't question her. I'm too drunk on the feel of her against me. She grinds her hips down and my pulse speeds, blood pounding in my ears and my skin. The only cure for this fire is the cause of it.

Her delicate fingers brush hair out of my face and her glowing eyes lock with mine. A little eyeliner remains around her lashes, but the rest of her face is scrubbed clean so I can see the lightest spray of freckles across her cheeks and the bridge of her nose. She's stunning.

"Hey, I need to go see my brother," she says. Not exactly what I was expecting her to say. She eases off of me.

My pounding heart starts to calm. If she doesn't want to take things further right now, that's fine with me.

"Sure, let's go."

Her hand flattens against my chest. "It's something

I need to do alone. Why don't you chill and enjoy your games. I bet you haven't gotten to play since I arrived."

Lifting her hand, I press a kiss to her fingers. "I've been occupied with better things." Before releasing her, I bite down on the meat of her palm, below her thumb. She jolts, her hips pressing forward against me. "Give me five more minutes," I say, skimming my hands up her thighs to her waist.

"Five minutes? Give yourself more credit than that," she says, kissing my cheek before she climbs off of me.

"Hey!" I say, flushing. "That's not-" She laughs. "When that happens, you won't be going anywhere for hours. Maybe days."

Grabbing her phone, she heads to the hall. "Seriously, just let me talk to my brother for a bit and then I'll meet you back here and we can pick up where we left off."

The promise leaves me adjusting my pants and taking deep breaths before I can get up.

Without her here, nothing holds my attention.

After getting a snack, I wander out of my cabin. Maybe I'll meet her in between the two cabins and we can go for a run and then have some quality time together out in the woods. The thought of her under me in soft grass is tempting.

I meander along the edge of the meadow, generally heading toward Jasper and Marigold's cabin, but as I near the south side, I catch movement through the tinted window of the tiny office I work out of. Maybe Vale is checking security camera feeds or something. I've been off duty for days now.

Jogging the distance, I pull the door open. Instead of Vale or Slate sitting at my desk, the chair is pushed aside and Ember hovers over the keyboard.

"Onyx!" she yips, spinning to face me. Her phone is clutched tightly against her breasts.

Confusion chokes me, anger burning it away. There are only a few reasons why she would be getting into one of our work computers, and none of them are good.

"Ember, what are you doing?"

Her mouth opens but no sound comes out. Fear oozes out of her and I hate that she feels any fear because of me, but it can't be helped. I wasn't the one who snuck into my office.

My approach slows, like she's a skittish animal. Making eye contact, I try to reason with her. "I was honest with you about everything. I need you to tell me exactly what's going on, and we can figure it out together."

Her breathing is ragged and she glances at the door. Gently, I take her elbow and lead her to the chair where I can pull her into my lap. She curls in on herself against my chest.

"I'll take care of it if you just tell me," I say, my anger

replaced with worry as I feel how her pulse flutters.

With shaky hands, Ember unlocks her phone and shows me a string of texts from her mother - demands for all sorts of information about our security and resources.

My eyes catch on the last text.

> If you can't do your duty, you aren't fit to be Heir. We will have to reevaluate your position.
> MOM 9:46AM

Glancing at the computer, I can see she hasn't gotten past my password.

"I'm sorry," she whispers. "She's my Alpha too. I was ignoring her, but I have to do something to help my pack."

"You didn't do any damage," I say, my arms banding around her protectively. It's true, even if she intended to.

Her next breath shakes like she's fighting off tears. "What if something happens to her? I already lost my dad, and I know they're shitty parents but they're the only ones I have. What if someone challenges her and kills her, and I'm not there?" Her voice is raw, rasping until it's just a whisper

"I'm sorry. I wish I could do something to help with that. But I'm not going to lie. I'm glad you're here safe with me. If someone wants to take her out, they'll probably go for you too. I can't let that happen."

"It's not your responsibility," she whispers.

"I hate to break it to you," I say, nuzzling into her neck. "But I care about you."

Despite her despair, she smiles.

"I know my mom is awful and I don't want to be like her," she whispers. "I don't want to pick a mate because of his rank and treat my children like tools to be exploited. I don't want to rule by fear. It makes me sick that I believed her for so long."

"You won't be like her. You are so much better than that," I say, my voice scraping over each word.

She looks up at me through dark lashes, her expression vulnerable. But I'm not the only one standing behind her now. She's always had Jasper, and now she's won over Hazel and Marigold too. I know even Slate would stand behind her. We aren't going to let her get hurt if we can help it.

The harsh truth is that she's tangled up in her pack's troubles and she won't be safe until it's over. Even here, Sienna is sinking her claws into her. And one day of trust isn't enough to undo eighteen years of conditioning.

"Are you going to tell Slate or Jasper what I did?" she asks.

"You need to talk with them about all of this."

She snuggles in closer, her nose bumping against my neck and her breath ghosting across my skin. "I will," she says, and I feel the movement of her lips.

"Come on, let's go home," I say. I want to get her out of this stuffy office before someone finds us here and starts asking questions.

Besides, the way she's touching me brings up fantasies of laying her across my desk, and there really isn't room unless I shoved my computer off, and that's not a good idea.

CHAPTER TWELVE

HEARTBREAK & HOOK UPS

Ember

Fear ebbs as Onyx walks me back to his home, replaced with a self-loathing that I embrace. How could I let my mother derail the relationships that I'm building here? I bury the thought that it's all temporary anyway. It's getting easier to pretend that this is home.

The cabin is warm and bright with buttery

afternoon light. Clove works in the kitchen, flour dusting her apron. Onyx's hand runs down my back reassuringly.

"Can you see when Jasper and the Alphas are free to talk?" I ask, my voice soft. Onyx nods and pulls out his phone.

Instead of fretting over the upcoming discussion, I ask Clove if I can help with her baking. After a few minutes, my shoulders ache with the repetitive motion of kneading the bread, but it's soothing.

Clove pulls the first batch of loaves out of the oven just as I set my second loaf into a pan to rise. The scent of nutty flour reminds me of Onyx, but also of his entire family. How would my life have been different if I had been raised in a supportive environment like this?

Onyx comes up behind me, putting his arms around me. I tense, glancing at Clove, but she wears a mild smile, her eyebrows rising as she focuses on her work.

"Everyone is heading over," he says into my ear.

"That was fast," I mutter.

"You are important, not just to me," Onyx whispers back.

"They've got to be sick of me taking up their time and energy."

Onyx's hands move to my hips, and I drop the loaf on the countertop as he spins me around to face him. He glares at me, and I swallow thickly.

"You are not a bother. You are worth it." His conviction makes me stammer, my skin flushing. Without hesitating, he leans forward and kisses my forehead before releasing me. Onyx settles into a kitchen chair, reclined with his feet out as he watches me.

Bemused, I turn back to my work.

"Here, I'll take over that," Clove says, taking my place in front of the dinner rolls I'm cutting and rolling. "Sounds like your brothers are here."

The door clicks open and familiar voices float through the house.

"Ready?" Onyx asks.

"No."

We take our discussion to the fire pit out back. Dappled sunshine highlights the rich, dark tones of Slate's hair, the same color as our mother's hair and what mine would be if I didn't change it constantly.

Jasper sits beside me on a bench, Onyx on my other side, while Hazel and Slate sit opposite in weathered Adirondack chairs.

Tension rises in my chest, choking me. I need answers, but this discussion is bound to be painful. It would be much nicer to play house with Onyx and ignore the reality outside our bubble.

"Ember, Onyx told us your mom has been texting you and pressuring you to send her private pack information?" Slate gets right to the point.

I glare at Onyx as he produces my phone and unlocks it before handing it to Slate. How the hell did he know the code?

Slate scrolls through the texts and holds it out to Hazel and then Jasper. Jasper lets out a low growl that somehow makes me feel better. Maybe he will be sympathetic.

"Sienna is going to turn on us if it keeps her in power," Hazel concludes.

"It won't," Jasper says, crossing his arms and scowling.

Slate runs his fingers through his wavy hair. "Look, I think we should send Ember back. It's becoming a risk to our pack."

My mouth drops open. I asked to go back, but I want it to be on my terms. Not exiled as a criminal. Beside me, Onyx is seething. I can feel his anger rolling off of him like heat.

"No, we just take precautions. Turn the phone off and take out the sim card. Let Sienna know we will keep her safe, but she isn't going to spy for her." Jasper says, frowning at Slate.

"How long until they take the fight here?" Slate demands.

"Will you guys just be honest and tell me everything?" I growl.

"She deserves to know," Hazel says softly, her hand squeezing Slate's forearm.

"If she decides she has to go home now, we'll have to lock her up." Jasper won't look at me.

I throw my hands up. "Fine, I'll just go now and find out for myself. Because I seriously doubt you guys will actually imprison me."

Onyx grabs my hand to keep me seated. When he finally speaks, it's cool and calm in a way that scares me. "See? If you don't tell her, it'll be the exact thing you were trying to avoid."

"Unfortunately, I think you're right." Slate says.

"What was that? I didn't hear you," Onyx says.

The Alpha curls his lip, staring Onyx down until the lower ranked wolf drops his gaze.

Jasper pinches the bridge of his nose and exhales slowly. "I got word this morning that someone challenged Sienna for Alpha. She killed him, but she's not in the best shape."

"What?" I yelp, starting to stand. Onyx tugs me back into my seat again. My instinct is to snap at him and to free myself, but I hold it in.

"If we send anyone to help her, it gives the pack a common enemy and puts her in a weaker position," Jasper says. His words sound like he's been debating this for a while.

"I need to go, at least," I argue.

"I'm sorry," Hazel adds, "but if you go back now, they'll use you against her. She needs to be able to fight without worrying about your safety."

"You don't believe I could help?" I ask flatly.

Jasper locks eyes with me, a hint of pale blue flickering in his eyes. "Do you honestly think you could take down someone like Flint or Orion?"

The sounds of the forest break the tense silence. He's right, I couldn't win in a fight against any of the huge males that make up the ranks of Granite Ridge. I'm powerless if they decide to no longer respect my claim as Heir.

"I know this isn't fair," Hazel says slowly. "But we will figure something out that doesn't include you getting hurt."

"What can you do if you can't send fighters?"

Slate and Hazel exchange a look before Slate answers. "We don't know yet. Hawthorne and Jasper have been talking to Sienna daily. They're working on a few ideas, but nothing has come together yet."

"Will you tell me when that happens?" I ask.

Jasper nods. "As long as you're being reasonable, yes."

"I'm not the unreasonable one at the moment," I snap. With a sigh, I try again. "Fine. Keep me updated. Am I free to just hang around like I've been doing? Or do you want to lock me up?" Sarcasm edges my words.

"Stick close and keep Onyx with you. Not too close to the road either. I don't want to take any chances." Slate rubs the back of his neck.

"And you'll stay?" Jasper asks.

"For now." It's the only answer I'm willing to give.

"Watch her," Slate instructs Onyx. I want to slap him, but then I remember that Hazel was snatched from their territory once. It's possible he's worried about my safety instead of thinking I'm a flight risk.

"I'm going to head back to keep working on this whole disaster," Jasper says, shaking his head as he stands and brushes off his pants. "Hopefully we will have some answers soon."

Hazel's concerned gaze lingers on me, and I'm grateful when Onyx drapes an arm over my shoulder.

"What are you guys gonna do tonight?" she asks.

"Dunno. Hang out," Onyx answers for us. Stomach in knots, I'm not interested in questioning him.

Hazel and Slate excuse themselves.

"What can I do to make you feel better?" Onyx asks, turning to bump his nose into my temple.

"I just want to get away from everyone," I answer honestly. He removes his arm. "No, from everyone else. Not you."

His pleased smile eases some of my turmoil.

"So what should we do?" His whispered question holds innuendo that brings a blush to my cheeks.

"Want to just take a walk?" I suggest. "I know we are supposed to stay close, but maybe we can head east, further from my pack?"

"Yeah, up the creek is really nice, near our border with Raven and Ironcrest packs," Onyx says thoughtfully.

"Two legs or four?"

His gaze turns hungry. Four legs means less clothing at the destination, but he reigns himself in. "Up to you."

"Let's just hike it. Slower sounds nice." I shrug. He puts up no argument, except to make sure I change into better shoes.

Five minutes later, we are walking along a faint trail I can hardly see, heading north-east. My legs aren't as long as Onyx's, but he slows his pace to match mine, and I stay close behind him until the trees thin.

The light through the branches takes on a pink tinge, but I don't fear sundown in these woods with Onyx beside me.

A squirrel scampers on an overhead branch, and a robin flits past, doubling back to check on us. Onyx smiles up at it.

"Your part of the forest feels different than ours," I murmur.

"Oh, yeah?"

"More alive." It hurts to admit, but I'm done

holding back truths from Onyx. He's seen the worst of me.

"Strange," he says. "Do you guys have any forest management going on?"

"No." I frown at him. "What's that?"

"We have Ewan. He's a biologist and he focuses on managing our land and keeping it healthy. We've also got a retired gal who specializes in trees."

"Really? How interesting." His pack has so many jobs that our pack ignores. Someday I'll make sure we have something like that.

The trees part into a clearing. It's small, but the evening light streaming down paints the wildflowers in pinks and oranges. Grass bows under our feet as he leads me forward.

'This is one of my favorite spots," he says, hands going to my waist.

My neck cranes back as I take in the sheer magnitude of the trees surrounding us like a faerie circle. They must be ancient to be this huge.

"It's beautiful," I murmur.

"I've never brought anyone else here," he says, lowering his head to touch our cheeks together. My eyes drift closed at the feel of his skin brushing mine.

"I think I owe you five more minutes," I murmur.

"Five minutes," he echoes with a grin.

I lean back to look into his eyes. "You're the only person who has ever stood up for me like that. I've never felt like this with anyone else."

"I love the idea of you being only mine," he purrs suggestively, pressing a kiss to my cheekbone.

I give him a soft smack on his chest. "You know what I mean. Believing things can be better. Trying to help me."

His face goes from playful to intense, his gaze darkening. "I'm not going anywhere."

His mouth is hot on mine, insistent and rough. He nips at my bottom lip and I grab his shirt and tug it up. He slips it over his head and tosses it aside.

We fumble with our clothes, shedding items until just our undergarments remain. My limbs are clumsy as we sink down to the ground. With an arm hooked under the small of my back, he lowers me until my head rests on the soft grass.

Onyx sits back, his gaze exploring me. My skin flushes and I try to stay still, letting him look. It's difficult to not reach for him, but the satisfied smirk on his face makes it worth enduring the tension. And when he finally crawls toward me, I get a beautiful view of the muscles in his arms and chest moving under his skin. He is stunning. The curve of his cheekbones and the fullness of his lips are familiar to me now, and I find comfort in his dark eyes.

He breathes in against my collarbone and kisses up my neck until I can't stand it a second longer.

Cupping his jaw, I pull his mouth to mine. One kiss melds into another and my sense of time disintegrates. Pulse resonating in my skin, I press closer to him, feeling his heart pounding in response.

Breathing hard, he breaks away, looking down at me like I'm everything to him. No one has ever looked at me like that. Am I the only one for him? Maybe I'm just the newest in a string of girls for him. Once the thought hits me, I can't let it go.

"Onyx?" I ask. He pauses his work on my collarbone.

"Yeah?"

Nervousness rises in me, churning my stomach. I bite my lip, trying to sort through my thoughts. "Have you ever had another girlfriend?" I ask him.

With a thoughtful half-smile, he rolls onto his side, propping his head up in his hand like he's settling in for a good conversation. "No."

"Even a hookup?" I cross my arms over my bare breasts.

"Does what we did at that party count?" he asks. I shake my head. "Then nope."

"Are you serious?" I blurt out.

"I've never seen a girl I was that interested in until you." He states it like it's a plain fact, no big deal.

"Oh," I breathe out, shivering as his hand skims down my ribs and over my hips.

"What about you and Hawk?" he asks, nuzzling his nose against my jaw.

Exhaling sharply, I close my eyes and try to string words together. He's making coherent thought rather difficult.

"It was all arranged, and he was nice enough, but it wasn't like we were a real couple. I mean, he did the expected things like hold my hand and eat dinner with me, but I don't think either of us wanted more. He never touched me like you do."

When I open my eyes, he's staring into my soul. "I've hardly begun. I don't want a few kisses, I want all of you."

Every cell of my being tingles and I have to bite down on my lip.

He watches my mouth hungrily. "You're gorgeous," he rasps.

"You're a flirt," I say, the energy between us almost unbearable. It's a heavy pressure, and I feel like I'll burst out of my skin.

His brows furrow, his eyes boring into me. "I want you to be my mate."

My mind goes blank at his declaration. It's one thing to daydream about it, but another to hear him say he wants me in that all-consuming permanent way.

Without waiting for my answer, he kisses my jaw and leaves a trail down my throat to the crook of my neck. As he bites down lightly, I gasp, grabbing onto his arm. He doesn't break the skin and follows it with a lick that makes my toes curl.

"I'm not ready for that. Things are complicated." I manage to say, though my body screams yes.

He grins at me, his hair falling over his forehead. "That's not a no."

"It's a no for now. Ask me again when my life isn't falling apart around me."

"What about tomorrow?"

"Onyx!" I pinch the skin on his shoulder and he growls, snapping at my hand.

"Alright, I guess I can wait," he says, sighing dramatically.

I swat at him again, a laugh escaping me. He's so handsome with filtered light dancing across the bridge of his nose and the curve of his lips.

Threading my fingers through his hair, I admire him. On his brother, their square features look like an old movie star. On him, they're rougher with sharp edges. To me, he's perfect. And he wants me.

"So now that I have you alone, finally, what do you want to do?" he asks, a certain kindness in his voice. He's letting me take the lead and set the boundaries. That might be a mistake.

Looking boldly into his eyes, I say, "Everything."

He smirks. "Too bad you didn't agree to be my mate."

My lip curls into a snarl at the teasing.

"I suppose we can compromise. Call it a preview."

He's already moving, his hands gripping my ribs to keep me in place. I let out some sort of strangled whine at the words, and I can feel his dark laugh against my skin as he closes his mouth over the delicate skin at my waist.

"A preview?" I question with a hoarse laugh.

His hand slides between my legs, testing and teasing over the fabric. I let out another whine that destroys what's left of my dignity. It doesn't matter, all I need is him.

Slowly, his fingers slip up and down until I'm trembling and trying to press myself against him. His tongue licks below my belly button.

"Onyx, seriously," I beg in a desperate whisper.

His fingers thread under my panties and plunge into my core. The shock and pleasure overwhelm my senses and my back arches. He strokes inside me as he looks up to watch my reactions.

My thoughts scramble, unable to function under his onslaught. My hands close over his shoulder, my nails digging into his skin.

He pauses. "Do you want me to stop, or do you want more?"

"Don't," I gasp, "stop."

He chuckles and resumes, turning his hand and trying angles until he gets an embarrassing moan out of me. Eyes screwed shut, I only see stars, so I gasp when he flips me over and pulls at my hips until I lift up onto hands and knees.

"Can you stay like this?" he murmurs against my skin, his tongue dragging up my spine like my skin is sugar.

"Yeah." My back arches at the feel of him.

Bending over me, his hand curls under until he hones in on my clit. His soft but insistent touch threatens to shatter me, and I press my ass back into him.

It's overwhelming as he begins moving his hips, grinding his cock against my ass through his boxers. If we just removed the clothes between us... I can't get enough air, gasping as he ruts into me.

His movements slow as he focuses on what he's doing with his hands. Two fingers dip back into me, and I almost fall forward. Only his growled command keeps me from faceplanting.

With his other hand he slides his finger over my clit over and over, working me into a frenzy. Pleasure burns hotter through me, becoming an unbearable pressure. His fingers against me, inside me, the weight of him pressing into me. I'm so close to release.

I want to live in this moment forever, but I can

barely tolerate it for these few seconds. His teeth clamp down on my juncture of neck and shoulder, holding there and barely pricking the skin, showing he could mark me as his mate - and I know in that moment if he broke the skin with his teeth, the magic would take and I would be his.

But he doesn't. Instead, he sucks the skin to leave a hickey. The hint of pain layered over the immense pleasure of his touch is the last thing I can take.

Cursing like a sailor, I break, shaking and tensing against the onslaught of pleasure. He groans as I squeeze his fingers and he presses into me.

He braces one hand on the ground, the other under my chest to keep me from collapsing. With whispered praises and peppered kisses, he stretches out on his side and tucks me against him.

"Goddess, I wanted to claim you so badly," he says. With a bashful grin, he scoots back and discards his boxers. I stare, realizing he came in his clothes. My cheeks prickle like I'm blushing, but my skin is already flushed. Tugging his sweats on, he cuddles up against me again.

The grassy earth shouldn't be this comfortable, but with his biceps under my head, I could easily fall asleep. Either Onyx feels the same, or he knows how tired I am.

"Get some rest," he instructs. "You need it. Especially with what I plan to do with you once you finally agree to be my mate."

"Dream on," I shoot back, barely able to string my words together.

He chuckles and presses a kiss to my ear. It's so tempting to drift off as he settles against me. His breathing soothes me and his touch makes me feel safe.

I'm lost in a haze, coming down from what he just did to me. I turn in his arms and kiss the tip of his nose. He smiles without opening his eyes.

"Rest," he rumbles, and I go still.

It's so peaceful, Onyx curled around me, his arm across my stomach. Time slips by and he dozes. Sunset melts into darkness, but the almost-full moon lights up our woodland haven. There are no predators around here except us, so it's safe for us to sleep if we wish.

Eventually someone will wonder where we are, but it's easier to pretend the rest of the world doesn't exist.

Onyx snuggles closer in his sleep, nuzzling into my chest. My hand goes to his head and I drag my nails through his hair. It's entirely possible I love this man.

I'd leave my pack for him.

The realization sends ice through my veins.

What would that even look like?

If I left, my mother would have to name another Heir, and by default it would be her new Beta, Orion. That would give him more power, and he already oversteps and stands against her every chance he gets.

Since things are already shaky, my mother will likely lose her position. She could be killed or maybe exiled.

If Orion or another of the males in the pack became Alpha, they would want revenge against Onyx's pack. My mother's lack of retaliation from our last battle is a sore spot for many of my packmates. Without her standing in the way, it's only a matter of time until they decide to move against the Bracken Creek pack.

I have to go back. The alternative is too risky.

Onyx moves in his sleep, his arms tugging me tighter against his chest. Heat radiates off of him.

But what if I went home and he came with me? I dismiss the thought as soon as it occurs to me. My pack would see him as the enemy. His life here is wonderful, and I can't force him into a new pack. He would be miserable and my pack would probably try to kill him.

How could I have been so stupid?

My heart hurts, pain stabbing through me worse than a physical wound. I can't have him. There's no way to make this work. At least, not right now. Once I am Alpha, I can repair my pack and change the culture until we can be together safely.

This bond between us grows stronger with every touch. The longer I wait, the more it will hurt to sever it.

If we will ever have a chance, I have to go back and demand the power I am due. The emotional hurt weighs me down, making planning difficult.

Watching him sleep, I can't bear the thought of telling him. He will insist on joining me. If I'm facing my treacherous pack, I need to know he is safe here.

Slowly, I move his arm across me until it lays between us. He barely twitches. Somehow, I know if he wakes up and asks me to be his mate again, I will accept, no matter the consequences to our packs.

As softly as I can manage I move away from him and rise. There's no need to gather my clothes, I'll just lose them when I shift.

Hand to my chest, pressing in as if I could reduce the pain of a broken heart, I look over Onyx one last time, memorizing the shape of his mouth and the way his lashes lay against his cheeks. His hair has lighter streaks from the time we've been out in the sun together this last week. His breathing stays slow and even.

There's no doubt about it. I am in love with him.

I can't stay here a minute longer. I'll lose my nerve.

With one last lingering glance, I sink into my wild instincts. My anger at the injustice of the situation drops away. Black fur covers my skin and in a split-second, I am a wolf.

In this form, I am graceful, weaving through the trees as I run downhill toward the border between Bracken Creek and Granite Ridge. In the back of my mind, every step leaves me screaming to go back to him, but it's effortless to ignore.

My animal side senses every little creature in the brush around me. The night is illuminated, making my journey easy. I'd never manage as a human, but in this shape, I leap from rock to rock and cross this deeper section of creek without hesitation.

It's time to go home and face this mess.

CHAPTER THIRTEEN

RECKLESS RESCUING

ONYX

Crickets chirp when I wake. From the warm moonlight, it's obviously still early evening.

Ember and I should head back. But her warm shape is no longer curled against me.

My entire body goes stiff, tension through every muscle.

Where is she?

There are a dozen reasonable explanations, but

somehow I know it's the worst one. She's gone. Her clothes litter the ground, so either she left naked or she shifted.

No.

This can't be happening.

The onslaught of violent emotions triggers my shift, and before I can think anything through, I'm in my gray wolf form leaping into the trees.

My wolf senses try to track her, following her scent northward. I lose it in the creek. Pain cuts through my panic. My paws stumble, and I throw my head back and let out a heartbroken howl.

Granite Ridge is on the other side of the creek. I cannot cross into that territory unprepared.

I don't know how I manage to get home. My paws shift to feet as I stumble up the steps to the front door. It's only by habit that I grab a pair of sweats and tug them on.

Cedar steps into the entry, his eyes wide with concern. I crash into him, pushing both of us against the wall. My twin grabs me, holding me up.

"She left," is all I can choke out. He muscles me toward the sofa, and I collapse, gulping down air to control my panic.

A few minutes later, Hazel bursts through the front door. She wraps me in a tight hug and I feel my head clearing. Slate enters behind her.

"Okay, what happened?" he asks.

Guilt eats away at me. I could have prevented this.

"We were out in the woods, and we dozed off. When I woke up, she was gone." My throat is raw, each word scratching. "I tracked her to the creek."

"Oh, Onyx," Hazel says, her hold tightening again.

Slate lets out a growl. "How could you have let this happen?"

"Slate," Hazel says softly. "That's not fair."

"It was his job to watch her. We shouldn't have let them leave the cabin."

Anger cuts through my haze of anxiety. It hones my mind and gives me something to focus on. Shrugging Hazel off, I stand to face my best friend. "You wanted her to leave so you should be happy."

"I wanted our pack safe and her to be safe too, and that would all be possible if you weren't too busy thinking with your dick."

I swing at him before my brain registers the decision. My fist connects with his jaw and he reels back. A split second later and he's on me, pressing me to the wood floor. The ringing pain in the back of my skull feels deserved. This is my fault.

His voice is dark and dominant. "Do not do that again, understood? You're not helping her right now."

My brain finally regains control and I stop struggling. The realization I just punched my Alpha horrifies me. I was thinking of him as my childhood friend, not my leader. He lets me sit up and I keep my gaze on the ground in submission.

"Understood."

"You two fighting really doesn't help the situation," Hazel says, crossing her arms. "We have to figure out what to do about this."

"I'm going to get her," I say without thinking.

"You can't do that." It's Hazel who stops me and I blink at her in surprise. "They'll treat you like an enemy, even if it's Sienna who catches you. She needs her pack to like her, and killing someone they see as an enemy would help her. I don't trust her to uphold our alliance right now."

"She's right," Slate adds. "We have to be smart about this."

"I can't-" I start to argue.

"I'll get Hawthorne and Jasper. We can get a hold of Sienna and sort this out." Slate heads to the door.

"Just hang tight. It'll be okay," Hazel says, smiling sadly.

Cedar watches from the hallway. I brush past him and head to the bathroom. It takes a while for him to go back to bed and fall asleep. It's just past two in the morning when I sneak out and head toward the parking lot.

While I'd prefer to shift and run, carrying clothing

in my mouth is hard enough. I can't carry any weapons. For once, I'm grateful to be the son of the Delta, because I know the codes for all the locks in the training building.

I'm able to slip on a tactical vest and a couple of guns loaded with wolfsbane. To be safe, I also tuck in four small daggers. My black hoodie goes over the top so I can appear somewhat peaceful.

I grab the keys from the sun visor of my dad's beat up pickup truck and promise myself I'll save up and buy myself a decent vehicle soon. The gravel crunches on the drive out, but I timed my escape to when patrol is on the north side of our commune and shouldn't hear it. Even if they do, it'll be too late to stop me.

This is reckless, but I don't care. No one else is going to help. They'll put our pack first. But I can't live without her.

Pulling off the freeway, I park on the road that leads to Granite Ridge's pack buildings. I'm not sure how far it is to their buildings, so I stop closer to the freeway than I would have liked. It'll be a farther distance for our escape, but it's just as likely we will ditch the vehicle and run as wolves across the border.

I leave the truck unlocked with the keys ready, in case Ember is the one to reach it first.

The march toward Granite Ridge feels like miles and my heart races the entire time. There's no way to know what I'll find, except that Ember is there.

Cinder block buildings rise up in uniform lines. Two dozen identical houses line a street with a large and luxurious modern ranch at the end. The Alpha's house. Everything is quiet and I can't even hear a patrol. It's been at least three hours since Ember returned home, and it seems that everyone has gone to sleep.

The front porch of the Alpha's house is too exposed, so I creep around to the back. My footsteps are deafening with only the rustle of leaves to drown them out.

I pause at the back door, listening for any noise inside. A tense discussion, yelling, anything. It's silent.

The door comes open with a little work with a dagger. I step in, waiting for alarms to blare, but nothing happens. It's a kitchen, sterile and white with a double stainless steel fridge and eight burner stove my mother would love. But there is no warmth here. It looks like a catering kitchen, not a family's. But then again, Sienna doesn't seem like the type to cook.

Cautiously, I move through the kitchen into the hallway. It splits in two directions. The scent of Ember is faint and old, but I catch a stronger trail down the left hallway. I pass an office and finally reach a closed door that definitely smells like her.

The door is silent as I ease it open at a glacial pace. Ember sprawls across the bed, eyes on the ceiling. Her face is red and puffy like she's been crying.

When the door latch clicks behind me, she bolts up.

"Onyx!" she hisses, scrambling to stand and darting toward me. I open my arms, wanting to sweep her up romantically. But she grabs my wrist and drags me forward so she can reach the door behind me and lock it.

"What the fuck are you doing here?"

"You ran away," I say dumbly. "I came to get you."

For a moment, she flounders, her mouth working silently. Not exactly the reaction I was expecting.

"I left because I didn't want to be there with you," she says. "Clearly, I didn't want you following me."

"No, that can't be why," I argue. The adrenaline running through my body is the only thing keeping me going, and my thoughts swirl together into mud. "You don't want to be here. You want to be with me."

Her lips purse for a moment and her brows furrow, like she regrets what she's doing, but she shakes her head. "No, you need to leave. I don't know what they'll do if you're caught, but it won't be pretty."

"I'm not leaving without you," I say stubbornly.

"Argh, you guys have my phone so I can't even call Jasper to come get your dumb ass." She turns away, pacing the length of her room.

The walls are white, her bedding is ivory, and all of the furniture is pale wood. It doesn't feel like Ember. She belongs somewhere comfortable and cozy.

"I need to be here to help my mom. Once that's handled, we can revisit *us*." She motions between us, back and forth.

"Then I'll stay to help."

"You're going to ruin everything!" she says, her voice still hushed but rising.

Pounding on the door makes both of us leap. "Ember, open up. We have an intruder." A masculine voice sounds through the wood.

"Shit!" Her face pales, all of the blood draining out in panic. "You need to go out the window and run. Please, for me."

She shoves me toward the window and slides it open with one hand.

Before I can argue with her, she grabs my shoulder and forces me down and half out the window. I have to grab the sill to keep from tumbling out head first.

Her door blows open with a splintering crack, and I push off the window frame to get between her and the attacker.

"No, Onyx!" Ember yelps, clinging to my arm.

Hands shaking, I draw a gun and level it at the three men bursting into her room. They're taller than I am, filling the entire space. They close the distance between us before I can react.

"Back off, I don't want to shoot you," I say.

"What are you doing?" Ember screeches.

They don't stop. My finger tightens on the trigger and the gun fires, striking the first man. He staggers back and then drops as the wolfsbane hits his bloodstream. Before I can fire again, hands clamp around my upper arms.

Something strikes my head, and my vision swims, pain splintering me apart. Desperate to get back to Ember, I struggle against my captors. Their hold bruises as they jerk me back and down onto my knees.

My vision tunnels, black seeping in around the edges.

Another strike, and I lose consciousness.

Chapter Fourteen

TRESPASSING & TRAITORS

Ember

A guard keeps his palm on my shoulder, pinching the muscle to let me know he will restrain me if needed. I'm being detained until Sienna and Orion can be roused.

"Get your fucking hands off of him," I snarl.

Onyx lays across the ground, blood seeping from his hairline. I grit my teeth so hard it feels as if my jaw will crack. I won't show them weakness, because then I will be truly powerless to help him.

My mother fills the doorway, her hair twisted into a bun on the top of her head and a crimson robe billowing over her shoulders.

"You've been back for mere hours and already you're causing problems?" she drawls.

Her words sting, but I wonder if they're more for the benefit of the pack. Things are more complicated than I realized. She strides to Onyx and nudges him with her black satin slippers.

"Do you know who this is? He looks familiar." Her eyes barely glance my way.

"He's my friend. He was worried about me leaving in the middle of the night, so he came to make sure I was safe." My fists clench, aching to hit the men still holding me in place.

"I've been getting far too little sleep tonight. Someone one string him up and we can deal with this in the morning. Flint, you're in charge of his guard. Keep him in one piece. I want to know what he was doing in detail."

"Stop! He's my guest," I yell.

My mother pauses, looking me over. "Guests are announced and welcomed. They do not sneak into the Alpha's house."

My mother's men grab Onyx's upper arms and tug him out of the room, his legs dragging across the carpet. Jerking away, I slip from my captor's hold and follow them.

Out front of our cold concrete training building, they handcuff him to a steel pole. His head lolls as he sags to the ground.

Sienna has already disappeared back to bed. I clutch my arms around my middle, feeling vulnerable as the pack members dissipate.

Flint, a thin man with greasy dark hair, sits on a bench and watches me with beady eyes. I bare my teeth at him. I'm ranked far above him, so he should look away, but he leers at me.

Anger heats my blood, making me sick with the cold fear churning my stomach. Hours ago I was lost in my own world with Onyx. He was safe, and I was trying to keep it that way. Why didn't Slate and Hazel stop him?

My eyes burn, but crying will only make this worse. Glaring at Flint, I walk to where Onyx sags, his arms pulled back behind him. My knees sting as they hit the concrete and my fingers brush back his hair to see the wound underneath. Blood mattes his scalp and a single thin line of crimson runs down the side of his cheek to his jaw.

"Hey," I say softly. His breathing is ragged, so I can tell he's conscious, but his eyes are screwed shut in pain.

With a small groan, he opens his eyes and raises his face to mine. Pain flashes across his features.

"I'm sorry," I whisper. "This is exactly what I was

trying to avoid."

His voice cracks. "You could have warned a guy."

I can't bring myself to berate him, even if he deserves it. "I thought if I left like that, you'd be angry with me. Not *follow* me. I didn't want anyone to stop me. I have to help my mom."

"I'd follow you anywhere," he rasps, his eyes closing and lines creasing his forehead and cheeks.

"I'm going to get you out of here. But I need you to swear you'll stay away until it's safe."

Running a hand down his stomach, I feel tactical gear under his hoodie. They didn't even bother to check him. Moving around to his side hidden from Flint, I lift the edge of his hoodie and slide out a small dagger. Keeping my back to our guard, I inch around to his hands and start picking at the handcuffs.

"Hey, what are you doing?" Flint says, leaning forward in his seat.

The blade slides into my waistband, the metal cold against my skin. "Checking his wrists. You guys were sloppy," I spit.

He sneers, crossing his arms and flexing, but doesn't take his eyes off me. There is no way I can get Onyx free with him here.

"Flint," I say, "what would it take for you to look away for a few minutes?"

His eyes narrow but he doesn't outright reject my

offer. I can see the thoughts spinning in his slimy head. "It would take a lot to be worth it, but I think we could figure something out." His gaze drops lower, making his intentions clear.

Onyx snarls, pulling against his restraints. "If you touch her, I will gut you and feed you your own kidney!"

"Oh, did you find yourself a loyal puppy?" Flint says with a chuckle. "That's good to know."

I'm done negotiating and playing it cool. Rising, I focus my gaze on the older wolf. He's not much taller than I am and has always looked half-starved. I'm confident in a fight I could take him down.

Stepping closer, I draw the dagger out and touch the tip to my finger, rotating it.

"This wolf is mine," I say, my voice a threat, "and if you interfere in me getting my way, I will do far worse than he said. You will have wished someone would have killed you."

"I doubt you could do anything to me," he says, putting on bravado. But I can see the hesitation in his eyes. We've sparred before in training, but never with weapons.

"Will you keep your mouth shut?" I ask, drawing close enough to strike him.

"Why should I?"

Nervousness floods me, but I ignore it. I wish I could snap and go to a place where I have no control. This is so much harder with a clear head.

I let the dagger tip forward until it's pointed at his chest. He moves to take it, exactly what I was hoping for.

As he reaches up, I go low, slashing across his ribs as they turn toward me - shallow enough to draw blood but not cause serious harm. A warning.

He jerks back, his hand going to his side. The cut runs from the bottom of his ribs almost to his armpit. His shirt billows open and blood drips down his side. I smile at him.

"Will you keep your mouth shut?" I ask again, calm and cold.

He sits back down hard, baring his teeth at me. "You bitch, I can't wait until someone puts you in your place."

Why couldn't he just cooperate?

With my left hand, I swing and connect with his jaw, knocking him sideways across the bench. He wildly grabs at me, and I slice across his forearm, holding the knife sideways in my fist. He recoils, curling in on himself defensively as blood seeps between his fingers.

"Stay there or I will end you," I snarl before turning to free Onyx.

"The little wolf has bite," a deep voice says, making me jump. Onyx growls, unable to see past me as I spin to face Orion. He melts out of the shadows, moving too gracefully for a man that large.

"Beta," I address him coolly. Straightening, I block

Onyx from him the best I can.

I'm never sure what Orion will do. He accompanied Hawk to join our pack, but stayed with us even when my ex returned to his family's pack up north. Standing a head above most of our packmates and with a vicious temperament, it didn't take him long to move up the ranks.

"Is there a reason you are attacking Flint and trying to free the trespasser?" he asks. He doesn't seem angry, just curious.

"I am taking charge of him. The handcuffs are unnecessary. He will do whatever I say."

Orion moves into my personal space and I refuse to step back, even though I have to crane my neck to keep eye contact. "Is he a lovesick moron you picked up during your little vacation?"

"No. And that's not your concern anyway." I hold my hand with the dagger up between us, an idle threat.

"I want to know if you have any attachments," he says, his voice low. "I'll walk you back to the Alpha's house. You shouldn't be out here."

Onyx lets out a snarl that sounds entirely animal. I half expect to see him shifted, but shifting with cuffs pulled tight and arms bound behind him would result in serious injuries.

Orion chuckles, placing a hand on my upper back. With a jerk of my shoulders, I shrug him off and move away.

"If this stray is a problem, I'm happy to eliminate him," he says quietly.

"If you touch him, I'll kill you," I say, rage in every syllable.

Orion shoves me forward, his hand brushing the back of my arm to let me know he'll grab me if necessary. "I'd love to see you try. Maybe I'll get my way tomorrow when we deal with him."

I allow myself to be herded back to the Alpha's house, and lock myself in my room with my heart pounding in my ears. With Onyx tied up outside, I can't possibly sleep.

Low voices in the hall tell me that Orion has posted a guard to keep me contained.

He's undermining me, but it's clear now that I've never been given any true authority. I'll have to seize it. But a fight against Orion won't end well. Strategy is my only strength against a brute like him.

It takes all my willpower to not scream and cry into my pillow. I feel so helpless, like every decision I've made has blown up in my face.

Eventually light filters in my window. I dress in all-black workout gear and pull my hair back into a bun. After some thought, I apply eyeliner and a red lip in the same style as my mother. It's time to take my birthright in full, and if all goes well, the man I love will walk out of here safe.

Sienna sits in the formal living room, holding court with her top ranked wolves. I ignore them and address my mother directly.

"I want the wolf from last night freed. He was my host during my visit and he was concerned for my safety. We are endangering our alliance by detaining him." With my shoulders back and my head high, I feel confident and my words come out strong.

She frowns, tapping a manicured nail against the glossy wooden table beside her chair. "Dear, he destroyed our alliance by breaking into the Alpha's home. He could have been assassinating you. He may have meant to for all we know."

"Absolutely not. I will vouch for him. It was the middle of the night when I left, and he was simply following me. The pack was asleep and he came straight to see me. You should be rewarding him for taking my safety so seriously."

"I'm afraid your word doesn't weigh enough in this situation," she says, her gaze flicking to the other wolves in her circle. "We are debating what to do with him. You are welcome to join the discussion, but you will not be overriding my counsel."

My nails dig into my palms hard enough to break the skin. In the past, I would have thought my mother was simply tormenting me. But now I see she's controlled by those around her. She's lost all her power in this pack, and she's clawing to keep her position.

With a huff, I sit in the nearest seat, leaving space between the other wolves and myself.

"As I was saying," Sienna continues, "I don't feel it's necessary to question him. There's no sign of any other trespassers, and if he was a scout, he wouldn't have come right in."

"I say we execute him. He threatened our Heir and he arrived with enough weapons to take out half our pack," Orion says, leaning back with his hands behind his head as if this was friendly small talk and not a deliberation over the life of another. His gaze goes to me and he smirks.

"You only want him dead because I want him alive and free," I growl, unable to help myself.

"So you prefer we just let him go?" the Gamma, Aster, a woman just older than my mother, questions.

"I've explained already, and the fact you can't accept my word is ridiculous and offensive," I say, my anger building.

"If we can somehow verify his intentions, hence the idea of questioning him, I am okay with sending him back to his pack," the Delta says. He's the oldest of the bunch, with gray threaded through his black ponytail.

Sienna crosses her arms and sighs. "Well, we have

two strong opinions. I see the merit in what my daughter says, but also the wisdom in Orion's choice."

"I believe imprisonment until we can negotiate with his pack would be best," Aster says, rubbing the back of her head where her hair is buzzed short.

"No," I say, exuding every bit of dominance I possess. "You are going to release him into my custody, and he will stay with me. I am completely confident he means me no harm. He's been protecting me for the last week. He's showing loyalty by coming here, and we're treating him like a criminal. This ends now."

"He is a criminal, and now is not the time to be forgiving toward those that threaten our pack," Orion says, drawing out his words. His presence presses down on me, causing my anxiety to rise. "But if you feel so strongly about it, you're welcome to challenge me."

"I don't have to do that. You're the only one demanding blood here."

"I outrank them. Dearest Ember, you've been weakened by your time in that pack. This is for your own good." His smirk is ugly.

"I am Heir and hold power over you," I say, my hands clenching into fists.

"Prove it."

My mother's face pales, but if I reject his challenge, I've already lost. He'll kill Onyx. If my mother tries to stop him, he'll use it as a reason to depose her. I've made this so much worse.

"Fine."

ONYX

After Ember is taken away, two ugly fuckers give me a beating until the world goes dark.

When I come to, it's light and I've been stripped of my gear and weapons.

Shit.

No one speaks to me, but the entire pack has gathered. Far more wolves look at me with hatred than I would have expected. Things are worse between my pack and Granite Ridge than I realized.

The crowd's noise drops as Sienna approaches, followed by Ember and the huge man from last night. The Beta, Orion.

With great effort, I press my back against the pole and push myself to stand so I can follow their progress. They stop in the training ring which is just paint on concrete, without even mats for safety during sparring.

"Beta Orion would see the trespasser executed as a dangerous stray," a man with graying hair and beard says, "and Heir Ember wants him freed. A challenge has been issued."

No.

My heart drops. He is three times her size and twice her age. Without a weapon, I doubt I could take him. She's vicious, but this is insanity.

"Stop, let me fight," I yell, my voice giving out. "I challenge for myself!"

A nearby man thumps me in the stomach and I barely stay standing, sagging against my restraints. From the needle-like pain in my side, I suspect they broke a few of my ribs earlier. Shifter healing is fast, but not that fast. It will take a few days before I'm back to normal.

Shoulders close in, and despite my height, I can't see the ring. But I can guess when the fight starts. The crowd roars to life, crying for blood and yelling disgusting, suggestive taunts to my girlfriend.

A growl rumbles low in my chest as I listen for the sounds of strikes landing or pained gasps. Through a gap in the crowd, I see Ember darting out of Orion's reach, landing a kick against the side of his knee. He falls to one knee, but the crowd closes in before I see her next move.

She's holding her own, if the noises her packmates make is any indication. I want to cheer her on, but it hurts to breathe.

A deep masculine grunt echoes through the space, followed by a feminine yelp. It's killing me not being able to see. The distinct noise of a fist connecting with flesh sounds, once, twice. Two wolves snarl.

Legs part for a second and I see Ember on the

ground, scrambling for a hold on Orion. He's gotten above her.

A whimper from her throat hurts me worse than the injuries I've received. I'll make his death slow for daring to hurt her. The crowd closes in and I pray she finds a way to knock him down and make him wish he was dead.

"Beta Orion is the victor!" A voice calls out.

No, no, no.

How is she? Black edges my vision as I strain to see her.

People part, and Sienna, Orion, and Ember stand in front of me. Ember's lip is split, and she holds her side. From the tension in her muscles to the way her posture covers that side, I have no doubt she's nursing broken bones. Her cheekbone is red and has started to swell.

Orion is leaning all his weight on one leg, but otherwise looks unharmed. He grins at Ember.

"Alpha, if I may?" he asks, bowing his head to Sienna.

"Yes, Beta?" She picks at her nails like this boring to her.

"Although I still believe he should be executed, I will offer his life to Ember as a gift. A mating present."

Who does this asshole think he is?

Ember clears her throat. "I'm flattered, and I will consider your proposal only if you set him free. I could never be mated to a man who kills someone I've asked to be spared."

"Fine," he says with a shrug, like it's nothing.

I should be relieved, but instead I can barely breathe. She can't possibly be considering him. The only upside is that I'll now live long enough to make good on the silent promises of pain and death running through my thoughts.

"Wonderful. He's been taught a lesson, and we can send him back to his pack with a warning," Sienna says as she saunters closer. With a cruel smile, she grabs my chin. Her spiked nails dig into skin, but I hardly feel it with all my other injuries. "Our alliance is broken, and any other interference from your pack will be considered an act of aggression."

Her pack cheers and howls around us, and I look into her eyes, like darker versions of Ember's. Instead of worry and warmth, I see ice and death.

I'm cut free and escorted to my truck by a handful of guards. Ember doesn't follow. Numbly, I allow them to push me into my truck and fumble with the keys. It takes all of my willpower to pull the vehicle onto the road.

Driving with one eye swollen shut is a bitch. The world swims around me and the truck keeps slowing as I lose focus. But somehow, I manage to get home.

The parking lot buzzes with activity. Hazel and Slate talk with packmates while Cedar and Jasper load equipment into a truck. At the sound of the engine, the group turns.

A dull sense of relief fills me, loosening my grip. Throwing the truck into park, I shove the door open and tumble out. Slate catches me, hoisting me up with help from my twin.

Hazel appears in my dimming vision, her eyebrows pinched and lips parted as she surveys my injuries. Everything sounds muffled, like I'm under a heavy blanket.

The rough hands grasping my body cause me to flinch, making me think I'm back at Granite Ridge enduring their punishments. My mumbled words do nothing to stop the blurring chaos around me.

"You idiot!" Hazel's voice breaks through, her words thick as if she is crying.

Cool wood presses into my back. The change triggers nausea, and I jerk sideways in time to throw up on the floor. It's darker in here, giving some relief to my pounding head.

An older voice speaks nearby, along with Hazel's worried tone. The words "Concussion," and "Broken Ribs," are repeated.

I must be in Sable's cottage. Good, the healer can patch me up so I can get back to Ember.

"Alright, you can sleep now. I'll keep an eye on you," Sable says, brushing my hair back and pressing something to my head. Instantly, the nausea subsides and the pain lessens. Relief soaks through me and my body finally relaxes. Sable fusses over me as I fade into a shallow sleep.

CHAPTER FIFTEEN

IMPRISONMENT & UNLIKELY ALLIES

Ember

The next couple of days go by quietly, and I spend most of my time resting in my room and letting my injuries heal. Dark thoughts overtake me, stripping away the hope and joy I had found in Onyx's pack.

My heartbreak seems trivial after Onyx almost lost his life. We are lucky Orion agreed to spare him, even if it was some kind of sick proposal to me. Joke's on him. I will

never accept him as my mate.

After I tire of cold cereal and my ribs have healed enough I can breathe without pain, I walk to the cafeteria to get some hot food.

"Hey Ember, I'll sneak into your room if that's what you like," a man jeers at me. I ignore him and load my tray with meatloaf and powdery mashed potatoes.

A strangled yell startles me and a body thumps to the ground.

"Apologize," a deep voice commands. I spin to see Orion pressing his boot to the man's throat.

"S-s-s-sorry!" he says, choking on the word. Orion steps off his airway and raises an eyebrow at me before stalking off. He's waiting for his answer.

Feeling sick, I turn back to my food.

No one else bothers me while I eat the swill our pack serves. I would give anything for Clove's fresh bread right now. Although I'd give up bread for the rest of my life if it meant I could go back to Onyx.

There's no use in wishing.

I force myself to focus on the discussions at the tables around me. Orion's name comes up often and it seems he has the support of most of the pack, if the dozen wolves around me are an accurate sample.

He's the biggest threat to my mother, and he's asked me, the Heir, to be his mate. That is a clear path to becoming Alpha.

What will he do when I reject him?

Or should I set my pride aside, let my heart shatter, and agree to be his? It would keep me safe. He might refrain from challenging my mother and wait until she steps down. Either way, he would end up in power.

It's too much to handle. I hide away in my room for the rest of the day. My mother never visits me. Maybe, if she was honest with me, we could find a way out of this mess together. But that will never happen. Some rifts are too deep.

My best option is somehow eliminating Orion. And since my daydreams of being with Onyx are now intermixed with visions of murdering Orion, I have a head start in brainstorming solutions.

Unfortunately, I'm not fast enough.

That evening, as the sun lowers behind the trees, the roar of a crowd pulls me from my solitude. It starts as a hum that I almost ignore, but rises in intensity until shouts emanate through my windows and down the hallway.

With stiff legs, I scramble from my bed and push off the wall as I cover the distance. The pebbles prick my bare feet as I rush down the stairs and out onto the dirt.

The entire pack is gathered. What the hell?

With this level of uproar, I expect a formal challenge within the painted ring in the training building. Instead, the jostling pack circles around figures in the center of the main road.

Muscling my way in, I snarl as someone elbows my chest. Dust stings my eyes as dozens of feet shuffle around me. Throwing my weight forward, I push further into the mob.

"Ah, there she is," Orion says, his voice yelling over the din.

The wolves part, letting me through. I wish they hadn't.

Orion stands in the center with blood spattered across his shirt. He grins at me, his teeth red.

At his feet, my mother sprawls out. Her chest rises and falls, but her eyes are closed. Crimson streaks her face from a broken nose and her wrist bends at an unnatural angle.

"Mom!" I cry, dropping to the ground beside her. Reaching for her neck, I feel for her pulse. It's steady, and I exhale in cursory relief. Even with a shake, she doesn't wake.

Rising, I face him. "How could you do this?"

"The pack wants a strong leader," he says with a shrug.

"You're disloyal! Why would anyone follow you?" I growl, wishing I had a weapon.

"There's my feisty little wolf," he purrs. Without even glancing down, he steps over my mother. I flatten back until I bump into the wolves surrounding us. Still, he comes closer. "Are you ready to accept me as your mate?" he asks.

"Why would I do that?" I growl.

"I'm the Alpha now," Orion says. The wolves around us whoop and howl in approval. "You are mine now. I'm wondering if you'll give in, or if you'll fight. I love when females fight."

My heart races, in a way that makes me sick. Tingling spreads through my limbs, panic overcoming me.

"It's okay, you have time to change your mind," he says with a dark laugh. "Why don't you spend some quiet time thinking it over?"

He gestures to his cronies and hands seize my upper arms. There's no use in struggling as I'm led back into the house and roughly pushed through the door to our basement.

Stair treads cut into my ass and thigh as I slide down a few steps before grabbing the railing and halting myself. I deserve this. Without bothering to rise, I lay my head against the step and give up.

I can't even find the willpower to tell myself everything will be okay. Orion won't be a good Alpha. He won't be a tolerable mate. There's no silver living, because eventually war will come for Onyx and his pack.

Hopefully they can defeat us. But the bloodshed will be my fault. He will never accept me again, marked by another and responsible for even more death.

Eventually, I limp to the sofa and curl up, grim images of the future playing in my head.

When I wake, all is quiet so I suspect it's night. It's fully furnished like an apartment, but the lack of windows is disorienting. At least there are frozen meals in the kitchenette from when Hazel was locked down here two years ago.

It seems poetic that I'm now the one imprisoned down here.

I force myself to eat and clean myself up. There are a few spare clothing items, but even that doesn't make me feel any better. There's no way out. And what's the point?

ONYX

Two days later and every bit of me still hurts, but none of it matters when I had to leave Ember behind. My soul aches, distracting me from the work before me. Grabbing the arms of my chair, I force my focus to the screen in front of me, where Sienna looks down her nose at us.

Jasper shifts his weight, clearing his throat as he addresses his mother. "Please, I need to know everything you can remember. Any detail might help.”

Sienna sits straight and proud, despite the purple bruise across her cheeks and the medical tape over her swollen nose. A small, vicious part of me is gratified to see her hurting like I am, but considering Ember is now in greater risk, my feelings toward Sienna are moreover apathetic.

“The details aren't important.”

“Ember is still there,” Jasper says patiently.

“Who knows what's happening to her right now,” I snap, unable to stay silent.

“She's most likely preparing to become mates with the new Alpha,” Sienna sniffs.

“You can't be serious.” Jasper scowls at his mother. She ignores him.

“I will do whatever it takes to get her back,” I say, desperate to get her to care.

“You're not capable of what it would take,” Sienna says, her cold, dark eyes meeting mine through the screen.

I growl, rising and slamming my hands down on the desk. “There is nothing I wouldn't do for her.”

“Jasper,” Sienna says, her voice light and unconcerned. “Tell me about this pup.”

I bristle, but Jasper pats my hand. With a forceful exhale, I settle back into my seat.

“He's the son of the pack's Delta. He's ranked as a

Zeta and is responsible for all of our digital security. Onyx is also the closest childhood friend of our Alpha and has his support."

Her gaze flicks back to me, contemplating my resume. It shouldn't matter. She's wasting time. What kind of mother wouldn't want to help her child?

Flexing my hands, I lock eyes with her. Time to lay everything on the table. "I am in love with her, and I believe she is with me too."

"It's easy enough to say that, but much harder to prove it," she quips. I want to throw the screen across the room.

"Give me a chance," I growl.

"What would you do?" Sienna asks.

"We'd like to remove Ember from the situation, just like you originally intended," Jasper explains.

"But what if she prefers to stay with Orion? That's the quickest and perhaps only route to power available to her."

"I was just informed she's currently locked up in your basement, so I doubt she's on board with Orion's proposal," Jasper says with clenched teeth.

My hands tighten on my chair so hard my knuckles pop. Jasper neglected to tell me that detail. No doubt feeling my anger through the pack bond, Jasper looks over at me with raised brows. With a slow exhale, I relax my posture, though my heart still pounds.

"Alright, what do you want to know?" Sienna finally says.

"What happened after Ember came home?" I ask.

"You came bursting in like a stalker and put everyone on the warpath," Sienna says, crossing her arms gingerly, avoiding her broken wrist.

"I was talking with her and we would have left together quietly," I say.

"Good job with that." The disdain in her voice raises my hackles. This mother-in-law relationship isn't off to a great start.

"You could have let us go. Those were your men."

"Unfortunately, it's not that simple," Sienna says.

"What do you mean?" I keep my tone civil, despite the venom I feel.

For a moment, Sienna purses her lips. I don't expect an answer, but she surprises me.

"Orion has been waiting for any excuse to challenge me. If I did anything outside of the pack's expectations, it was an opportunity for him."

"You were his Alpha," I say.

Sienna sniffs, picking at her manicure.

"After I left, what happened?"

"Ember hid in her room after Orion asked her to be his mate."

"So why did he challenge you?" Jasper asks, gentler than I can manage.

She sits back, her lips in a thin line. We both stare at her, waiting it out. After a moment, she huffs. "I told him he couldn't force her to be his mate."

"And he challenged you." Jasper fills in. "And now she's locked in a basement."

"We need to get her out of there," I say.

"Okay, let's talk strategy," Jasper says, smiling when his mother sits forward attentively. Somehow, we won her over. If we are lucky, she'll have the missing pieces we need to put together a rescue mission.

PROVIDE, PROTECT

Ember

The day slips by and I spend it staring at the ceiling. Only the hope of violence against Orion drives me to eat a frozen meal and drink water from the sink.

When the door at the top of the stairs swings open, I expect Orion to come in and ask if I'm ready to become his mate. If I don't agree, the magic of the mate bond

won't work and he can leave me to rot or perhaps try a little light torture.

I've resigned myself to my fate.

Aster stands there, clothing drapes across her arms. I watch her coldly as she makes her way down.

"What do you want?" I ask.

"I'm the only one coming to help you, so perhaps you could be polite." Her words are clipped, and there's an undercurrent of exhaustion.

"What's going on up there?"

"Orion has banished your mother, but he's not going to let you go."

"Is she okay?"

"She's alive."

Aster drapes a simple white dress over the banister and smooths it with her weathered hands.

"The sooner you agree to be his mate, the easier this will be for you."

"I can't do that. He's a monster."

"You're the only one who has a chance to curb him. We need you." Her gray eyes stay on the ground. I've never felt much emotion through our pack bonds, but I can feel her regret.

"I'm being sacrificed, is that it?"

"You're doing your duty to your pack," she says simply. "He's going to come for you soon. I recommend you get ready."

"Thanks for the warning," I say, bitterness on my tongue. "I don't need a dress. I need a weapon."

"I'm sorry, Ember." She finally meets my eyes. I only see resignation in her gaze.

"If you can't help me, go away."

She does.

I pace anxiously, my nails digging into my palms. In a few hours, Orion will come for me. I'll have to accept to even have a chance at getting my hands on a weapon. Will that be enough for the magic to take? The idea of his claim mark on me makes me want to throw up.

Ignoring the dress, I tuck a fork into my waistband. It's the closest thing to a weapon I can find in this basement.

For too soon, the door at the top of the stairs creaks open.

"Ember, you're wanted," a guard calls.

Preferring to walk instead of being dragged, I march up the stairs and face my fate. Two younger men stand at the door, their heads bowed.

The front door stands open, and I pass through it, shoulders tense. Orion's broad frame is outlined against a lowering sun, the pack spread out before him.

"You summoned me?" I say, my eyes scanning for a weapon, an escape, anything.

Orion looks over his shoulder, beckoning me forward. Arms crossed, I step diagonally, forward but out of reach. Let everyone know how much I despise him. His lip curls and fear twists in my gut. Those eyes promise retaliation.

Engines rev in the distance, and dust plumes from a line of SUVs pulling level with our compound. Orion snags my wrist and tugs me against him.

The crowd turns, facing the newcomers.

The first door opens and Zephyr steps out. The Alpha of the Ironcrest pack smiles wide, his short, silver hair glinting as bright as his teeth.

"I heard we had a new Alpha to greet," he says.

Orion lets out a low growl, moving closer to me.

The older man strides forward, his guards falling into step behind him. The crowd parts as he approaches us.

An echoing boom sounds from our right, away from Zephyr's convoy.

Orion's hand seizes my wrist as dust sprays across us. The sounds of gunfire ricochets off the concrete block buildings.

Zephyr throws his arms out, steadying his people. "What the hell is going on?" he yells, just as Orion shouts, "Everyone down. Find them!"

Hands drag me back as the entire pack breaks into chaos. I'm pulled into the house, the noise dulling as the front door slams shut, closing me in. I scramble to get my feet under me.

"Who?" the guard yelps.

I don't care what the distraction is. This is my only chance. Jerking against his hold on my arm, I pluck the fork from my waistband and stab the tines into his side. He doubles over, releasing me.

Another set of hands catch me, and I thrash and struggle against the hold. "Hey, it's okay," a familiar voice says.

Twisting to see, I meet Cedar's soft blue eyes.

My panic clears, and I turn to see Onyx leveling a wolfsbane gun at the guard. Before the bleeding man can react, Onyx fires. The poisoned ammo takes seconds to render him unconscious. Cedar releases me now that I am steady on my feet.

"Hey, I heard you needed a rescue," Onyx says with a grin.

"Are you kidding me?" I cry, launching myself at him. He hoists me up, my legs hooking around his hips as I bury my face into the crook of his neck. The world falls away as I breathe in his scent. I thought I would never get to touch him again.

Far too soon, he lets me go. Standing back, I gaze at him in wonder. He looks perfect, all visible wounds healed. Terror grips me. I can't go through seeing him almost die again. "Why did you come back? What were you thinking?" I whisper.

"I was thinking I couldn't live without you," he says

before he tugs me forward and captures my lips with his.

The dull darkness of the last few days falls away, my body coming to life again. Energy surges in every cell of my body. I kiss him like he's my oxygen and I'll die if we stop or even slow for a second.

"Now's not the time!" Cedar hisses.

He releases me. "As much as I love this, and love you, we need to go." Without wasting another second, he grabs my hand and leads me toward the kitchen.

"We need to hurry," Cedar says, taking up the rear and scanning behind us as we rush through my house.

"How did you manage this?" I hiss.

"A lot of wolfsbane and calling in favors," Cedar says.

"Zephyr was the distraction. We followed his group in," Onyx explains, pausing at the back door and peeking out. "Looks clear."

"And the explosion?"

"Drones and fireworks," he says with a grin.

Two guards lay unconscious between the house and the tree line. As we pass, Onyx kicks one in the leg and mutters, "Oops, motherfucker."

"Hurry, they're just up ahead," Cedar snaps, keeping pace behind us. Jasper's black car idles on the access road, just out of view of the main compound.

Marigold stands by the passenger side, a crossbow peeking over her shoulder. "Come on, you guys!"

Onyx wrenches the door open, pushing my head down as I leap in. The twins pile in behind me and Onyx pulls me up in his lap as he slides across the bench seat. I have no complaints. In fact, it's not close enough. I want to burrow into his skin.

Jasper sits in the driver's seat, another gun in his lap. "Hey!" he greets me, before turning the steering wheel and feeding gas to the engine.

The car spits pebbles with a sound like rain as he peels out and drives northward. Marigold's arm reaches across the center console to grip his thigh, her expression tense as she stares past us out the back window.

We hit the freeway and Jasper speeds, increasing the miles between us and the pack as quickly as possible. After twenty minutes or so, he eases off to the speed limit. We are all breathing easier and even smiling.

"Alright, I'd say that went pretty well," Marigold says, leaning her head back against the headrest.

"Much more successful than my first attempt," Onyx says, nuzzling against my temple.

"I can't believe you guys came for me."

"We weren't going to leave you there," Cedar says plainly, like it was the most obvious fact in the world.

"Why? I left on my own, and then..." I trail off, unable to verbalize what Onyx went through because of me.

"We heard shit hit the fan," Onyx says, kissing my

shoulder.

"I suppose that's accurate," I say, my mind whirling through everything that has happened and what to tell him. Jerking upright, I glance at Jasper. "Do you know what happened to Mom?"

"She's recouping at Ironcrest," he says calmly. "But that's not where we are going."

"How is she?"

"She's doing pretty good, all things considered."

Marigold looks over her shoulder and gives me a supportive smile. "She's fine, just worried about you. She's the one who convinced Zephyr to play decoy actually. Turns out, he doesn't care for Orion or the northern pack."

"Neither do I," I said darkly.

Everyone is quiet for a moment. The road splits, and Jasper turns West, away from both his pack and mine.

"What happened after I left? Did he?" Onyx starts to ask, but can't seem to finish his question.

Looking up at him, I attempt to smile despite the choking feeling in my throat. "After he challenged my mom, he demanded that I become his mate and when I said no, he locked me up until right now."

I feel like I barely escaped a train crash.

"He'll never get near you again. And I'm going to make him wish he had never even looked at you," he promises. It's the best thing I've ever heard and I reward him with a soft kiss.

"So seriously, what's the plan? Where are we actually going?" I ask, feeling lighter than I have since leaving Onyx in the woods.

Jasper sighs, keeping his gaze on the road. "You guys are going to lay low for a while, and I am going to work with Slate and Hawthorne to put together a plan. Not totally sure yet what that'll be, but we need you out of the way. No more idiotic schemes to run home and challenge anyone."

His words sting. It felt like the right thing to do at the time. If I had known the consequences then, I would have made a very different choice.

"We'll drop you off at a vacation rental nearby. You'll hang out for a few days and then when everything is safe, you'll come home," Marigold says, looking pleased with herself.

"I'll be staying to give you back up, and keep you out of trouble," Cedar grumbles.

I reach over and squeeze his hand. "Thank you, Cedar."

Onyx kisses my forehead, and I fold my arms in until I am cocooned in his embrace. Everything has fallen apart, but somehow I'm more than alright. Alone, I had no chance of helping my pack and my mother. With Onyx and my friends, maybe there's a chance.

ONYX

The rental is a brick house at the end of a small neighborhood two towns over. Being ninety minutes away from everything makes me nervous, but it's worth it for the safety. Granite Ridge will never find her here.

Jasper's sleek, black vehicle pulls into the driveway and we climb out. Now I have her, all of the stress from the last few days dissolves, leaving me exhausted and a bit sore from wounds still healing. Sable said I had several fractures in addition to a nasty concussion, but shifters heal quickly and she helped it along with her salves and tonics. My bag in the trunk holds several of her concoctions. I wasn't sure Ember would be okay when we found her.

Jasper inputs the door code and we step into a silent house. I note the security camera at the door. What must the owner think, seeing five young adults arriving together, two of us limping in and clinging to each other like they just survived the apocalypse? At least we left our weapons in the car.

"We can't stay long, but I'm going to order some groceries and make sure you're all set for a while. Better to be safe than sorry." Marigold disappears into the kitchen.

Cedar and Jasper explore the other two bedrooms and hall bathroom. I open the interior door to the garage through the laundry room, revealing a ping pong table and a set of bicycles. Maybe our stay here won't be too bad. Frankly, it wouldn't matter if the house was completely devoid of entertainment. I have Ember back.

She brushes against me, peeking out. "Oh, don't tell me you love ping pong," she says, scowling at me playfully.

"It could be fun," I say, wrapping my arms over her shoulders in a hug. "We could try making it strip ping pong."

"Or not," Cedar yells from the hall.

Ember's nose wrinkles as she laughs silently.

"He's going to be a total cock-block isn't he?" I mutter, leaning down to kiss her.

"As much as I can't wait to test that theory, it's been a rough few days and I'm not feeling my best," Ember murmurs, allowing me to support her weight.

My instincts to protect roar to life, and I lift her up, one arm under her knees in a bridal hold.

"That's overkill. I just need a nap and some real food," she says against my shirt. But she nuzzles down against my chest and allows me to carry her to the master bedroom. Cedar will be fine in the kids room.

Gently, I lay her out across the bed and pull a coverlet over her.

"I'll rest here a bit, but I really am hungry," she says, a yawn breaking her words in half.

Food, provide, protect.

Marigold sits on the kitchen counter with her phone in her hand.

"I've almost got the grocery order done and it'll be here in an hour. I'm glad they have delivery. One of the benefits of a bigger town, I guess." She looks up and smiles at me. "You look happy," she notes.

"Yeah," I say. "Everything's going to be fine now."

They had to tolerate my incessant worries over the last few days as we put together a plan, negotiated with Zephyr to help, and I healed from the beating I took.

"Thank you, Goldie," I say quietly.

She slides off the counter and pats my arm fondly. "She's your mate, so she's family." My stomach swoops at hearing her called my mate. It's not official, not yet, but I love the sound of it. "Hazel is probably going crazy right now. We'd better text her."

The Alphas had to stay behind. They couldn't be involved in our smash and grab plan. And despite his grumpiness, Slate was supportive. Somewhere along the line, Ember won him over, or he knew Hazel would strangle him if he didn't help get her back.

"I even got you s'mores supplies," Marigold says with a wink before walking into the living room where Jasper sits perched on the edge of the sofa, texting on his phone.

"Oh, here," Jasper says, pulling Ember's phone from his pocket and tossing it to me.

"Thanks," I say, tucking it away for later. Right now, I need to secure sustenance for my girl.

There isn't much in the house, just a few basics the host was kind enough to stock, and a few random items previous guests had left. I find a box of crackers in the pantry that weren't expired and didn't seem too stale. It's better than nothing and I'm not about to leave her to go pick something up, not when food will show up on our doorstep in fifty minutes.

Clutching my box of crackers in front of me like I had gone out and hunted wild game for my beloved, I stride back into the bedroom.

Ember is sleeping peacefully. She's thinner than she was before. I hate the dark circles under her eyes and the hollowness of her cheeks. She's still beautiful and always will be, but the signs of her mistreatment make my stomach clench.

Setting the box on the side table, I stretch out beside her and tug the blanket over my own chest too. She lets out a tiny noise and turns in her sleep until she's tucked up against my chest.

A short nap won't hurt. Especially right now when Jasper and Marigold are here too. With her in my arms, it's all too easy to drift off.

"Dinner," Marigold calls, waking us. Ember startles in my arms, looking around wildly. I run my hand down her arm, soothing her until she locks eyes with me and relaxes.

"It's okay," I murmur. She lets out her breath slowly, her brows furrowing. "Come on, I know you're hungry."

"Yes, please," she says, climbing off the bed and rolling her shoulders.

Marigold, Jasper, and Cedar sit at the little kitchen table. Cedar is perched on a stool because there are only four chairs. Ember presses her lips into a thin line as she picks up a plate from the counter and slides into her seat.

She devours two grilled cheese sandwiches before she slows down. Marigold happily piles more tater tots and carrots onto everyone's plates. She must have used an entire loaf of bread to make enough sandwiches for five shifters.

"There's lots of easy-to-make frozen stuff in the fridge, like chicken tenders and lasagna. You guys should be fine," she says.

"Thank you," Ember says.

"Of course!" Marigold chirps, beaming at her.

Ember sets a tater tot back down. "So what did I miss while I was gone?" Her eyes meet mine, wide with guilt.

"I made it home and they patched me up," I say gently.

"He was yelling about going back for you pretty much the entire time," Cedar adds.

"We had to convince him a little strategy was needed," Jasper explains.

"Yes, because rushing in worked out so well the first time," Ember quips, her hand slapping over her mouth when she realizes what she said.

I chuckle. "No, you're right."

"I'm so sorry," she says, "I can't believe they hurt you like that."

"Not the worst beating I've had," I say with a shrug.

Cedar washes the dishes while Ember cuddles up to me on the sofa. Marigold and Jasper sit opposite us, hands linked over the side table. Jasper's thumb rubs circles over Marigold's wrist absently.

"Anything you can tell us would be helpful," Jasper says, pulling out his phone to take notes. "I don't think Sienna was being entirely honest with us and we don't know enough about Orion or the situation."

Ember pinches the bridge of her nose, gathering her resolve. Her bright hazel eyes move from me to Jasper. "It seems like most of the pack supports him. I don't know what he's been doing to win them over. Maybe they just respect his strength. After everything with my father,

Sienna definitely lost their favor. I didn't really pick up on it, but I've always-" She pauses.

"I know it's been hard," Jasper says softly. "Becoming Heir suddenly, trying to prove yourself especially when the pack is in so much turmoil."

"Guess what, I'm not Heir anymore," she says, her voice a little too high. My hand goes to her thigh. She's not in this alone.

"So everyone seems to like him?" Jasper asks.

Ember nods, sinking her teeth into her lush bottom lip. It takes her two tries to speak again, as if she's scared of what she's going to say.

"I don't think he desires me. He wants me as his mate to solidify his position as Alpha. So there has to be some dissent. But I honestly couldn't tell you who or how much."

My hold on her thigh tightens, and I have to flex my hand open before I hurt her. The reminder that he is demanding she become his mate heats my blood. I'm so ready to hurt this dipshit.

Sending my anger, she takes my hand and draws it to her mouth, pressing a sweet kiss to my knuckles. It feels so natural, like nothing at all, even though it's everything to me. I'm crazy about this woman.

"We can use that," Jasper says, leaning back in his seat. "I noticed a handful of wolves that seemed unhappy with him becoming second to Sienna. We might have a few allies."

"Why?" Ember asks. "Your pack won't want to interfere."

"You know just as well as I do that Orion's wolves will want war. Better to face them now than wait until they're stronger and prepared."

"Are you serious?" Ember says, her lips parted in surprise.

"Orion can't stay in power. We worked too hard to become allies with your pack again. Zephyr agrees, as Cashel. We just have to find the right way to do it," I say.

"I didn't realize." Ember breaks off her words with a yawn.

"It's getting late. We should head back, babe," Marigold says. "We can go back over our notes and make a list."

Jasper nods absently, still lost in his own head.

Jasper and Marigold both hug Ember and she squeezes them back. My heart is full.

Cedar retreats to the secondary bedroom until it's only Ember and I standing in the little living room.

"How are you doing there?" I ask softly.

She lets me wrap her in my arms, her chin tucking to her chest as she leans into me. "I can't believe I'm here. I thought it was over. Seriously, I had lost hope."

"No," I murmur, gathering her up.

"You almost died."

"Nah, it would take way more than that to take me out. Remember, you even tried to kill me and it didn't stick. They didn't stand a chance."

"Onyx," she says sharply, and I drop my playful smile. "I can't go through that again. Seeing you unconscious and bleeding. It was the worst moment of my life."

"Hey, hey, it's okay. It looked worse than it was." She probably knows I'm lying, but I don't know what else to say to make it better. It wasn't a great moment for me, and I definitely thought I wasn't going to make it out of there alive.

"Don't ever-" she starts to say.

"Come for you?" I interject. "Try to save you? Follow you?"

She scowls at me and pushes away, but I keep a hold of her waist so she can't move far.

"I'd go through all of it again for you." Her eyes widen and her mouth opens to argue. "It wouldn't be my first choice. If I could help you by taking a little vacation or maybe save you by getting a massage, that would be much nicer."

Gurgling laughter bursts out of her, and she wipes at her tears with the back of her hand.

"But don't think for a second I wouldn't do absolutely anything necessary to protect you." My voice drops, threatening all kinds of dark things.

"I'd do the same for you," she whispers. "In fact, I'm already planning several scenarios that involve torture for the men who hurt you."

"There's my beautiful, bloodthirsty girl," I say before lowering my head to kiss her. She tangles her fingers in my shirt, kissing back with the ferocity I love in her. We break apart just long enough for her to pull my shirt over my head.

She shoves me backward and we stumble toward the master bedroom. Finally, I have her alone in a proper bed, and this time she won't disappear in the night.

This isn't a distraction, it's devotion.

The door clicks shut and I press her back against it hard enough her emerald hair falls across her face. She lets out a low laugh. I tuck it behind her ear tenderly, running my fingers over the shell of her ear. She tips her head toward my touch.

"Be my mate," I say simply. No teasing, no speeches, just my heart laid out before her.

Her hand rests against my chest and her fingers tap while she picks her words. "I'm not a safe person to be with."

Grabbing her wrist, I move her hand to the scar across the bottom of my ribs. "I can take it. We already established that."

Her expression darkens. "I am going to reclaim my pack and be Alpha."

"Okay," I say immediately.

"Onyx," she says slowly, "it's what I have to do. And if you are my mate, you'd be Alpha too."

It's not a surprise. That's how it works for every pack. Yet, it hadn't crossed my mind that becoming Ember's mate would mean I became Alpha when she did. I've never wanted leadership or power.

Before, I thought she'd give up her position, but I know her better now. Looking into her determined gaze, I know she will make it happen. Nothing could stop her.

So do I want her still, if it means becoming an Alpha?

Yes.

Without a doubt.

"I'm sure Slate can give me a few pointers," I say, dipping my head to brush my lips against her cheek.

"Seriously, Onyx, I need you to be completely sure."

I fix her with an unflinching stare. "Yes. I will be your partner and mate, even if it means learning to be an Alpha."

Her eyebrows shoot up, her gaze softening and mouth parting. "Really?"

"I'll be your trophy mate," I say with a snicker. "Every strong Alpha needs someone pretty on their arm."

She slaps my chest, but her smile widens, her dimple visible. "I'm trusting that you are completely sure. Because I can't have you hold me back from my position."

"Ember, I would never hold you back."

"Okay," she says. When I don't react, she repeats, "Okay, I'll be your mate."

Her words don't sink in. Did she just accept? Is this happening?

"Onyx, did I break you?" she asks, tilting her head and pursing her lips.

"Wow," I say, "I thought I would have to beg for at least a week before you gave in."

"Are we going to make this official?" she asks, a nervous edge to her voice.

"I want to mark you and you mark me. But it can wait until you're ready," I say, my hands brushing down her ribs and waist before moving to her hands. Clasping both of her hands in mine, I pull them above her head, like when we first kissed.

"No, I don't want to wait. We should face this together, as mates in every way. And then my pack can't question you or treat you like that again."

"Like you'd let them get away with that," I murmur, admiring the way she's stretched out. Her back arches, her head tipping back against the door.

"Are you ready to become a Granite Ridge wolf?" she asks softly, as if that revelation would change my mind.

"I guess we will have dual citizenship, because it

goes both ways, my little hummingbird." My words are nonsense, but I can't help but poke fun.

"Mmm, I like that idea. When I claim my position, I'll need help from your pack to clean house and rebuild the pack's structure. Make it healthy."

"Jasper will be thrilled," I say.

"Stop talking about my brother," she teases. "Stop talking about everything. I need to make you my mate like I need air."

"Yes, Alpha," I say a split second before our lips crash together.

CHAPTER SEVENTEEN

SMOKING S'MORES

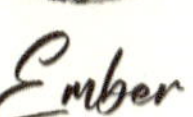

Ember

There's no more talking. Everything that needed to be said was said. Every worry I had laid out, and Onyx soothed all of them. He's willing to give up his life for me. Together we will rebuild my pack until it's a wonderful place to live. But thoughts of planning and strategy will have to wait, because Onyx is undressing me.

He tosses my shirt over his shoulder and reclaims my wrists in his left hand, keeping me upright against the cool wood of the bedroom door.

I struggle against his hold, wanting to touch him, but he grins and resumes kissing me. The world falls away as he coaxes my mouth open. The feel of his tongue against mine sends heat flooding my body, flowing from my fingertips to my toes and gathering low in my stomach.

This man makes kissing an artform. The slow brush of our lips, the way his teeth nip at my skin as he moves down my throat and lowers his mouth to my breasts. No amount of twisting deters him. His hand only tightens and pushes my wrists up, until I'm desperate, drawn out and panting.

His head comes back up, a wicked grin on his face. "I'm going to bite you," he says, "Right here." He gives a demonstration, fangs pressing into the crook of my neck hard enough to sting but not break the skin. This time, I'm confident I want it, and I let out a whimper at the sting.

"I want to claim you, too," I say, my words breathy. I gasp as he bites a second time, this one harder, as if he is testing the limit. "Do it," I say.

He lets out a low laugh. "Not yet. You didn't think I'd go this easy on you?"

I'm not sure if I'm about to melt or burst into

flames, but it's becoming unbearable. As if sensing my impending implosion, he finally releases my wrists.

It's all the urging I need. I launch myself at him and he grabs my waist, hoisting me up until I'm wrapped around him, my hands threading into his hair. Biting his bottom lip, I drag my nails along his scalp, earning a groan that makes my stomach flip.

He inches backward until we're falling onto the bed, his arms banded tight around me. My hair splays around us, enclosing his face, nose to nose with mine.

"I love you," I murmur.

"I've loved you for longer," he responds with a smirk.

"It's not a competition."

"No, 'cause I'd be winning."

I silence him by biting his neck, not low like a claiming, but high on his throat. He growls at the pain and pleasure as I suck at his skin. "I love when you're rough with me," he admits. A shiver runs down my spine.

Electricity buzzing under my skin, I push away until I have room to pull my leggings off. Onyx sheds his own pants and boxers and then helps me tug my leggings over my ankles. He nips at my ankle hard enough to leave a mark, and as I pull back, he hooks a finger into the edge of my panties and draws them down my hip, kissing the side of my thigh as he removes them entirely.

I watch his progress until my gaze strays to his naked body. My breathing goes ragged. He doesn't stop me or protest as I close my hand over his cock and slowly stroke down.

His eyes close, a look of ecstasy on his face. I stroke up and then back down harder, watching his reaction. He lets out a growl, his eyes opening, glowing a brilliant sapphire. "If you keep doing that, we'll miss out on other *more important* activities."

My hand withdraws, a flush burning from my cheeks to my neck.

"Fuck, that felt good," he rasps, crawling over me. I lay back, running my hands over the corded muscles in his arms, from his biceps down his forearms.

His mouth goes to my breasts for a short moment before he licks the curve of my stomach. I'm proud of my curves, but I still squirm under him. His fingers sink into the soft skin of my ass and hips, holding me still as he swirls his tongue over my clit. My vision goes white. He repeats the move until I can't remember my own name. Every muscle tenses, my back arching.

"Holy hell," I say, my voice trembling.

"You look magnificent," he whispered as he moves up my body and reaches between us. His cock nudges my entrance, ready for him. Slowly, gently, he pushes in with shallow thrusts, each one slightly deeper until he fills me entirely. My mouth falls open in a silent scream at the feeling of fullness.

"Even better than I imagined," he murmurs, the words almost inaudible, as if his thoughts are escaping without him realizing.

As he resumes moving, tenderly, attentively. My thighs close over his hips, pressing against him as my head turns sideways and my eyes squeeze shut to block out everything but the feel of him inside of me.

He picks up speed, growing confident at my soft moans as he strokes against my inner walls, sending sparks through my body. I'm so sensitive, and that burning pleasure intensifies.

My hands scramble for a grip on anything stable, my fingers curling around the bottom edge of the wooden headboard. He groans louder. "I'm not going to last long, you feel too good," he warns, the words broken and slurred.

Feeling my own orgasm looming again, I force my eyes open. His throat is bared to me as he moves against me. I want to kiss, bite, and mark him so bad it takes my breath away.

Releasing the headboard, I reach for him. His pace slows as he lets me pull him closer. Kissing down his neck, I find that juncture with his shoulder where the tendon is taut. It's tempting, and I lick across the skin. His inhale is audible, encouraging me.

He's mine, and I'm claiming him.

My sharp teeth close over his skin, tightening until the skin breaks in a dozen tiny wounds. His blood hits over my tongue and the magic hits me.

Adoration, arousal, and possessiveness fill every fiber of my being. I can't untangle his emotions from mine, and my nails dig into his shoulders as a whimper escapes me. Pleasure barrels over all of it, sweeping me up, and I don't know if it's mine or his.

His teeth cut into my skin, the pain nothing compared to the intense onslaught of feeling. It's as if every emotion is mirrored back, a reflection of a reflection until infinity.

I'm shaking, cursing, tears falling from the corners of my eyes into my hair. His forehead drops to my sternum as he sucks in deep lungfuls of air.

The emotion ebbs, until I can separate his feelings from mine. How does anyone adjust to this? He lifts his head and grins, and happiness soaks into me through our mate bond.

"This is crazy," I finally manage to say.

"Yeah," he replies, withdrawing and stretching out on the duvet cover beside me.

Reluctantly, I climb out of the bed and cross to the bathroom. After I clean up, he flips off the lights and tucks the covers around us.

"I can't believe we did that," I say with a laugh. "Everyone is going to freak when they find out."

Onyx brushes my hair back and nuzzles against the nape of my neck. He doesn't answer for a while, but then he says, "No one is going to be surprised."

"Will they be happy for you?" I ask tentatively.

Onyx chuckles. "They'll be thrilled for *us*." Affection bubbles up in my chest and this time it's mine. The hand draped across my waist tenses, and he drags me flush against him. He must have felt the warm fuzzy feelings reflected through our bond.

In the darkness with my mate holding me, I've never felt so safe. For once, I don't fight sleep but let it overtake me. It's short-lived, because my mate wakes me after a time, and we come together again before falling into a deeper sleep.

ONYX

A trail of smoke wafts from the oven when Ember cracks the door open. She lets out the cutest little squeak and scrambles for oven mitts.

"Everything going okay over there?" I ask, restraining myself from jumping up to help.

"Shush, it's fine."

Propping my chin on my fist, I suppress a smile. She insisted on making a surprise for us and wouldn't even let me see the ingredients. Teeth biting her bottom lip, she lifts a glass casserole dish out of the oven. The top is golden brown, not blackened, but smoke trails off of it anyway.

"Did you burn something?" Cedar asks, leaning against the doorway with his arms crossed. After three days stuck in a house with us, he is as grumpy as we predicted.

"Not you too!" Ember grumbles. Glass clinks as she dishes up her creation. She spins with a plate in each hand, a bashful smile lighting up her gorgeous features.

"What is it?" Cedar asks.

"S'mores!" she says.

Melted golden marshmallow flows over graham crackers on the dish I accept from my mate. She sinks down beside me and blows on her serving.

"I know you aren't super familiar with them, but that's not really how s'mores are supposed to be made," I tease.

She narrows her eyes in a playful glare. "Well, we don't exactly have a proper fire, and you said microwave s'mores aren't acceptable. So here we are."

Indulging my feisty mate, I pick up the graham cracker and take a bite. The top layer crunches beautifully and chocolate oozes out from under the marshmallow.

"Actually, this is great," I mumble between sticky

bites.

"Are you just being nice?" she asks, eyeing her own s'more like it might poison her.

"No, seriously. Cedar, get one, you'll love it."

As Ember takes a tiny, testing bite, she lets out a little moan that has me thinking of carrying her out of the kitchen, but there's plenty of time for that later.

Cedar loads up two on his own plate and sits opposite us. "Any word from Jasper?" he asks.

"Nothing today," Ember answers glumly.

"What about from your mom?" he asks.

Ember licks sugar from her fingertips before answering. "She has been making all kinds of new friends over in Ironcrest. I'm a little afraid Zephyr will be my new step-dad." She looks slightly green at the idea, and I have to agree.

"I doubt it," my brother answers with a shrug.

"So what if they don't find a solution?" Ember asks, not for the first time. Through our mate bond, I feel her spike in anxiety. My hand brushes up her forearm. I love the way her emotions settle under my touch.

Instead of offering platitudes about trusting Slate and Jasper, Cedar fidgets with his fork. "I think we all know someone is going to have to challenge Orion for Alpha. I know you guys want to find another solution, but short of invading and taking over the pack, I don't see any other viable option."

I could punch him. Ember's heart starts to beat wildly and her emotions rollercoaster through fear, worry, and anger so quickly my head is spinning.

"Well, fuck," I mutter. "That's exactly what Jasper said not to do."

Ember grabs my hand, her nails pressing into my skin. "Onyx..." she says, seemingly unable to finish her sentence.

'It's okay," I say quietly, wishing my brother would leave. Or at least shut his mouth.

"We know he's right," she finally says, tipping her chin up as she regains her composure. I'm so proud of her. Despite being terrified, she's ready to face the wolf who beat her in a challenge just a few days ago.

I won't let that happen again.

"We don't know that," I argue.

"How long do we wait for another solution, then?" Ember says, barely above a whisper.

"Realistically, you have time. Things can't get that much worse in Granite Ridge in the next week or two," Cedar interjects with another shrug.

"See, we can give it time," I say, threading my fingers through hers and flipping her hand over.

She sighs. "If there was another solution, they would have found it by now."

"Fine. I'll challenge him for Alpha. I'm the mate of the pack's rightful Heir. He can't deny me."

"No!" Ember blurts. "I can't let you do that. What if he hurts you worse?"

I scowl at her. "I resent that. It took three of them and a set of handcuffs to take me down last time."

Cedar's mouth presses into a line, but he doesn't say anything.

"I'll do it," she says.

"No," I say, fisting my hand on the table.

"It's our only option," she argues.

"I can take him."

My brother lets out a dramatic sigh. "I'm not sure either of you can take him on your own, unless you find some advantage over him."

Ember taps her index finger on the table, her nail making a hollow clicking noise. Her lips purse to the side, looking adorable while she contemplates taking over a pack.

"Let's say we can find a way to defeat him in a challenge," Ember turns to me, reluctance written all over her face. "But would they respect us? Even if we beat him - what if they all just followed him anyways?"

"They'll follow you. Especially if Jasper supports your claim."

That's one thing I'm sure of. She is Ferris's daughter, so even if the pack has turned on Sienna, they have to bow to Ember if she claims her birthright.

"Not everyone will," Ember says.

"And those are the ones we have to get rid of. We already knew we had to clean house if we wanted to build a healthy pack. This way, we can cut out the worst of them right from the start."

Cedar stands and clears his throat. "I suggest you call Jasper."

Ember's gaze is distant as she turns over scenarios in her head, but her emotions remain calm with a touch of something warm swirling in our bond. Hope?

"I love when you're plotting," I say, pulling her hand to my mouth. Gingerly, I place a kiss over her wrist.

She bites her lip again. "I still don't like the idea of you fighting Orion."

My jovial mood falls away. "He dared to put his hands on you. And he tried to take you from me. I'm going to kill him."

She smiles as if I didn't just threaten murder. Challenges aren't supposed to be to the death, but it seems deserved in this case.

"As much as I'd like to see that, I think it needs to be me. I want to prove myself. And the pack won't respect me if you just swoop in and save the day."

"Don't let him land a hit on you or I'll go fucking crazy," I threaten, my voice lowering dangerously.

Her eyes are lit with a faint glow, her smile feral.

I love when she is sweet and nurturing, but I also love when she's feisty and demanding. I love every side of my beautiful mate.

"Are we really going to do this?" she asks, her cheeks flushing.

"We don't exactly have any other ideas. And I think it could work. But Cedar's right, we don't stand a chance unless we have some sort of strategy."

"Then we better figure it out." she murmurs, her eyes dropping to my mouth.

We can figure it out right after I take her back to our bedroom.

"You two are gross," Cedar mutters, dropping his plate in the sink. Shaking his head, he strides out.

"Poor guy," I say, leaning forward until I can kiss her cheek.

"He'll be fine." She wrinkles her nose as I nibble at her ear.

"But we better go back to our room instead of defiling the kitchen." Her giggles soothe my worries as I brush her hair off her shoulder to kiss over the pale scars that mark her as mine.

Chapter Eighteen

BUBBLE BATHS & EX BOYFRIENDS

Ember

"Mom?" I ask, crossing my legs under me as I sit on the bed.

Her voice sounds distant, maybe irritated. "Ember, what do you need?" she says sharply.

"Um, how are you doing?"

"I'm fine." She sighs audibly, bringing a flush of embarrassment to my skin.

My hands curl into fists. "Last time I saw you, you were unconscious and looking half-dead."

"I'm sorry you had to see that. You don't need to worry about me." Her words are clipped. I can almost picture her picking at her nails in this moment, as if I am the least interesting part of her day.

"Okay," I say, trying to keep the sarcasm from my tone.

"Jasper tells me you're staying away... with that boy," she says, her casual tone anything but kind.

"Onyx," I snap. "His name is Onyx."

"What are you thinking, running around with him?" We've moved from dismissive to reprimanding, and things are about to get so much worse.

My shoulders tense, the anxiety spiraling through my body. "He's my mate."

"Please tell me you didn't."

"I love him and it's done," I blurt, recklessly adding, "I don't need your approval."

"And you don't have it." She's not angry. I'm not worth her anger, just her half-hearted disdain. But after everything I went through trying to help her and my pack, I'm not accepting it.

"Orion locked me up after I refused to be his mate," I hiss, a cold sweat prickling across my skin. I'd give anything to be less emotional - it's like I'm fighting my own reactions as much as I'm fighting her.

Her next words cut deep. "That would have been wiser than that boy."

How can she say that? "He almost killed you," I say dumbly. "Onyx has done nothing but protect and support me."

She huffs. Clearly that's not good enough in her eyes.

"Orion would have *used* me, and he's way old. He would have treated me horribly."

"Possibly," she admits, like it's an interesting possibility.

"How are you not concerned about that?" My question slips out, and to my surprise, she answers it.

"You are safest when you have power, Ember. And if I can't protect you, you need to find someone who can. Since you've chosen a mate who has no notable ranking, you've given away any future position you could have had. So I suppose it's best you stay away and not come back."

"I can stay with his pack and Jasper," I point out, the idea tempting me.

"If you like," she murmurs, distracted again.

"Actually, that's why I'm calling." I clear my throat, needing to recapture her attention.

"Yes?" she asks wearily.

"I'm going to retake the pack."

There. It's out there.

Silence rings through the line. Finally, she asks, "How on earth do you intend to do that?"

"I'm going to challenge Orion."

"You can't do that." She sounds horrified, her pitch jumping.

"I'm pretty sure I can," I say, taking a slow breath to steady myself. We don't need her approval.

"Ember, you will not win. You and your little mate will be slaughtered." She finally sounds worried.

"Geez, thanks for the confidence, Mom."

"I know you don't think I love you, but I have only ever wanted you safe," she says, acting like the concerned mother she isn't. It's too much. I want to scream at her.

"You didn't give a shit about me until Jasper left and you were stuck with me as your Heir." My words shake.

"That's not true."

"Look, I didn't need to tell you any of this." I say, the sting of her rejection turning my words bitter. "I don't know why I thought you'd support me."

"I support you making wise decisions," she argues. I cut her off.

"You support me doing what you want me to do. Regardless of how it hurts me. Consider this a courtesy warning of what I'm going to do. If you want to help, like actually help me, you can talk to Jasper about it."

"There's nothing to discuss!" she says, her voice growing louder. I've finally cut through her facade. But now that I have her full attention, I want nothing more than to end this wretched call.

"Mom, I need to go."

"You aren't going anywhere," she snaps back.

I ignore her. "Be safe. I'll talk to you when it's over and we have our pack back."

"Ember!"

I hold the phone away from my ear as she says my name again, louder. My fingers tremble from the confrontation, but I press down the red button to hang up and let out a long, slow breath.

"That sounds like it went well," Onyx says from the doorway, a half-smile on his face. He's so damn handsome, even with sympathy in his eyes.

"Come here. I need a pick-me-up after all that."

It's too much to handle, and his hands on me transport me to a higher plane, where my mother's bullshit doesn't exist.

He leaps on the bed, an eager puppy. I welcome his arm across my chest, pushing me down into the mattress. My legs unfold and my hair fans out around my head.

"You're so beautiful," he murmurs, lowering his face and trailing his lips across my forehead and down my nose.

"I don't know what I expected, but she just wants to control me." My fingers curl into his shirt in my frustration.

I love that he doesn't try to justify Sienna's behavior

or argue with me. Sighing, I turn my head so he can nibble down my neck and run his tongue over my claim mark. He happily scrapes his teeth over the spot, forcing a soft groan out of me.

He pops up, a grin on his face. "It doesn't matter. You don't need her. She's not the Alpha anymore. You're about to be."

Before I can protest, he brushes his lips against mine and then presses firmly, encouraging my mouth to open. All my worries fall away as he kisses me, as fervently as the first time.

A contentedness settles over me, and I happily scratch my nails down his chest, hoping to leave red lines under his thin shirt. He grumbles, nipping down on my bottom lip.

I want nothing more than to slip out of our clothes and ravage each other until he's whispering my name like a prayer, but there's too much to be done and I'll be brainless for an hour afterward if we do that.

"As nice as this is," I say, hating every word, "I have one more call to make, unfortunately."

His hands knead over my shoulders, squeezing down my arm. "Want me to leave?

"Fuck, no," I say, closing my eyes and straining my neck at the pinching pleasure he's inflicting on my tendons. With one more kiss his hands drop away, leaving me desperate for more.

"Let's get it over with. I have a list of things I want to try with you, and it'll be really hard for you to make any calls while I do them," he whispers against my skin.

"You're not going to like this one."

"Why?"

Hawk picks up the phone after the fifth ring, when I'm about to give up and end the call. My stomach jumps into my throat and I lean harder into Onyx. The warmth of his chest feels good against my side, banishing the shivers of anxiety.

"Ember? Is everything okay?" His voice sounds odd, unfamiliar. It's been months since I spoke with him, but he feels like a stranger.

"Hi, Hawk." My voice falters, and I feel Onyx's hand tighten on my waist. "Well, not really. That's why I'm calling."

I should have called him months ago, to try and reconcile politically, even if we would never be mates. We could use his support right about now, but I doubt his family will give it.

"What's wrong?" His voice is sharp.

"Orion."

"What?" His voice lowers, sounding angry, as if he already knows what's wrong with that one word.

"He challenged my mom and took over the pack," I admit, praying he will help and that I'm right in trusting him.

"Oh, shit."

"Yeah."

"Sweetheart, I'm so sorry," he says. I prickle at his pet name for me. There was never any affection behind it and I know that now.

"Hi, Hawk." Onyx butts in, unable to help himself. He leans his cheek against my fingers gripping the phone, making sure his voice is heard. I press my lips together to keep from laughing at him.

"Uh, hi? Who is that?" Hawk sounds baffled. With a sigh, I press the button for speaker phone.

"It's Onyx, remember me?" My mate puts on a friendly tone, like he's reconnecting with an old friend.

"Sorry, no."

"I'm the one Ember stabbed during the battle at Bracken Creek."

Hawk coughs. "Oh, I don't think I saw that."

"Whatever, it doesn't matter. But I'm Ember's mate," Onyx continues, the words tumbling out. My mouth falls open and he gives me a wink.

Hawk takes a beat to process and when he speaks again, his tone is formal, as if he knows more distance is needed. I'm not his to protect.

"Congratulations. I hope you two are really happy."

"Thank you, I hope you're happy too," I say sincerely. " But I was hoping you could help me with the Orion problem. I need to challenge him and get my pack back."

"Ember, are you sure about that?" I can picture Hawk's face and the way he would raise a single eyebrow. No doubt he is making the same expression now.

"Yes."

"How can I help?"

"Tell me anything you can about Orion. We don't know much about his weaknesses. Anything that could help. Please."

"Of course. Let me think," he says, trailing off.

"I really appreciate it," I say, closing my eyes as Onyx trails his hand down my hip and thigh.

"He always liked it if he could manipulate people into doing what he wants, and honestly, he's always been cruel," Hawk says.

"That tracks with how he's behaving now," Onyx replies.

"But he's charming when he wants to be."

"We've seen that. Thanks." Onyx's words are edged with sarcasm. "Why the fuck did you bring this guy along with you?"

"Sorry, I know this doesn't help, but I do know my Dad sent Orion with money to buy gifts to win people over. I guess he's used that to his own advantage."

The idea of this powerful Alpha miles and miles north of our territory who may or may not support our enemy layers more fear on top of my undercurrent of anxiety. But we have to focus on the enemy in front of us, so I push it out of my mind.

"What are his weaknesses?" Onyx cuts in.

"His ego," Hawk says without hesitation.

"Can you think of anything else?" I ask.

"Let me talk to my sister and I'll get back to you."

"Thank you," I say, feeling less optimistic than before.

"I'm glad you've got someone who loves you," he says quickly. My eyes flick to Onyx, and he's already watching me with an intensity that sets my body aflame.

"Yeah, he's pretty great," I say with a smile.

"Good. Take care of her, man."

"I am," Onyx says, hanging up without looking at the phone. Gently, he rolls me onto my back. "That went better than the first call, right?"

"Yeah," I have to agree.

"See? Things are already looking up." I need his optimism right now. My mother's negativity rattled me more than I'd like to admit.

My mate's hair tickles my jaw as he kisses down my throat. When this situation becomes too much to handle, he's the perfect escape. It's easy to lose myself in his touch while his citrus scene fills my lungs.

With scattered kisses, he pulls my shirt off. I return the favor, forcing him to stop kissing me long enough to pull it over his head. The second it hits the floor, he jumps up to lock the door before leaping back on the bed with a playful grin.

"Everything is going to work out," he says, framing me in with his arms as he hovers over me. Instead of answering, I pull him down and nuzzle into the crook of his neck.

"Think about the future when we have our own house, all to ourselves," he whispers. The picture is beautiful, and my heart jumps. His teeth nip over my claim mark. "I can't wait to show off this to everyone."

My fingers skim over the place I know his mark is, even if I can't see it while he overwhelms my senses. "You're so tense," he says. I don't feel that, not when he's turning me boneless.

With a sharp exhale, Onyx sits up. The cold air washing over my chest makes me scowl at him. "What?"

"You are too stressed," he says, his eyes roaming over me hungrily.

"Yeah, but we were..." I reach for him, but he holds up a hand to silence me.

"Wait, I've got it."

My breath comes out harsh as he climbs off the bed and walks away. What the hell? My irritation keeps me from following him, and instead I open my phone back up to see if anyone has texted me an update. There's nothing.

The sound of a faucet sounds from the bathroom.

Cabinet doors clang as he does whatever he's doing. Exhaling slowly, I lay back and close my eyes.

"Okay, my love, it's time to relax," Onyx says. I jerk up and my phone drops my chest and bounces across the duvet. Ignoring it, he takes my hand and ushers me to the bathroom.

The garden tub is steaming with bubbles piled on top. "You made me a bath?" I ask stupidly.

"I found bubble bath under the sink," Onyx says, his grin crooked. "Do you like baths?"

"I don't really do them." My arms cross over my breasts, my shoulders hunching.

"You'll like this one, I promise." He could convince me of anything when he smirks like that. My annoyance falls away as his clever fingers pull my shorts off and then his own sweats. With a steady hand, he guides me into the tub and then steps after me.

"Oh, it's a two person bath?" I ask with a laugh.

"Yes, strict quality control. How else would I know you're enjoying yourself and destressing properly?"

"Good to know my mate is a bath connoisseur."

"I'm a lot of things."

"A man of mystery," I tease as my toes dip into the hot water. "Oh, that's nice." Pausing, I look up at him. "Do we need to get a hot tub?"

"Only if it's private," he says, his dark eyes promising pleasure as his hands guide me into the tub.

We settle into the water and the steam caresses me. My back rests against his chest, my head leaning back until my temple rests against his jaw.

It's a little strange, but as his hands brush over my skin under the water, I find myself calming. The lavender of the bubbles obscures his scent, so I turn my face against his neck and breathe him in. He lets out a rumbling chuckle, and impulsively my tongue darts out to taste his skin. His laugh turns to a groan.

"Oh, sorry, am I interrupting your special bath?" I ask, leaning back and giving him an innocent smile. "I better control myself."

Water sloshes as he dives for me, crashing our mouths together. Bubbles splatter on my face and neck, his wet hands digging into my hair to keep me where he wants me.

Feeling victorious, I drag my nails down his soapy back. "So much for a relaxing bath," I hum.

"Damn, you're so..." he pauses, his teeth closing over my lip. My hips buck, pressing against him. "Slippery." It's my turn to tip my head back and laugh.

"I don't think we can do what we want in here," I say, breathless. "Maybe we relocate?"

"Not yet." Onyx's answer is a growl as he slides me back against his chest. I open my mouth to argue, but he silences me with fingers reaching between my thighs.

"Is this normal procedure for a bath?" I ask him, my

teasing sounding desperate as he starts to explore my body.

He bites my shoulder firmly for a few seconds and says, "Time to stop talking." As if he knows I'll argue again, his other hand goes to my breast while he continues to rub soft circles against my clit.

There's no way I could speak again if I wanted to. An embarrassing moan escapes me. My body burns, the hot water intensifying it until I'm gasping and gripping the edge of the tub.

I want to reach for him and give him some of the attention he's lavishing on me, but I can hardly control my limbs. My knees fall open, giving him as much access as possible.

His free hand moves from my breasts up to my throat. My breathing hitches as he collars my neck, gripping softly without squeezing.

Whimpering pathetically, I surrender to his control. His thumb swipes down the column of my throat while he gently strokes my core. I'm lost in each movement, the waves of pleasure of his touch rising until I'm gasping and shivering. My back arches and I press my head back against him, my vision dancing with stars. My mate's soft voice murmurs against my ear. "You're so perfect. I fucking love you."

I've barely come down when he scoops me up and sets me on the edge of the tub. My mate dries me off and then dries himself with rough drags of the towel. I bite my lip as I watch his muscles flex while he contorts to dry his back.

"Enjoying the show?" he asks.

"It's okay, I guess," I quip back. With a playful snarl, he hauls me against his chest and walks us back to the bed.

Still blissed out from his ministrations in the tub, I stretch out and grin at him. "I believe I was promised an entire list of things done to me."

Onyx's wolfish grin rekindles my lust. "You sure you're up for that?"

I've barely nodded when he lifts my hips and lines us up. Our bodies fit together so perfectly, and I find myself murmuring how much I love him while he's buried inside of me. Murmurs turn to gasps and moans as we try new positions and angles. I'd like nothing more than to hide away with him for the next month. But after we're both spent, I know we have to face all the unspoken worries.

But for a moment, we rest quietly. Onyx brushes my hair back so he can press kisses along the curve of my ear. His arm loops over my waist, his chest against my back, our legs folded together.

"Is there any chance I can convince you to let me be the one to fight Orion?" he asks softly.

I wish I could say yes. It would be so nice to let him

face this for me. There's plenty of good reasons to agree. But I just can't.

"Sorry, I've got to do this myself."

His breath ghosts over my neck. "Alright," he says with a sigh. I can sense how worried he is through our bond, and I love him for respecting my choice.

Turning in his arms, I face him. His stormy eyes are full of conflict, and I can't help but brush his hair back and run my hand down his striking face. "I've got this. With you backing me up, I know we can win."

Perhaps he can tell I'm lying, but regardless, he kisses the tip of my nose and nuzzles down into his pillow.

"I don't think we have time for a nap before dinner," I say with a chuckle.

His answer is a rough tug on my hips to drag my closer. I almost miss his response, mumbled into his pillow. "Just let me hold you, for a while." Feeling treasured, I comply.

ONYX

Jasper and Marigold fetch us the next day.

Cedar answers the door, and Marigold greets him loud enough we can hear her clearly in our bedroom. Ember tucks the last few items we have into a backpack.

"Ready?"

She eyes my extended hand. I wiggle my fingers, trying to make her smile. With a deep breath, she squares her shoulders and threads her fingers through mine.

Jasper and Marigold stand in the living room, talking quietly with Cedar about pack updates. The second we come into view, Marigold lets out a gasp.

"Hey, guys," Ember says, her iron grip on my hand betraying her nervousness.

"You're mated!" she squeals, flinging her arms around Ember in a violent hug that pulls her away from me.

Ember's eyes widen and anxiety bleeds through our bond. "Careful, Goldie," I say with a chuckle, prying Marigold off my mate. She transfers to me, nonsensical words of happiness tumbling out of her as she squeezes me.

Jasper hugs his sister next and congratulates her softly while I work on extracting myself from Marigold's hold. She spins toward my twin.

"How could you not tell us?" Marigold swats at Cedar and he raises his hands defensively.

"It was bad enough being here at the time. They're not the most quiet pair," Cedar grumbles, his ears turning a red that matches the blush spreading across Ember's cheeks.

Her embarrassment burns through our mate bond,

butting up against my own pride at showing off my beautiful mate. "It's okay," I whisper, landing a kiss on her cheek.

"Yeah, I know," she murmurs.

Clearing my throat, I regain the room's attention. "As much fun as this is, we need to get the show on the road."

We only have a few bags with us, so it's easy to load up Jasper's trunk and pile into the sporty vehicle. A moment later, we're pulling onto the road.

Ember leans against me in the back seat, anxiously swirling her thumb in circles around my knuckles. Cedar sits on the other side, staring out the window.

"So before we get into our plan," Ember says, taking the lead, "do you guys have any updates to share? Any new ideas?"

Jasper's pale hair shakes. "Sorry, no. Slate and Hazel haven't been able to find any common ground with Sienna or Zephyr."

"I don't think there's much they can do to help," she says. "We are going to have to handle this ourselves."

Marigold twists around, a line between her brows as she frowns at us. "What are you thinking?"

"I'm going to challenge Orion."

"Ember!" Marigold snaps, eyes going wide. "Do you think that's a good idea?" Jasper's knuckles are white across the steering wheel.

"I'm not going in unprepared. We need something to even the playing field, which is why I asked to come back to Bracken Creek."

That's my feisty girl, standing up for herself while being mysterious and irresistible. I hide my smirk in her hair by nuzzling against her neck.

"Oh, and Jasper?" she asks. "Can we borrow your car? I want to make a good impression when we go back. You can sit in the back seat and let Onyx drive, if you don't mind."

She's incredible. I don't even attempt to hide my grin as I peek at Jasper's reaction. His mouth thins and his jaw ticks. After a moment, he answers. "If it'll help, that's fine."

A small smile curves Ember's mouth and she meets my gaze in the rear view mirror.

Pulling into the gravel lot, we are greeted by several pack members. Cedar unfolds himself and heads straight to our parents. Ember moves to follow him out of the back seat, but I hold tight.

"What?" she whispers.

Reaching up, I tug the neckline of her shirt slightly askew, revealing the circle of tiny, pale scars. "I want everyone to see that you're mine."

"You're ridiculous," she says, rolling her eyes, but I can feel through our bond that she likes it.

Once I've retrieved our bags, I hold them both with one hand, keeping the other free to hold Ember's hand. No one will doubt our relationship. I don't want anyone to question or disrespect her.

My mother hugs Ember tightly, and tears glitter in her eyes as she steps back, holding Ember's shoulders firmly. "I'm so glad you are back. I missed you, dear. And now I get to keep you."

"Mom, I'm sorry, but it's just a quick visit. We have a situation to handle in Ember's pack." She pales at my words.

"Can we go see the healer?" Ember asks quietly.

Slate and Hazel stand in our path. "Am I seeing correctly?" Slate says.

"What are you seeing?" I tug Ember closer, squeezing her hand.

"You've claimed each other?" Hazel asks. A hopeful smile curves her mouth, though concern furrows her brows.

"Looks like it," I say with a smirk.

Slate opens and closes his mouth, emotions warring in his eyes. It's Hazel who reaches out to embrace Ember. "Congratulations."

"Thank you," Ember murmurs, smiling at her.

Slate relents, his face relaxing. "I'm happy for you guys, but maybe we should focus on the issue at hand."

"Stop being an ass," Hazel says. "After things are

settled, we should have a party to celebrate."

"So what's this plan you mentioned?" Slate asks me.

"We are going back to Granite Ridge. I'm going to challenge Orion," Ember answers, raising her chin.

Hazel's intake of breath is audible, but Ember isn't done. She inches closer to Slate. "And let me be clear. If you even think about stopping me, I will consider the alliance between our packs to be null. I'm taking my pack back with or without your help."

Facing each other, the similarities are obvious - the same straight nose and intense gaze, the way they clench their hands when they're nervous and determined.

Slate's shoulders slump minutely and his head ducks. "I'm sorry you'd even worry that I would do that. Tell me what I can do to help."

"Thank you," she says softly, giving him a grim smile. "Can I see your healer?"

"Are you hurt?" Hazel asks.

"No, I just need her help with our plan," Ember explains.

"Alright, let's go to Sable's cottage." Hazel waves us forward. Jasper and Marigold trail behind, and the six of us make our way across the meadow to secure that advantage that my brilliant mate came up with.

CHAPTER NINETEEN

FANGS, FIGHTS, & FEAR

Ember

Onyx drove Jasper's fancy car into Granite Ridge territory, just the three of us. Marigold, Hazel, and Slate all wanted to come, but I can't risk accusations of Bracken Creek manipulating the situation. Jasper is family and the former Heir, so his presence cannot be disputed.

We drive straight into the compound and park in the dirt between the Alpha's house and the cafeteria.

Dozens of people pour out of the buildings and surround us.

While the small gathering that we met in Bracken Creek was friendly and curious, the group that circles us in Granite Ridge is decidedly hostile.

Onyx and Jasper climb out of the car, boldly meeting their accusatory gazes. I wait until Onyx comes around to open my door. It's another calculated move and a way to show respect.

A few of the wolves drift closer, testing our boundaries.

"Back the fuck off," Jasper snarls, pulling his favorite dagger out. The lazy charm is gone, replaced with the promise of violence our parents modeled for us from our births. It's oddly validating to see him revert back, even if it's for show.

Onyx's expression is stony and his hand rests on the handle of his gun tucked in his waistband.

"So nice of my little wolf to come back willingly," a tall figure croons. The crowd parts for their new Alpha.

"Orion," I say, raising my chin and pretending I'm not two heads shorter than he is. "I challenge you for the position of Alpha, as is my birthright as the daughter of the late Alpha Ferris."

He lets out a booming laugh. My jaw snaps shut so hard it hurts, every muscle tensing.

"Why should I accept your challenge? You're not

strong enough to force it. I could just let my pack have their way with you."

Onyx's hand tightens on his weapon and Jasper turns to face away from us defensively.

"I thought you were demanding I become your mate, just a few days ago. You wanted my claim to the position then. Defeat me, and you'll prove yourself."

He sneers. "Maybe I just wanted the youngest, prettiest thing in this pack. But I'm confident better options will present themselves."

"Funny, I'd rather be claimed by a guard from another pack than let you touch me." To make my point clear, I tug my neckline to show off my mark. Onyx smirks, not minding in the least that I downplayed his ranking.

Orion's sneer melts into a snarl as he bares his teeth at us. "You're nothing. I could kill him and take you if I wanted to."

"See? You're a fraud. An Alpha would never do that," I declare, my voice rising. "The pack cannot trust a leader who has no respect for our laws and traditions."

He growls, stalking back toward us. Gritting my teeth, I hold my ground, biding my time until the right moment.

"I challenge you, Orion, for the position of Alpha of Granite Ridge."

He stops a few feet away, glaring at us. "If you need

to learn this lesson a second time, I'm happy to help. When do we fight?"

"Sorry, did you need time for a pep talk? Because I'm ready now," I drawl, my heart leaping as I hear a few snickers from pack members around us.

"Fine." He storms away, a few wolves stumbling back in their hurry to get away from his anger.

The entire pack has gathered, and they move loosely with us. Expressions range from disgust to curiosity, but it's the tinge of hope through the weakened pack bond that causes me to straighten as we walk toward the center of the street.

Orion stands ready, shaking out his hands like I'm not his first fight of the day. As I stop a few feet away from him, he looks up with a chilling smile.

"I can't say I'm disappointed. This way you'll still be begging me."

A savage growl rolls out from my mate. With glowing eyes, he paces on one side, keeping my packmates back. Jasper stands behind me, his intelligent gaze trained on Orion.

"Ready?" I ask. Fear flashes through my mate bond, my terror mixing with Onyx's frustration as the challenge begins. He'd give anything to stand in my place, but I'm not powerless.

Flexing my own hands, I prepare to cut this wretch down to size.

Orion moves first, like I expected. He's fast for someone that large. He barrels toward me, reaching to grab me, and I easily slip aside.

With a wide swipe, I scratch my nails into his forearm, drawing blood. The dried wolfsbane and rowanberry powder under my fingernails won't incapacitate him, but it should slow him down if it gets into his bloodstream and prevent him from accessing his shift. Hopefully it's enough to give us a chance.

Jasper shouts a warning and I spin back toward my opponent. His fist flies toward my face and I duck. Shifting my weight, I land a swift kick against his knee.

Orion's breathing quickens and he lets out a small grunt with each step. It's working.

He comes for me again and I can't dodge in time. The strike glances off my shoulder and pain explodes down the nerves in my arm and across my shoulders into my neck.

I stumble but regain my balance quickly. Orion faces me, his stance low and ready, but he doesn't attack again.

"Are you going to dodge me and hope for the best? Or are you going to try and take my rank from me?"

His words make me flinch. I can't afford to look weak, but if he gets hold of me, he could kill me in seconds.

"It's not my fault you're so slow," I shoot back,

darting forward and swiping at his face with my other hand. His reaction is slower than it should be, thanks to the poison in his system.

Angry red cuts streak down his cheek and across his jaw. His roar shakes my bones. Before I can retreat, he grabs my wrist.

No!

With a twist, he forces me to the ground. My knees splinter, sending pain up to my hips until my entire body is stabbing needles. Tears blur my vision.

Orion's huge knuckles connect with my cheek, and the world turns white. I gasp for air on the ground. Dirt and rocks embed into my hip and arm, and my hair has slipped its bun, falling around me in a tangle.

Instinctively, I curl over my wrist. Crimson liquid drips onto the dirt, and I numbly realize it's coming from my nose.

A shadow covers me and I tense, waiting for the kick.

ONYX

Blood sprays from Orion's hit, and I cannot stand back and watch. Ember lays in the dirt, her eyes squeezed shut. The brute laughs as he stands over her petite form.

With an inhuman snarl, I leap at him. His eyes gleam as he takes me in.

My strike lands on his chin, sending him back into the edge of the crowd. He straightens, working his jaw. "Do you want to die? That would free up the girl for me." Blood shines on his teeth as he grins at me.

"You accept my challenge." It's not a question, but Orion grunts in acceptance. There's a hunger in his eyes, a desire for violence that makes my hands shake. I clench my fists to keep the tremble from showing.

He's slowing, stopping. If she got enough into him, he won't be able to shift. It's unlikely I can defeat him in my human form, even in his current state, but as a wolf, I stand a chance.

The panic and turmoil drops away as I fall to four legs. My tail swishes behind me as I gather my haunches under me and prepare to leap.

Orion's face scrunches, his eyes glowing with rage. He just figured out he can't shift. I won't waste this chance. All the tension in my body uncoils at once, launching me toward his chest.

Orion's defensive pose cannot withstand a huge wolf landing on his chest. He goes down, wildly attempting to block me. My jaws close around his arm and I snap the bone down by his wrist. The scream from his throat is sweet to hear.

Sharp and sudden pain blasts through my body,

overwhelming me. Jumping back, I realize there is a blade embedded low in my chest by the joint of my front left leg. Clamping my teeth over the handle, I pull the knife free and toss it aside.

Orion laughs, spitting blood on the ground beside him. He still cradles his arm, but clearly he thinks he's won already. Blood flows through my fur and down my leg from the wound I can't even see.

My growl warns him to stay down, but the stubborn bastard kneels, struggling to pull himself in a standing position. Crimson coats his collar and seeps across his chest.

Gathering my strength, I leap again. But this time he's ready for me. His fist connects with the wound he already gave me, and the pain blacks out my vision for a second.

An undignified yelp escapes me, and I bite wildly as my legs give out. Orion grabs my front leg and pulls me sideways, squeezing and twisting. Memories of the beating they gave me last time I was here fill my mind, overwhelming my control. Snarling, I thrash and snap my jaws, connecting with his unbroken hand. Blood hits my tongue, but I can't see the damage.

The pain of my leg wrenching and stretching the stab wound is too much. Fear of what is coming next overpowers my wolf, and humanity comes rushing in. My body shifts back without my permission.

Orion's low laugh sends icy terror through me as he breaks my arm. I struggle to suck in air and stay conscious. If I don't protect myself, I'll be abandoning Ember.

His grip on me is too strong. My strength is fading as blood flows from my wound.

Something hits Orion, a blur of black fur, sending him sprawling. Blinking to clear my vision, I watch my beautiful little mate close her jaws over his neck and shake her head. Orion screams, yanking at her fur and trying to get a grip on her body.

With a vicious growl deep in her chest, Ember stays locked on him, her jaws clamped down with ruby liquid gushing between her fangs until Orion stills.

Ember's shift flows over her as she turns and moves toward me, landing on her knees on the dirt as I try to push up to sit. Pain screams through my chest and arm and I land back on the dirt with a strained noise.

Red coats her face, her bare chest, her hands. We're a matching set, bathed in blood. Her eyes shine wild, glowing like the wolf she is.

Reaching up with my uninjured hand, I brush her hair back. "You're incredible," I say, my mind swirling. But somehow I know it's important to tell her how beautiful and amazing she is.

Her smile is everything. I could die in this moment, seeing her happy. Black crowds the edges of my vision and I push it away. I've got plans with my girl.

"Onyx!" her voice says, sounding far too worried. I try to answer, but my throat isn't cooperating anymore.

"Onyx!" I yelp, seeing his eyes unfocus and his muscles slacken. A new terror grabs me by my throat, strangling me. I can't lose him. He's been through worse; he needs to hold on long enough for his natural healing to kick in.

Jasper crouches beside me. "You just won back your pack. You need to address them. I'll take care of him." He

forces a shirt into my hand.

"Are you fucking kidding me?" I snarl. His eyebrows rise, imploring me. "Fine!"

Standing, I yank the shirt over my head and then I look across the faces of my pack. Respect, shock, and anger reflect back, but I don't give a shit. "Get him into the Alpha's house," I growl, motioning to Onyx. "And get first aid supplies."

People shuffle where they stand. How dare they hesitate. My anger spurs my natural dominance, and I press down on all of them with my will, demanding their obedience with every part of my being.

Two men to my left step forward and reach for Onyx, lifting him up between them. Jasper steadies him, holding his seeping wound, as they walk toward the house.

Pointing to a female wolf I know wasn't fond of Orion, I demand, "Go get all the healing supplies we have." Of another, I say, "You, gather up anyone with medical experience. He is your Alpha and we will do everything to make him well and comfortable." They bow their heads and rush to obey.

Taking a breath, I look over the rest of the crowd. "Anyone who doesn't want to follow my rule, I suggest you leave now because I will not be merciful of any disloyalty. The pack will be changing. We are no longer at war with those around us. They are our allies. I will build a healthy pack where you can be happy. No more assigned mates. No more beatings during training. But I will not tolerate any disrespect to me or my mate."

Jasper returns, his hand going to the small of my back. "Sister," he rumbles, "tell me which trainers you remember punishing you like we discussed."

Do I want to hand those wolves over to him? They're older, and I know they won't respect me, not after how they treated me growing up. They enjoyed causing pain. Not wolves I want to build a pack with. With a shrug, I point to a couple of the trainers who were always bloodthirsty and ready to take consequences too far.

Jasper confirms their names, and I nod. With a smile that almost scares me, he grips his dagger and stalks toward them. I don't care what he does with them, as long as they're gone.

Addressing my pack again, I say, "I'm going to attend to my mate. If you don't want to support my leadership, pack up and leave now. Anyone still here by sunset, we will begin building a new pack together. Understood?"

The group lets out a mix of agreement and grumbles.

I leave them to make their decisions. Onyx needs me. Gritting my teeth, I jog toward my childhood home, bracing my aching wrist against my stomach.

Onyx lays across the sofa, and three packmates tend to him. His wound is clean and one man carefully sews up the wound. Jasper's bag sits on the ground at my feet, and I tear it open, hunting for the jars we retrieved from Bracken Creek's healer. As soon as the stitching is done, I apply a thick layer of salve.

My strong mate hardly makes a sound as we align his broken arm and wrap it loosely, leaving room for the swelling that is just beginning.

They offer to wrap my own wrist, but it's already feeling better. Just a sprain.

Jasper crouches in front of me and wipes the blood from my face with a damp cloth. "You did great."

"Thank you," I say with a weak smile, ignoring the fresh blood splatter across his shirt. "Will you stay and help me evaluate the wolves we have left once the disloyal have cleared out?"

"I'll stay for a day or two. And then I'm going to go home and come back with reinforcements. We aren't taking any risks while you establish yourself as Alpha."

My impulse is to argue that I can do it all on my own and his help is unnecessary. But after everything my brother and Onyx's friends went through to help me already, I find myself agreeing. "Alright."

Onyx's head turns, his eyes clearing as he focuses on me.

"Hey, you." I say softly.

Jasper stands and motions those around us to leave.

"You were magnificent," he says.

"You liked all that violence?" I ask, scrunching my nose when I smile.

He reaches up with his good hand and cradles my cheek. "I like everything you do. Didn't I tell you?"

"You might have mentioned it." I press a kiss to his fingers, despite the dirt coating them still.

"So we won," he says, sounding in awe of what we accomplished.

"Yup." Brushing his hair back, I sigh. Relief mingles across our bond. "How's it feel to be Alpha?"

He huffs a laugh and then winces. "At the moment, rather painful."

"It'll get better, I think. These wolves are so lucky to have you. I'm lucky to have you."

He shushes me. "Go see your pack. I'm going to lay here and focus on healing myself so I can help you."

"Promise you're feeling good?" I implore him to be honest. I need him healthy and whole.

"Great." Color is returning to his face already and his voice is clear. We're going to be alright.

Standing, I clench and unclench my hands. It's time to get to work cleaning this pack out.

ONYX

My fists clench as I stare at the security system's back end controls. It's almost perfect, but a couple of components aren't doing what I want. Considering I am updating three outdated systems and merging all the controls, it's a miracle that most of it's working.

Pushing my chair back, I stalk out of the cold office. I don't mind Ferris's taste in dark marble, so we haven't made any updates to this room yet.

I can hear Ember singing along to alt rock that is

older than she is as she works on the family room. My feet slow in the doorway, admiring the sight. Hair now a vivid purple and tied up in a messy bun, Ember's hips sway as she drags a paintbrush down the built-in bookcases that span one side of the room. The bright white is covered by a sweep of dark emerald. Previously, the shelves were lined with expensive but soulless decor items. Soon it'll be actual books and a rather impressive record collection, all currently stacked across the two sofas while she paints.

Piece by piece, she's transforming this house into her own style - dark, rich, and colorful. I love it. It's cozy and feels like home.

Hands going to her waist, I lean down and kiss below her ear. She leans into my touch. "Hey, ready for a break?" I ask.

My hopes of luring her back to bed are dashed when she turns and says, "Yeah, I'm almost done here. Then we should go check on how everyone's doing today." Sighing, I make myself useful, cleaning up her painting supplies as she touches up the edges.

Ten minutes later, she's picking dots of paint off her wrists and forearms while we step off the porch and survey our pack. The cafeteria boasts a bakery case of treats, along with an updated kitchen in the back. Bracken Creek's chef, Crickett, has been training the two cooks to prepare food with seasonings and flavor. Meals have been steadily improving.

In the training building opposite, my father stands with his arms crossed, surveying the wolves sparring. He's teaching them to disable instead of harm, preparing the pack for any future conflicts we hope never come. A younger man and woman follow Fisher as he works - our replacement trainers. As a mated pair, they will both be Deltas, once Fisher is satisfied with their abilities.

Other wolves bustle around, completing various projects. Marigold stands in the center, giving out instructions and directing movements. One of the houses is being converted to a school. There's no teacher yet. There also aren't any children, but we want to be ready. A nearby empty house is being gutted so it can become a health clinic. We also need to acquire a healer, but perhaps Marigold's brother Indigo could take the position someday.

I hug Ember around the shoulders and give her a squeeze. "Look at everything you've accomplished."

"It'll be good when it's all done," she mutters, her gaze tracking the work going on around us.

As we wander forward, she points out two houses now sport wreaths on their front doors, and someone has even painted their front door a cheery yellow. The renovations at the house have inspired pack members to start personalizing their homes.

"Hey, I had an idea," she says, scuffing her feet

along the dirt. "What if we took that empty house on the end and turned it into a rec center?"

"Yeah?"

"We could put in pool tables," she continues, "maybe some arcade games. One room could be a movie theater."

"That's brilliant," I say, kissing her temple. "Everyone already loves you, but imagine how much they'll love their Alpha after you give them a whole game *house*."

She laughs softly, a soft blush coloring her cheeks. "So are we going to the inter-pack gathering tonight?" she asks, a vulnerable look in her eyes.

"Yeah, I think we should. It'll be a chance to see your other brother," I say, pulling her closer. Her shoulders rise and drop in a sigh.

"I guess I need to change out of these painting clothes," she says. "Should I dress up for this party?"

"I love you in anything and nothing at all," I growl, hesitant to release my hold on her. But if we are going to the event, I've got work to get finished.

Ember

I cling to Onyx's hand as we arrive at the party in an old pack car. Eventually I'll buy him a nice vehicle worthy of an Alpha. Maybe a sports car. Jasper can help. I'd like to see the two of them car shopping together.

Wolves from every pack mingle in the Valley Pack's central lawn. Onyx leads us toward the circle of Bracken Creek wolves. Marigold sits on Jasper's lap, and Hazel stands behind Slate with her arms draped over his shoulders, one hand playing with his dark curls.

Cedar stands and thumps his twin on the back. "How's it going?"

Onyx's smile is proud. "Great. I think everyone is taking to our changes faster than we hoped."

"That's wonderful," Hazel says, darting around Slate and throwing her arms around me. I'm getting used to hugs, and I even hug her back. As she pulls away, I see her wiping at her eyes before she plops into Slate's lap. His arms band around her waist, pulling her tight against him.

"I can't believe you guys are Alphas," Marigold says dreamily, cocking her head. "Seems surreal."

"You're telling me," I mutter. Onyx sits and pulls me

down across his thighs. My breathing slows to match his, soothing me.

"Well, now that we're all here, there was something we wanted to share," Hazel says, clapping her hands together.

My eyes narrow at the nervousness in her voice. Slate's expression is smug. What on earth? Onyx and Cedar seem as puzzled as I am, but Marigold's hands cover her mouth, her eyes going wide.

"Are you serious?" Marigold squeaks. I'm definitely missing something.

Hazel's lip quivers, her mouth curving into a watery smile, but she nods. Marigold launches herself off Jasper's lap and squeezes her best friend around the shoulders.

"Okay, what the hell, guys?" Onyx asks.

Jasper's expression shifts from confusion to surprise. "Are you pregnant?"

My mouth falls open.

"Yeah, we are having a pup. Maybe two," Slate announces. My hands come up to keep my mouth falling open, mimicking Marigold's reaction.

My little nephew or niece. And a new Heir for the Bracken Creek Pack.

"Congratulations," Cedar says, looking happier than I've ever seen him.

"You guys! A little Hazel, or a little Slate if we're

unlucky!" Onyx says, teasing his best friend. Slate shoves him half-heartedly.

"Wow, that's amazing," I say quietly. Hazel turns, taking my hand in hers.

"Thank you. They're coming into a safer world because of you. I know you're going to be an auntie, but I'd like it if you and Onyx were also godparents."

"Godparents?" I ask, blinking.

Hazel nods. "It's something my family does. Someone else to care for them and help guide them."

"We'd be honored," I manage to say, feeling tears burn in my own eyes.

"You too, Marigold," Hazel says. Her best friend squeals and bounces on the balls of her feet. I step back, tucking myself into Onyx's side, safe from flailing arms and being wrangled into group hugs.

Word of Hazel's pregnancy spreads outside of our group in minutes, with dozens of shifters around with excellent hearing. A line of well-wishers forms, and Onyx suggests we get a drink.

Wandering around the outskirts of the gathering, I notice my mate has a shit-eating grin forming on his face.

"Oh, no," I say, scowling at him. "What are you thinking about doing?"

"Nothing," he says.

A moment later, he's tugging me behind the nearest

building. It's the darkest corner of the party, and thankfully devoid of horny couples making out. For the moment, at least.

"Wow, you take me to such nice places," I say.

"Maybe I just like it when girls are mean to me," he says, his voice caressing me. He leans against the wall with a devilish grin. The chill in the air nips at my feverish skin, and I step closer.

"You're such an idiot," I murmur, smothering my laugh by closing my lips over his neck.

"Yet you love me," he says, tipping his head to the side with a dramatic sigh.

"Why is that again?" I tease.

With a smirk, Onyx scoops me up, hands against my ass, and turns us until I'm pressed against the rough wood. His chest is solid, his grip stable.

He kisses me until I've forgotten where we are and what my own name is. The party continues on without us, and I don't care. I've got everything I need right here.

Finally Onyx pauses, sucking in air. "Let's go home," he says. Without waiting for my agreement, he grabs my hand and leads me toward our vehicle.

Digging in my heels, I pull him to a stop. "Hey, it's a nice night out. Do you want to run instead?" His eyes light up.

Stowing our clothing in the truck, we turn toward the forest. Black fur sweeps down my arms as I shift, and suddenly the forest is brighter. Night creatures scurry away as our paws grip the earth, propelling us into the trees.

The moonlight filters through branches as Onyx chases me northward, toward our home. Through our mate bond, I can feel adoration, desire, and playfulness as he snaps at my tail. As we cross the border, I slow. The trees are denser here in this corner of our territory, and I know patrol has the night off.

Halting, I glance over my shoulder at the dark gray wolf a few steps behind me. He cocks his head in a silent question. Closing my eyes, I reach for my human side, and let the shift change me back. When I open my eyes, Onyx stands just a few inches away, his hair mussed.

With a sweet smile, I reach up and run my fingers through his hair to untangle it. The intensity in his gaze takes my breath away.

"I've been thinking about getting you alone in the forest again," he rasps, lifting a hand to brush along my neck and push my hair over my shoulder. My whole body shivers.

"I had a feeling," I say, excitement rising as he closes the distance between us. His desire warms me through our mating bond, meeting my own.

"Did I mention purple is my new favorite color?" he murmurs before his mouth closes over my skin. My laugh is cut off by the feel of his teeth nipping the sensitive spot under my jaw.

The night's chill prickles along my back and his body heats my front, his handing rove down my ribs to my bare ass. We're wild things in the night, a tangle of limbs and unending kisses flowing into each other. Promises whispered against heated skin and soft moans mingle in the air. He is mine and I am his, and when we're done, we can return to the home we claimed together.

FAMILY TREES

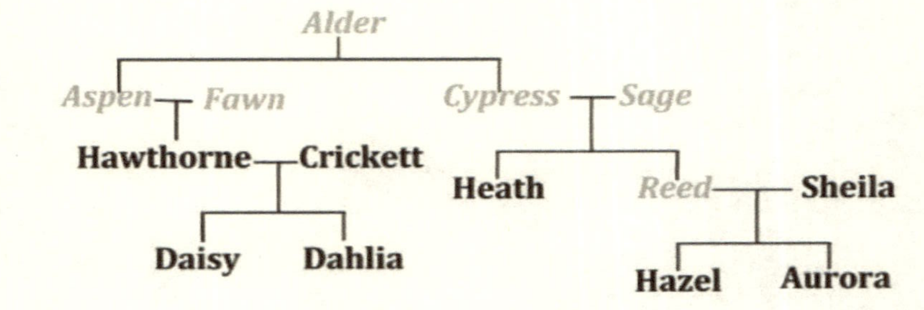

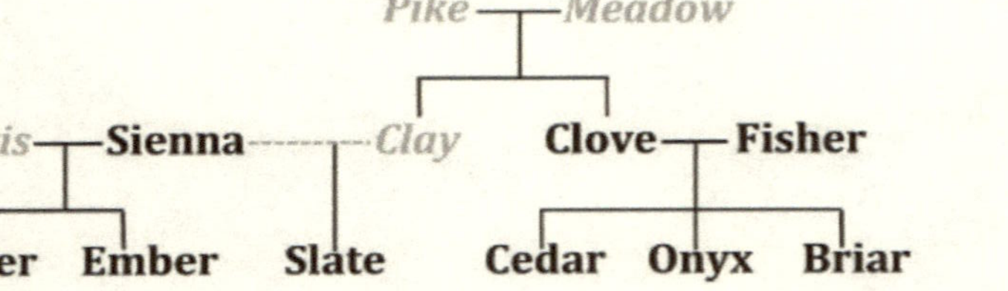

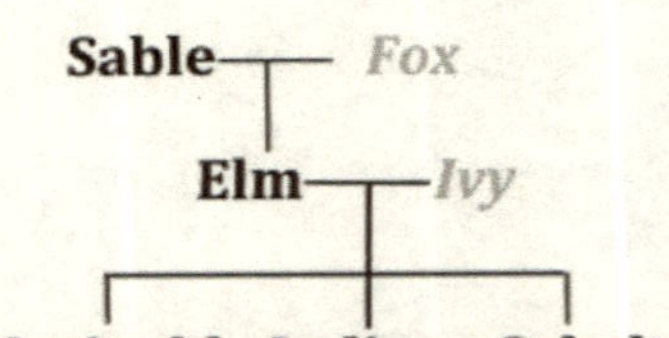

BRACKEN CREEK PACK

Alpha – Hazel and Slate
Beta – Jasper
Advisor - Heath
Gamma – Hawthorne
Delta – Fisher
Zetas – Elm, Lazuli, Cassia, Onyx
Thetas – Vale, Aven
Healer – Sable
Business Manager – Linden
Supply Manager – Fern
Teacher – Marigold
Chef – Crickett
Baker – Clove
Gardener – Cedar
Others – Ewan, Ginger, Yarrow, Daire, Laurel, Violet, Briar, Indigo
Elders – Oren, Tansy, Raven, Zeren
Youth – Cobalt, Dahlia, Daisy, Elwood, Juniper, Oliver, Starling, Willow

GRANITE RIDGE PACK

Alpha - Sienna
Beta - Orion
Heir – Ember
Delta – Bear
Gamma – Aster
Zetas – Flint, Aries

BRACKEN CREEK WOLVES
WOLVES AND WATERCOLORS
ALY HOLLIS

The story continues...

WOLVES AND WATERCOLORS

Aurora

Heath asked me to hang out in the cabin until he came and fetched me for dinner. But screw that. As cute as his vintage cabin is, I need to be outdoors. The clear air caresses my skin, soothing my lungs with sharp juniper and the musty scent of pine needles decomposing underfoot.

Slipping back out the kitchen door, I take a proper look around. Rough tree trunks rise around me, reaching toward the sky. Unable to resist, I run my fingers down the bark, savoring the texture.

Wildflowers and trailing scrub cover most of the ground, with worn paths through the underbrush snaking out in several directions. Everything feels so fresh and green and my soul soaks it up greedily, as if I had been starving for life until this moment.

With my sketchbook under my arm, I settle cross-legged on the edge of the porch. Delicate white flowers burst from dark greenery around the closest tree. My eyes follow the winding footpath as it darkens in shade and then brightens in sharp relief when the boughs part and sunlight streams down.

My pencil skates over the paper, the shape of the landscape forming with soft lines curving and crossing. The scale of this viewpoint is interesting. Close enough for details while still maintaining the towering scale of the aged trees.

A twig cracks and my pencil jolts from my hand.

Taking a steadying breath, I turn to search for the source. A man stands a few feet away with a sheepish expression on his face. The dappled sunlight gilds his short, messy hair and highlights a square jaw. He doesn't have the refined features of my sister's partner, but there's something classic about him.

He moves with a grace I don't expect from anyone that muscled, his triceps flexing as he scoops up my pencil from the dirt and presents it to me. Not that I was looking.

"Sorry I startled you," he says, soft and low.

"No, it's fine," I stammer, forgetting all of my social skills in that moment. Sliding the pencil into the spirals of my sketchbook, I set it aside and wipe my palms along my torn jeans.

"You must be Aurora," he says, his gaze meeting mine. Gray-blue eyes like a brewing storm hold me captive. His pupils widen, swallowing up the blue.

"Yeah," I say, my mouth finally remembering how to speak. "I figured I'd get a head start with being a good

Auntie and be here for the little one's arrival. Plus I haven't seen Hazel in like two years. A girl needs her sister sometimes, you know?"

This man listens to my babbling without moving or even changing his expression. Anyone else would have shifted their weight to signal that I'm making them uncomfortable. He stands still with those stormy eyes fixed on me like I'm sharing secrets of the universe. When he speaks, it's tentative and thoughtful. "I get that. I miss my brother when we go too long between visits."

"Yeah," I say, thrusting my hand toward him. "It's nice to meet you..." I trail off, hoping he takes the hint.

A calloused and warm hand envelops mine. "I'm Cedar. I'm cousins with Slate, your sister's m- partner." His mouth twitches into a frown for a fraction of a second.

I narrow my eyes, looking for the resemblance. His hand releases mine and cool air washes over my warmed skin, leaving a trail of tingles.

"I'd better get back to work," he says, ducking his head as he turns away. The back of his hair is just as messy as the front, short caramel waves going in different directions, streaked with platinum. My fingers ache to touch, but he's a stranger and I will definitely not be touching his hair.

On instinct, my eyes flick to his swinging left hand, looking for a flash of metal. Nothing. He seems older than me but not by much. Maybe he's Hazel's age.

"See you later!" I yelp, nerves rising up and tightening my throat.

Looking over his shoulder, he smiles at me. Full lips curve, hollowing dimples in his cheeks. Freaking dimples. My stomach clenches and I forget how to smile back until it's too late and he's already striding through the trees down a path I can't see.

Maybe it's all the exposure to nature, but he looked so vibrant and healthy. Hazel did too with her glowing skin and gleaming hair. If I stayed longer, would I start to look that lovely?

Exhaling slowly, I tip my face up and savor the sunshine across my skin. The soft rustle of leaves relaxes me as a breeze brushes against my cheek. Already, I feel better, like the nature around me is soaking into my soul.

"Hey, you," Hazel greets me. She moves slowly, somehow graceful even when her walk has become a bit of a waddle.

"Are you mad I came?" I ask, setting aside my sketchbook and pushing off the porch steps.

Hazel scoffs, her nose scrunching as she shakes her head. "Of course not. Sure, more notice would have been nice, but I could never be angry when I get to see you."

She supports her belly with a hand while the other rests on her hip. Instinctively, I reach a hand out, withdrawing before I touch her.

"Here, come feel. Baby is kicking a ton today."

My palms go to her belly. It feels hard, not squishy at all like I imagined. Hazel raises an eyebrow and then guides my hand to her side. The skin ripples under my fingers. I jerk back with a yelp.

"Was that the baby?" I cautiously reach for her again.

She laughs at my surprise. "Yeah, it's pretty weird, right?"

"So weird." I don't pull away the second time I feel it.

"They must like you," Hazel murmurs.

"How are you feeling?" I ask, dropping my hands.

She continues to rub her belly. "Pretty good, considering. I mean, this is getting rather uncomfortable, but I know it won't last that much longer."

"When exactly are you due?"

"Next week." She shrugs, unconcerned. "But first-time mothers usually go late, from what I've been told."

"Are you going to a hospital?" I ask, biting down on my lip as I realize that healthcare access might be a problem out here.

Hazel shakes her head. "I don't have any complications and we've got a nurse here who is more than qualified for a delivery. Actually, she's delivered most of the kids around here."

"That makes it sound more like a cult," I tease.

"That's what I said when I first got here."

"But, to be clear, it's not a cult. No weird rituals I'll

need to watch out for?"

Hazel's smile is uneven, giving me the distinct feeling she's holding something back - not the reaction you want to get when you're worried your sister is a cult leader.

"Of course not. Just people working and hanging out. I think you'll like it around here. I did."

"Yeah," I say, my brows furrowing as I watch her for other clues.

"So, are you hungry? It's about time for dinner."

"Cool, where are we eating? Your cabin?" I ask, stepping back onto the porch to retrieve my belongings.

"Oh, actually everyone eats together most days. We have a chef and a baker, and it's just easier for them to make big meals for everyone," she says.

"Sounding a bit cult-ish again," I mutter, laughing dryly when she rolls her eyes at me.

"You'll want to grab your sweatshirt, Ror. It'll get cold once the sun goes down."

"Alright, *Mom*." Popping inside, I toss my sketchbook onto the dresser of the guest room and grab my sweatshirt off the bed.

Hazel waits at the steps, her arms crossed over her belly. "Come on," she says, seizing my hand and tugging me forward.

When she said everyone, she meant the entire community. Thirty or forty people meander around a clearing. The trees are sparser here and buildings form a wide loop. A vintage-style diner sits on the opposite side, where most people gather.

Dozens of eyes follow me. "How often do people visit? I'm getting weird vibes," I whisper to my sister.

Hazel sighs, her elbow jostling me as she unlinks our arms. "It's not that common, but I think most people know you're my sister so they're just interested because of that."

"What have you been telling them?" I ask, wrinkling my nose.

She leads us toward the door where Slate waits, talking with Uncle Heath. "Come on, it's a buffet," she says, allowing Slate to open the door for her.

"Wow," is all I can say as the smell of garlic and cheese hits me. A gleaming countertop stretches the length of the building, stacked high with platters of pasta, meat, salad, and bread.

Hazel grabs a plate and begins to load it with breaded chicken, pesto pasta, and fluffy slices of garlic bread. I follow her example and even take a serving of salad.

Slate and Heath trail behind us. It's as if everyone is waiting for Hazel to go first before they get their own food. As we step out of the far door, I spy a line forming out the door.

Picnic tables surround the diner, stretching into the forest. Hazel heads to a table on the south end and plops her plate down before sliding onto the bench with a soft grunt. Suppressing my smile, I take the seat beside her. Slate is right behind us and claims the spot on her other side.

"This all smells amazing," I mutter, drooling over the parsley-speckled garlic bread oozing with butter. I'm so enthralled with my food that I hardly notice as others join us.

"Hey there," a young woman says. She sits across from Hazel, wearing a vivid emerald sweater and a dainty daisy headband threaded into her reddish-gold hair.

"Hi," I say automatically.

"I'm Marigold. I'm sure Hazel has mentioned me, but I'm her best friend," she says with a confident wink. Positive energy radiates off of her, and I instantly like her.

"Oh, good to know she's got you and it's not a total testosterone fest over here," I say, tipping my head toward Slate.

Marigold lets out a giggle. "I'm so excited to finally meet you." She glances around the table. "Normally, my boyfriend, Jasper, would be here too. He's Slate's brother, but he's visiting their sister."

Nodding, I pick up my fork and pop a spiral of pasta into my mouth to have something to do.

Another person walks toward us, and I recognize the boy from earlier. Slate's cousin? Cedar? He walks with his head down, eyes on the ground. As he settles onto the bench beside Marigold, I clear my throat.

"Hey, nice to see you again."

"Again?" Marigold asks, looking between us with a smirk on her pink lips.

Cedar is unbothered. "Yeah, I walked past the cabin and she was outside."

"I was sitting on the patio drawing. It's gorgeous outside, I couldn't stay indoors," I explain, feeling a blush creeping up my neck even though I did nothing wrong.

"Oh, that's right, you're an artist!" Marigold chimes. "What's your medium?"

"Watercolor, but I like to switch it up sometimes. Pencils, pastels, gouache, but watercolor is my favorite."

"She paints landscapes," Hazel says.

"Oh! Are you going to paint while you're here?" Marigold asks.

"That's the plan," I say, reaching for the phone in my pocket for the question that always comes next.

"I'd love to see some of your work," Marigold says. With a shy smile, I hand over my phone with the photos app queued up.

Marigold swipes through, her face growing more animated. "These are freaking gorgeous!"

"Thanks."

"Slate, I think she's better than you are!"

"I don't doubt it," he rumbles, his eyes not leaving my sister.

"It's not the same thing," I mutter. "You know, I'd love any advice on finding good views for painting.

Anything scenic or interesting is great."

"I'd love that, but I'm usually busy during the day. I'm the local teacher and those kids keep me busy." She shrugs and gives me an apologetic half-smile.

"I can take you," Cedar interjects. Those gray-blue eyes rise to mine. "I manage our garden, so my schedule is flexible."

"If you don't mind," I say, my whole body tensing. "But I'm sure you're busy. I'll be fine on my own, or you can just point me in the right direction."

"I'm ahead of schedule because of how warm it is. The spring planting is almost done, so I've got plenty of free time." He doesn't pressure me, just states the facts in that calm way of his.

"You definitely shouldn't go alone. I'd take you myself, but now's not a great time for hiking for me," Hazel says with a light laugh.

Heat creeps up my neck as I hold Cedar's gaze until he glances down. "If you are going to help me with finding locations to paint, I can help you in the garden. It's only fair, and I really like gardening."

The edge of his mouth quirks, like a smile is breaking through. Warmth stirs in my stomach. I'd love to see those dimples again. "Do you do a lot of gardening at home?"

"No, I wish."

"I've got everything handled, but you're welcome to come see it."

"I'd like that." I tear my eyes away from his and feel my blush redouble when I see how high Marigold's eyebrows are arching. A small smirk twists her lips. What did I do? I wasn't flirting. Maybe things are just so boring around here, anyone new is entertaining for them.

Scowling to myself, I stab another bite of pasta and look away into the trees as I chew. I must be reading the table wrong. This isn't a group of starving artists and actors in Los Angeles.

Hazel and Marigold discuss baby things while I disassociate. When Hazel stands, I blink in surprise. Our plates are mostly empty.

"I'd better get her home," Slate says, his hand on Hazel's lower back.

She lets out a yawn and then nods. "Yeah, I'm wiped. Rory, I'll see you tomorrow, okay?"

"Goodnight, Mama," I say, giving in to the urge to pat her belly.

Marigold rises and stacks our plates. "I'll drop these in the kitchen. Cedar, are you on dish duty tonight?" He shakes his head. "Good, you can walk Aurora back to Heath's cabin."

"Um, that's okay. I remember the way."

Cedar's open mouth closes.

"It's getting dark quickly and the forest looks different after dark. There aren't city lights out here. It's pitch black. You need someone to help you, sorry." Marigold leaves no room for arguing as she walks away, balancing the stack of plates in front of her.

"Sorry," Cedar says.

"I really think I'll be fine on my own," I protest.

He huffs, shaking his head. "She's right about it being dark. My family's cabin is near Heath's, so let's walk together. Just to be safe."

My lips press together, keeping my arguments contained. I pride myself in being capable, so the entire situation irritates me. But this gorgeous man wants to walk through the trees with me, and that's hard to say no to. I feel my resolve slipping. "Okay, fine."

Cedar allows me to take the lead as we cross the clearing. I may think I have a general idea of where Heath's cabin is, but as soon as we reach the shadow of the trees, I am entirely lost. But Cedar doesn't tease me or point out my failure. Instead, he walks beside me, subtly directing my steps with his own. My ego purrs. When was the last time I met a man who doesn't jump at the chance to say *I told you so?*

That appreciation is replaced with an unnerving sense of disorientation as the trees swallow up all available light around us. The starlight through the branches can't reach us and taunts me as it paints the highest branches in silver.

Grinding my molars, I slow and step carefully, trying desperately to keep track of the man a few inches away from me. Surely he won't let me walk into a tree. Does he know the forest so well he can walk in the pitch black? Haven't they heard of a flashlight?

My foot catches, my body jolting forward as my momentum turns to falling. There is no time to cry out, my body tensing for impact. Before I hit the ground, hands close around my upper arms, halting my nose-dive so suddenly, I let out an embarrassing "Umph."

"You okay?" Cedar asks as he levers me back to standing.

"Yeah, totally," I say, doing my best to sound cool and collected. Never mind that my heart is hammering in my throat so hard, I'm sure he can hear it.

He sighs, clearly not fooled by my bravado. It's probably the shake to my voice that gives me away. "Aurora, why don't you hold on to my arm. We are almost there, but I know it's too dark for you to see."

Gently, his hand finds mine, guiding it to his arm. Holy biceps. My breath stalls as I wrap my other hand around his arm, feeling the muscles shifting under my fingertips.

"Thanks for catching me," I murmur, internally berating myself for feeling up his arm, even if he placed my hand there.

He doesn't seem to mind or he's too polite to react. I can't see his face, but his voice is casual as he says, "No problem. This is exactly why I wanted to walk you back. It wouldn't be a good vacation if you broke your arm on our uneven trails."

"I appreciate that. I don't want to be a burden for

Hazel. I'm worried I'm adding to her stress," I admit, though I'm not sure why I'm opening up to this almost stranger.

Cedar doesn't answer for a long minute, but his free hand covers mine. "Step up, there's a rock here," he says.

I ignore how his voice turns my stomach all gooey. He's my sister's new family, not someone in the city. She would have to live with the consequences if I hit it and quit it, and something tells me Cedar isn't on hookup apps.

WANT MORE?

Want a bonus short story featuring Hazel, Slate, Jasper, and Marigold?

Join Aly Hollis's newsletter for updates, or follow on social media! See all her links here...

THANK YOUS

Thank you to my husband for supporting my writing habit.

Thank you to Ilea and Anandi for your editing insights. This story wouldn't exist without your encouragement.

Thank you to my author community, especially Tereza Kane and Harlowe Savage, for late night brainstorming sessions and caffeine-fueled writing sprints.

And thank you to my mother for cheering me on and my story even when I told you not to. I will never get over the embarrassment of you sharing my spicy werewolf books with all your friends, but I appreciate the support.

ALSO BY ALY HOLLIS

Bracken Creek Wolves:

Campfires and Canines

Moonlight and Mischief

Secrets and S'mores

Wolves and Watercolors

Snow Drifts and Soulmates *novella*

Blood and Brambles *novella*

Sablewood Trilogy

Raven Rebel

Ember Queen

Fated Traitor

Standalones

Wish Me Freely

Selkies and Saltwater

Blood Sugar

Seasons of the Alphas

Shifters' Fated Summer

Breeding Meadow

Knotting Autumn

Winter's Heat

ABOUT THE AUTHOR

Aly Hollis lives in the Southwest with her family, two enthusiastic heeler dogs, two judgmental cats, and an adorable turtle. She's written fiction since she was a child, but Campfires and Canines was her first book to be completed, edited, and published. It received such a great response, Aly wrote and published three additional novels and a novella in the Bracken Creek world.

When Aly isn't writing, she loves crafting, drawing, and debating book tropes with her friends.